The
MELODY
of
SECRETS

ALSO BY JEFFREY STEPAKOFF

Fireworks Over Toccoa

The Orchard

The
MELODY
of
SECRETS

Jeffrey Stepakoff

THOMAS DUNNE BOOKS
ST. MARTIN'S PRESS ✳ NEW YORK

This is a work of fiction. All of the characters, organizations, and events portrayed in this novel are either products of the author's imagination or are used fictitiously.

THOMAS DUNNE BOOKS.

An imprint of St. Martin's Press.

THE MELODY OF SECRETS. Copyright © 2013 by Jeffrey Stepakoff. All rights reserved. Printed in the United States of America. For information, address St. Martin's Press, 175 Fifth Avenue, New York, N.Y. 10010.

www.thomasdunnebooks.com

www.stmartins.com

5254 8038 10/13

Library of Congress Cataloging-in-Publication Data

Stepakoff, Jeffrey.

The melody of secrets : a novel / Jeffrey Stepakoff. — Ist. Ed.

p. cm.

ISBN 978-1-250-00109-2 (hardcover)

ISBN 978-1-250-02271-4 (e-book)

1. Astronauts—Fiction. 2. Secrets—Fiction. 3. Astronautics—United States—History—20th century—Fiction. I. Title.

PS3619.T47649M45 2013

813'.6—dc23

2013020534

First Edition: October 2013

10 9 8 7 6 5 4 3 2 1

For my parents, Elaine and Joel

No human race is superior; no religious faith is inferior.
All collective judgments are wrong. Only racists make them.
—ELIE WIESEL

A man's reach should exceed his grasp, or what's a heaven for?
—ROBERT BROWNING

PROLOGUE

M aria sat in front of the mirror slowly buttoning up her light blue sleeveless linen dress when she heard the bombs falling in the distance. She paused for a moment, turned her head, listening as the explosions came closer, and then continued dressing. There was a time not too long ago when this sound would have sent her running, but not anymore. Though she was hardly eighteen years old and knew that the war would be over in a matter of weeks, inside, Maria felt dead already.

She thought about dashing out the door of her little cottage and sprinting through the forest to the old house and grabbing the children—her music students throughout the war—and running off with them in the night. But with the Russians coming in from the east, and the Americans from the south and west, where was there left for a German girl and half a dozen orphans to run?

The air-raid sirens in town wailed from afar. A pitcher of water rattled on her dressing table. Picking up a wide-tooth ivory comb, Maria ran it through her damp honey-blond hair. She could smell the lilac that had been in the bathwater.

Who was this person looking back at her? She didn't even recognize herself anymore. No bath in the world would ever wash away what she had seen.

A nearby explosion rocked the cottage, causing Maria to jump. These bombing raids were getting closer every time now. Drawn by bright flashes of tracer light and the distinctive staccato popping sound of antiaircraft fire, Maria went to the windows. She pulled the lacy curtains away to see a sky filled with fire and smoke and what looked like a sea of aircraft, a few falling from formation in trails of orange flames but most moving relentlessly forward, dropping their fat bombs in steady cadence as they flew over.

Boom! Another percussive blast shook the ground, rattling the cottage windows. A plate fell from a cupboard in the kitchen, hit the floor, and shattered. Maria gasped. It was no longer just the fuel depots in town they were after. They knew about the camp, and the underground rocket factory, and the officer's quarters in the houses all around the outskirts of town—she was in the target zone now.

There truly was nowhere left to run.

Barefoot, as though in a trance, Maria walked into the living area, reached into a recessed shelf, and removed a violin case and bow. She popped the latches on the sturdy old case, expertly removed the violin, thrust it atop her shoulder, pressed her face to the chin rest, and pulled the bow across the strings.

A beautiful melodious sound, steady and true, resonated throughout the room. Maria closed her eyes, shutting out the world, focusing intensely on the long soothing tone. Then with a quick breath she shot the bow upward hard across the strings and, her fingers on the other hand working along the neck—outside the bombs falling all around—Maria stood in the middle of the room, lithe and shapely in her thin A-line dress, and played her violin.

She played Sibelius, the Concerto in D minor, powerful and poignant and mournful. And as though she stood before an audience of ten thousand giving the final performance of her life, she played with absolute conviction and precision, the instrument's pitch always perfect.

Back and forth, Maria pulled the bow across the strings in varied pace and angle, chin parallel to the floor, fingers coursing over the strings, as the bombs fell closer and louder—but she could no longer hear them. Everything she felt, everything she had seen over these last few years, it all came pouring out through the violin, the music speaking volumes more than any words ever could.

Her hair flying as she moved her head in the building rhythm of the concerto, a few snapped strands of the bow's horsehair whipping around as well, tears began to pool in the lower lids of Maria's big wide-set eyes and then to stream down her soft high cheeks, conjured not by fear of fire or jagged metal or demise but by all that had happened, all that she knew. The music brought it out, as it always did, and she was lost in it now, protected by it, enchanted, and carried away to some place safe by it. The world had gone mad and she was ready now for the end. Ready for death. In fact, she welcomed it.

The door of the cottage flew open.

Maria looked up from her dreamlike state and saw a man with a gun rush inside—a soldier, his face smudged with grease and soil, close-cut dark hair filled with leaves and small twigs, hands and forearms and neck bleeding from innumerable cuts. From a patch on his leather jacket, she could see that he was an American.

She yanked the bow rigidly, producing a discordant screech, and then stopped playing. Empty and spent, she just stared at him.

And he stared back. Then, in an instant, he ran his eyes all across the room, finally coming back to hers.

"Don't scream," he said, aiming his handgun directly at her chest.

Screaming had not occurred to her, for there was no one near to hear her. Dress fluttering against her skin as the wind blew in, she did start to think about fighting.

Without moving his gaze or gun, he reached behind his back and slammed the door shut.

"Are you alone?" he asked.

Violin hanging from one hand, bow from the other, she continued staring at him, speechless, as though he were some illusory creature.

Several bombs exploded off in the distance, the planes dropping their payload on the factory.

Wincing in pain, he took a determined step forward, extending the large-frame pistol even closer to her. "Are you alone?"

She could hear the volatility in his voice but still said nothing as her mind raced, studying him. Broad-shouldered and rock-hard fit, he looked like he was barely a year or two older than her, and she could tell from the bars on the shoulders of his jacket that he was an officer. On the front, above a patch with silver wings, COOPER was sewn in dark threading.

He had fallen from the sky.

"*Sprechen Sie englisch?*" His accent was terrible but comprehensible.

Yet, still nothing from her.

He raised the gun and his voice. "Say something or I swear you'll spend the rest of the three seconds of your life—"

"Yes," she finally said with only a faint hint of her German accent, eyes never leaving his, jaw set, shoulders square. "I am alone."

His gun pointed at her chest, violin and bow swaying from her limbs, as another distant explosion gently rocked the cottage, but still neither moved.

THE LAST OPTION

We have sixty seconds to launch, sir," a nervous technician announced.

Air force colonel Mike Adams, a big man with an executive presence, nodded as he leaned forward on the control panel, looking out the thick plateglass window at the launch site below.

"Satellite beacon is active and operating," another tech said, and the steady *beep, beep, beep* of a small satellite—the payload atop the slender rocket on the launch pad below—could be heard transmitting over speakers in the control room.

"What makes you boys think this one's gonna fly?" Adams asked without bothering to look back at the half-dozen men in the small room. With his deep, low voice, at once folksy but commanding, Adams struck them as someone who in another life might have run a Nebraska cattle operation.

"My team has tested and retested every piece of hardware on that rocket," a navy lieutenant said.

"And that's *in addition* to the safeguards provided by each and every subcontractor," a white-coated scientist added.

Colonel Adams scratched his belly, pressing it up against the control panel, eliciting a glance from the navy lieutenant.

It was clear that the lieutenant didn't like his operation's being second-guessed by some Pentagon administrator, no matter how superior, and he wasn't going to make a secret of it—this project warranted Washington's full support. "We have absolute confidence in the Vanguard rocket, Colonel."

"You had *absolute confidence* the last two times you tried to launch her," Adams said, finally turning to the men.

"Did we hit a few snags?" the scientist asked. "Sure. And we found them and fixed them."

"Fifteen seconds!" a tech called out.

"Colonel Adams, that rocket down there is the sum of America's best minds," the navy lieutenant said, his tone deftly straddling reassurance and rebuke. "Have some faith, sir."

Beep, beep, beep, the satellite's transmission reverberated throughout the room. It was a sound filled with the promise of technology, the expense of tens of millions of dollars in funding, the dreams of a nation, and the security of a way of life.

"I have plenty of faith." Adams looked back down at the slender Navy Vanguard TV3 rocket, seventy-two feet tall, steam rising from beneath her as the launch sequence continued. "It's the people of this country that don't. They don't care about your snags and fixes. They just want to know why the Russians beat America into space. They want to know why they have a Soviet satellite flying over their heads right now when 'America's best minds' can't seem to throw a grapefruit over a barn, let alone get our own satellite up there. Gentlemen, this bird had better fly."

"Five, four, three, two, booster is ignited, and—liftoff! We have a liftoff! Vanguard TV3 is a go!"

All the men leaned toward the glass window, watching with rapt attention, the stakes of this mission apparent on their faces.

All across America, people watched the launch on their television sets.

In Sacramento, a family of five gathered in their living room eating breakfast on standing metal trays, gripped by the images of the launch on their bulky black-and-white set.

In Manhattan, a young man threw open the front door of his apartment, tossed his hat, and ran into the kitchen to join his pretty wife, an infant in her arms. Without turning her face from the television, she reached out and took his hand.

In Wichita, a farmer in dusty coveralls stood on his front porch and peered in through a wide-open window at the television set in his living room, his family congregated around it. He wiped his brow, a look of wonder on his face.

On an unfurling ball of golden flame, fueled by just the right mix of liquid oxygen and ethyl alcohol, the rocket began to defy gravity and rise, slowly, gracefully, like a ballerina going en pointe. It was a thing of grand beauty to behold.

In the control room, the glass window vibrating with the steady rumbling of the ascending rocket, several of the men began to applaud. A couple cheered.

About four feet over the launch pad, the pillow of roaring fire and smoke expanding underneath it, the rocket hung in midair, levitating, and then abruptly lost thrust, dropping back down to the concrete launch pad, fuel tanks rupturing and bursting, causing the entire rocket to explode and quickly burn up in its own flames.

Propelled out of their stupor by the oncoming debris, the men quickly ducked down as shrapnel flew up toward the control room window. A toaster-sized chunk of blackened rocket engine slammed into the glass, cracking it from top to bottom, leaving a web of wavelike lines in its wake.

Then there was silence, except for the *beep, beep, beep*.

Tentatively, the men rose, looked out the damaged window, and saw lying below in a nearby patch of tall grass, the small aluminum sphere that was supposed to be in the heavens above them. Thrown from the top of the rocket, it was dented and charred but still transmitting what now seemed a wretched earthbound sound.

Beep, beep, beep. It was mocking them.

Stunned, the men silently watched the widening trail of black smoke float out over the Atlantic in the distance.

Finally, Adams picked up a phone. "Get me the executive officer at Redstone."

"You're going to the army?" The navy lieutenant asked.

"We're done here."

The scientists and technicians immediately exchanged worried looks. No one wanting to be the first to object—it was common knowledge among them that former enemies were on staff at the highly classified Redstone army base.

"Sir—" The navy lieutenant raised his voice. "You can't put the Germans on this."

"I don't have any other options." Adams turned away, phone to his ear, looking down through the shattered glass at the disaster below.

Pushing aside the rolling chair separating their bodies, the navy lieutenant got in his face. "Colonel, with all due respect—and interdepartmental politics entirely aside—this is a matter of national security. The highest kind. *You can't put the Germans on this.*"

Adams met his eyes and held them until it was very clear who had the power in this room. "Actually, Lieutenant, I can."

BLOSSOMWOOD

From the air, there was cotton, field after field of it, rolling like whitecaps gently breaking on an endless sea. As one came up from the south, as the big cargo planes did on their way in from the cape in Florida, over the pristine Tennessee River, whose snaking tributaries fed the rich ruddy soil in the fields, Redstone Arsenal and the army's affiliated airbase sprawled over the entire southwestern quadrant of Huntsville—tens of thousands of acres of fresh gray concrete and low-lying government installations, smack dab in the middle of the cotton sea. Brown military vehicles buzzed back and forth along the skinny two-lanes between the fields to the west of town.

And to the east, past the sooty old textile mills and dry-goods warehouses and the small downtown encircling the yellow brick courthouse, just beyond the historic districts—Twickenham and Old Town and Five Points, with their lovingly maintained antebellum homes—spreading out into the horseshoed base of Monte Sano, a new suburban neighborhood was being rapidly built.

Welcome to Blossomwood read the hand-carved sign on one of the red brick posts at the entrance to the community. A tableau of a merry family of openmouthed hummingbirds was painted vividly on the sign.

The main street, paralleled by milky-white sidewalks, wound along carefully planned one-acre tracts, each one covered with spotless green turf, and multihued annuals and azaleas, and pines young and old. Set generously back from the street, each lot contained a brand-new one-story ranch-style house, some built as recently as within the year—a response to the steady rise in military personnel.

With their long, low roofs, wide, overhanging eaves, oversized windows with shutters, and simple exterior trim, these rambling red brick ranchers were sleek and restrained in design, evoking a confident charm, a certain elegance in their utility. It was an aesthetic that sparked first in California after the war and had now caught on, with minor regional refinements, throughout the new suburbs springing up in the Deep South. On the streets of Blossomwood, past the carefree children playing on expansive driveways, the sound of a dog barking brightly, the scents of sawdust and sod, there was a pervasive rightness to how things were—a living, breathing validation of a way of life where man was free not only to dream but to pursue his full potential.

Branching off the main street in the subdivision, down Monterrey Drive, to the very end of a cul-de-sac, Sierra Circle, workers installed several root-balled dogwoods in the front yard of a particularly charming new brick ranch home.

Penny Tucker, a full-bosomed woman in a satin pencil dress mercilessly cinched at the waist, sashayed past the landscape workers—their heads turning in unison. Pointy-toed heels click-clacking away, she floated past a grouping of azalea bushes still in containers, up the front steps, across the deep front porch, and rang the doorbell.

Maria Reinhardt opened the door, a tray of chocolate-covered Rice Krispies Treats in her hands. The waifish teen who had played that violin in the cottage in Germany twelve years ago was now a beautiful refined woman in her late twenties. "Penny! Oh good, you're just in time."

Penny stepped inside.

"Tell me," Maria said, her German accent barely detectable. "Too much chocolate?"

"Honey, there is no such thing as too much chocolate," Penny said with her languorous Lower Alabama drawl, picking out a perfectly cut square and popping it into her mouth. Chewing, Penny vocalized her pleasure, emphasizing her point.

Maria closed the door to her house and they walked through the foyer, passing the open living room to the left, stopping at the dining room on the right.

"I have proper strudel and Black Forest cake," Maria said. "But Peter is coming home from boarding school today and he loves these Krispies things." She put the tray on the table next to a cake on a glass stand.

"Your kid's got good taste."

"Who would think to cook breakfast cereal with marshmallows and butter?"

"American ingenuity at its finest." Penny spied a pitcher of martinis and began to pour herself one.

Maria popped a square into her mouth, closing her big eyes with pleasure as she chewed. "I love America."

Sipping from the martini glass in her hand, Penny took in the sight of her friend standing before the long, elegant living-room table, covered with bowls and dishes and platters of pretty little finger

sandwiches and frosted baked confections. It was a scene straight
out of a ladies' magazine.

In her full-skirted sleeveless tea dress, Maria was fine-boned
and feminine. Blond hair perfectly curled and set, soft-toned matching lipstick and nails, her creamy skin pastel and muted, she moved
like a dancer Renoir might have conjured.

Maria stepped back, surveying the table, her expression dropping when she noticed a burned-out lightbulb in the fixture above
the table. She shook her head and went to a cabinet.

"I had a leaky kitchen faucet for three weeks," Penny said. "I
asked Jimmy to fix it every day, and every day it just dripped and
dripped. One day he came home from the base after a long day of
test piloting looking for his supper. But all he found in the kitchen
was a monkey wrench. I had a steak at the officers' club that night
and when I came home my sink was fixed." Penny sucked a gin-
soaked olive off a toothpick.

Maria strode back to the table, chin high, a lightbulb in her raised
hand. Even doing the most mundane tasks, Maria Reinhardt was
poised as a princess. Indeed, if Penny was Marilyn Monroe, Maria
was Grace Kelly.

"Oh, honey, you can't get to that right now," Penny said, her
palm out toward the food-covered table. "Just give Hans a kick when
he comes home later. He designs rockets for the army. I'm confident
he can change a lightbulb in his own house."

"Yes, well, I birthed a baby. After that, I am confident I can do
anything." Resolve on her face, Maria kicked off her midheight
pumps and, bulb in hand, stepped up onto a chair.

"I'm telling you," Penny went on. "You are too sweet. Men are
like horses. You have to know when to feed 'em and know when to
kick 'em. Only way you'll ever get 'em to jump."

"I need jumping done right now." Maria hopped up onto the dining room table.

"Oh, watch the cake, dear!" As though she were watching a game show on television, Penny just leaned against the wall, sipping her martini, entirely amused at the spectacle. This was definitely not something you'd see in the *Ladies' Home Journal*.

In nylon-stockinged feet, Maria tiptoed across the slippery polished table, stepping over and around all the trays and bowls of food. She reached up high to the space-age-themed fixture above her head. A gleaming bronze base from which sixteen poles of varying lengths protruded, each holding a bulb at the end, it called to mind the structure of an atom. Stretching precariously, using her fingertips, Maria removed the burned-out bulb, replacing it with the new one.

"Bravo!" Penny clapped.

"Thank you for your support," Maria said with a grin as she gingerly stepped over the food. Feet arched, toes pointed, holding her skirt just above the frosted cakes, she made her way to the edge of the table and, old bulb in her elongated hand, leapt to the floor, landing like a ballerina in a third-position curtsy.

The doorbell rang.

"*Now* we are ready for tea," Maria said, stepping into her shoes, smoothing down her skirt, and walking with the calm of a thoroughly prepared hostess to the door.

"*Guten Tag, mein lieber Freund*," said Sabine Janssen when Maria opened the door.

"Good afternoon to you too, Sabine."

Sabine smiled, a bit sheepishly, as she stepped in and kissed Maria on the cheek. Both women knew the only way they would assimilate and truly make Alabama their home was to speak English.

But Sabine, her crystal blue eyes darting and nervous, had a much harder time with this than Maria.

Before Maria closed the door, another woman, conservatively dressed, her helmet of dark hair sprayed immobile, white patent leather purse swinging madly from one hand, a Tupperware container balanced in the other, flew past the landscape workers and ran up the steps to the door.

"Catastrophe!" Carolyn Propst exclaimed, easing right by Maria and Sabine and striding into the house as if it were her own. She threw the purse like a hand grenade onto a sectional sofa in the living room and dropped the Tupperware down on a coffee table with a thud.

"What happened?" Sabine asked, alarm in her guttural voice, stepping over to join Carolyn.

"We have a complete catastrophe on our hands is what happened!"

Maria closed the door and went to the open living room, where Penny had placed herself on the sofa, a fresh martini in hand. On the walls behind her were framed petit point works, finely embroidered landscapes that Maria had recently completed to try to make the new house feel like a home.

"What's the matter, honey?" Penny asked, drawing out her drawl as though trying to settle things down.

"What's the matter? What's the matter?" Carolyn stood before the women, nervously laughing at the scope of the crisis. "The hotel doesn't have chairs for tonight."

"What are you talking about?" Sabine asked, sitting down. When Sabine focused on expressing herself in English, she tended to speak concisely and seriously.

"I am talking about two hundred and sixty-five people standing." Carolyn plopped down on the sofa, every part of her slumping like a rag doll, except her bulletproof hair.

"For every problem, there is a solution," Maria finally said, hands resting on the back of a sofa. "What exactly happened to their ballroom chairs?" Unlike Sabine, Maria spoke eloquently, which only accentuated her composure.

"Apparently, they sent them to a church in East Memphis—"

"What?" Hands raised, Sabine cut her off. "The chairs for our event are in Tennessee?"

"No, the chairs for our event are in Oswego."

"Os-what-o?" Penny popped open Carolyn's Tupperware, curious to see what her friend had brought.

"Oswego, New York." Carolyn became even more exasperated as Penny started nibbling on a cherry shortbread cookie.

Tennessee, New York. Sabine looked back and forth between the two women. "Why would the hotel send their ballroom chairs *anywhere?*"

"Because they had to make room for the *new* chairs, the ones that were not on the truck with the new tables that arrived today because apparently the new chairs are still on the shipping dock—"

"In Os-way-go." Penny said, nodding her head in understanding.

"Which is most definitely not anywhere near Huntsville, Alabama!" Carolyn said.

"The event is in four hours." Sabine looked at her slim Swiss wristwatch.

"Does the hotel have a plan?" Maria asked.

"Standing buffet. That's their plan."

"Well, that'll work," Penny said.

"With prime rib?" Carolyn's voice cracked. "Twenty-four-ounce cuts of rare prime rib? How do you hold a plate with one hand and cut your two-pound slab of beef with the other?"

The women thought in unison, and what they envisioned wasn't a pretty picture.

On the hall table, under a polished chrome-framed mirror, Maria picked up a phone next to a sizable stack of unopened mail and dialed.

"I have to confess, sugar," Penny said close to Carolyn. "I thought you were being a teensy bit, you know, theatrical, and even though this might not be a full-on catastrophe it really could get rather messy." Penny picked a dried cherry off the cookie and plunked it in her mouth. "I'll tell you *my* plan."

"Oh, do tell." Carolyn leaned back. This was going to be good.

"We get more liquor."

"More liquor?"

"Precisely."

"I believe we have sufficient quantities ordered," Sabine said.

"Well, whatever the order, we double it, for starters."

"That's your plan?" Carolyn asked, rubbing her forehead.

"That's my plan."

"Major Sullivan, please," Maria said into the phone. "In base operations." Wrapping the rolled cord from the handset around her long, slender index finger, Maria simply tuned out the ongoing situation in her living room.

Carolyn just kept talking. "In four hours the entire arts-supporting community of Huntsville is going to be wondering why they paid fifty dollars a plate for a sit-down dinner they have to eat standing up, and your plan is to get 'em smashed?"

"Works every time," Penny said, reflecting on such occasions. "Well, mostly."

"Catastrophe!" Carolyn said.

"Besides, I don't hear any other suggestions, so we might as well make this heavy-hauling walking 'n' talking buffet affair as fun as possible."

"Major Sullivan, this is Maria Reinhardt." Her voice was cool, even serene. "Hans is fine, thank you so much for asking, Major. I have a problem with which I wonder if you might be able to assist me. As you may know, many of the rocket scientists on your team, as well as some of their wives, were trained in classical music when we were children in Germany, and many of us have formed a symphony orchestra here in Huntsville. Yes, the HSO. Well, the new Huntsville Symphony Orchestra board of trustees . . ."

Eyes forced wide, Maria gazed at Carolyn and Penny, the co-presidents of the HSO board, who, along with Sabine, were finally silent, fixated entirely on Maria.

Leaning on a sofa table, phone pressed comfortably to an ear, Maria smoothed her bouncy-set blond hair and continued. "They are hosting a fund-raiser tonight for the HSO at the Russel Erskine Hotel downtown—that is right, General Medaris will be there with Faye—and we seem to be missing some chairs."

Maria ran her tongue over her lustrous teeth, making sure they were entirely free of any errant lipstick.

Across the room, Penny gave Maria a thumbs-up, clearly impressed with her ingenuity and nerve.

"Well, while the board and I were racking our brains to try to solve this embarrassing predicament," Maria continued, "I remembered all those lovely padded white chairs that were arranged so neatly on the lawn at Redstone last month when Secretary Wilson spoke at the opening of the new missile command facility."

Her plan clear now, Maria exchanged upbeat smiles with the other women, her voice growing ever more confident as each woman sent nods of approval her way.

"Two hundred and sixty-five." Maria looked quite pleased with what she was hearing. "You are so kind, Major. I know the scientists will appreciate it, as will the entire town. And I will be sure to let the general know how helpful and supportive you were."

Maria hung up and turned to her friends. "The chairs are being deployed."

"Maria Reinhardt, I swear, you are cool as a cucumber in the fridge!" Penny exclaimed.

Carolyn rose, visibly embarrassed at how easily Maria had solved her *catastrophe*. "I'll call the hotel and let them know that—"

"He is taking care of it all." Maria motioned for her to sit as she went to the dining room table, ferrying teacups on saucers and the martini pitcher to the coffee table. "If they can split an atom and send a missile across the ocean, they can get some chairs to a local hotel. And considering what our husbands do for them, it is the least they can do for us."

"You are so right about *that*," Carolyn said, leaning back on the sofa. "They have Will flying virtually every day. It used to be just transport, but now he's test-piloting these new jets with rocket-assisted takeoff—"

"RATO jets," Penny said, imitating her husband's husky voice.

"Two feet of runway and, *whoosh*, straight up." Carolyn shot her open hand up into the air. "I don't even want to know what they're putting him in anymore. I just pray as soon as he walks out the door each morning."

"I say those same prayers every time Jimmy walks out," Penny said.

"They have Karl effectively living at the base, day and night lately, developing and redeveloping his rocket fuel," Sabine said.

"Which are probably flying some of those new jets," Penny said.

"Probably." Sabine nodded thoughtfully, pouring herself some tea from a porcelain pot Maria had set down on the coffee table.

"Hans is living there too," Maria said in her soft-spoken way, sharing a look of understanding with Sabine that was not lost on the two American women. "Designing and redesigning his engines. Sometimes I think he is married to his slide rule."

There was a charged silence in the room while all four women seemed to take a collective breath. Two German women, the wives of rocket scientists whose work had helped the Nazis, two American women, wives of American military pilots—in some ways the two sets of women couldn't be more different, but in the ways that really counted they were learning there was a bond.

Sabine felt she had to elaborate. "It is not that I am ungrateful." She sounded almost stoical as she struggled to produce the proper words. "But the hours he keeps, the demands on him, on us, from the army . . . I appreciate the U.S. government's bringing us here after the war, I really do, and everything they did for us, are doing for us, and I know he loves the opportunity to continue his work, but . . . This was not a simple act of good will."

The porcelain teacups rattled on their saucers as a rocket engine reverberated thunderously over at the base, just a few miles away. The women hardly noticed.

Sabine looked up, her eyes filling with tears, but she fluttered them dry. She looked back at her friends. Did she dare say more? Sabine turned to Maria, speaking much more comfortably in her native language. "*Ich sollte jetzt aufhören.*" But she knew she needed to repeat herself for the others in English. "I should stop now."

She wanted to say more. That was clear to the others. But Sabine clenched her jaw shut tight. Concern in her eyes, Penny glanced at Maria, who went to Sabine and put a supportive hand on her knee.

Sabine—and Maria—had left everything they'd ever known after the war and started new lives with their husbands here from scratch, initially under guard on military bases and finally, when they could be trusted, in these new houses of their own. The American women knew how difficult all of this must have been. But they also knew that the German women had not long ago lived in a country whose men shot at their fathers and brothers and husbands and meticulously planned and carried out worse. Were the German women's husbands, although just men of science, above the fray of war? Above accountability for how their work was used?

There were no easy answers and the past was complex. To explore it, ask questions about it, open up their hearts to one another about it could have terrible consequences. In their own ways, they all knew this. The future was full of promise, so the past was best left behind.

"Well, speaking for all of us pilot wives," Penny finally said to Sabine *and* Maria. "We're glad y'all are here. The past is past, and today is today. So thank you for putting up with so much for the men whose work might end up in the engines our men fly."

"Some things keep us *all* awake at night," Maria said, smiling soothingly at her friends.

After a moment, Carolyn nodded, and then a smile began to grow on her face. "Tell us your secret, Maria Reinhardt. How *do* you always seem to remain so steady and calm?"

Maria's mind filled with flashes of what she had lived through during those years of war in Germany, and for an instant she was that crazed, ragtag eighteen-year-old playing her violin in a final fit, ready for death. These memories that often ran through her mind like an old movie reel put matters like missing chairs into perspective.

But Maria decided to share something else. "Honestly, I think I owe a lot of my outlook on the world to Hans. After living with him for twelve years, if there is one thing I have learned it is to try to keep emotions out of things. Focus on what is rational and known. Not on what is felt."

"Ah, the wisdom of the rocket scientist's wife," Carolyn said, musing. "Keep passion in check."

"Good advice," Sabine said.

"Nonsense," Penny said, turning to Maria. "I've heard you play violin. That in itself is proof of the power of passion over science."

Maria crossed her legs, hands entirely at ease on her thighs. "Mastering violin is just mastering craft. It is really that simple. Following very specific principles and instructions. Like cooking."

Maria leaned forward and picked up a cherry cookie to gesture her point to the room.

"I haven't used a recipe in ages," Carolyn said. "I just trust my instincts. Not a lot of science in that."

Maria took a bite, considered it. "One cup of white flour, one *overflowing* cup of white sugar, half pound of cherries, a teaspoon of baking soda, and a quarter teaspoon of salt. Baked at 350 for twenty minutes. Even if you are not reading the recipe, you are following the rules. Cooking comes down to math and science. Like most things in life."

"What about sex?" Penny asked.

"Sex?"

"Yes. Good point." Carolyn laughed. "Is Hans all science in bed?"

Thrown off guard by that one, Maria labored a bit to find her words. She ran her tongue over her teeth a couple of times. She uncrossed her legs and then crossed them again, suddenly not so composed. "We choose our marriage partners for very rational reasons."

"Oh, don't try to give me a schoolbook lesson in human reproduction," Penny pressed on. "I'm talking about *real* sex, which

I propose has nothing to do with science and everything to do with dumb, stupid, entirely irrational, *rip-the-sheets-to-shreds* passion!"

Carolyn sighed. "I'd like some of that."

They all laughed, Maria not quite as much as the others, as the front door opened.

"Hi, Mom!" An eleven-year-old boy in prep school coat and tie bounded into the house.

"Peter!" Maria threw her arms around her son.

The other women watched, smiling. Despite what Maria might say about emotion, she was clearly overcome with it at the sight of her son.

"Let the boy go, darling." Dr. Hans Reinhardt strolled in, carrying Peter's laundry bag. "You have all weekend to hug him."

"Tell her, Dad," Peter said. He was a handsome boy with striking blue eyes, blond hair, and high cheekbones. "Tell them all. You can tell them all, right?"

"Tell us all what?" Maria asked, eyes darting between the two.

Tall, fair, strong-jawed, Hans Reinhardt broke into a huge smile. "Something has happened," he said with his erudite Bavarian accent. "Something that is going to change everything in Huntsville."

Outside the house, as a landscape worker watered the newly planted dogwood tree with a long garden hose, a dark sedan, its windows rolled tightly up, drove very slowly around the cul-de-sac and slowed in front of the house. The worker looked up at the vehicle, water splattering mud onto his shoes. The sedan hurriedly sped up and drove off, down Monterrey Drive, disappearing into Blossomwood.

A NIGHT OUT

The sun had been down for an hour or so. Along with the bright lights from the attached bath, several thin-shaded lamps lit the clean, neat master bedroom of the Reinhardt house.

In lacy conical bra and silk slip, Maria leaned over her dressing table, thoughtfully applying pale pancake foundation to her face. Behind her, Hans folded over the French cuffs on his pressed white dress shirt and began inserting fleur-de-lis cufflinks. In his forties, Hans looked even more distinguished in the elegant new formal wear.

"They have tried launching a satellite over and over on the navy's so-called research rocket and every time it has failed spectacularly," Hans said.

"Are you supposed to sound so happy about that, dear?"

"These poor American engineers. They can't get the oxidizer to mix without combusting. *Poof!* Up in flames every time."

He did try to contain his smile, but it was impossible.

Applying cherry-red lipstick, matching the color on her fingernails, she shot him a half-playful look.

"Oh, Maria, it is hard to have pity. We have been telling them to use our rocket for the space program for two years now, but they would not listen. They brought us over here after the war, told us to take our V2 rocket, which worked, and build more for the army, which we have done very successfully. Then they stick thermonuclear warheads on our rockets and install them back in Germany to threaten the Russians—which works, because the Russians know very well what the V2 did to London with only conventional warheads. So you see, darling, German rockets are fine for America's dirty work, but space must be conquered by dignified American know-how." Hans leaned over her shoulder, looking in her mirror as he straightened his black bow tie. "Which would be fine indeed, except for the little problem that Americans cannot seem to figure out how to keep their *dignified* research rockets from exploding on the launch pad."

"Hans! Be nice."

"Me? Have you read the papers here? The Russians call theirs Sputnik. The press calls America's last attempt *Kaputnik*."

Maria couldn't help but to laugh at that one.

Putting on his thin-lapel shawl tuxedo jacket, he continued. "Well, now that the Russians have managed to get a satellite up there, Eisenhower has decided that suddenly those classified German rockets the army has been quietly cranking out down in Alabama to use as warhead-tipped ballistic missiles—the rockets that actually work—might be fine to launch a satellite into space after all. It seems that being beaten into space by the Russians is worse PR than having America get there with nasty German science."

"Well, I know it feels good to be right, and even better that your work is getting the attention it deserves." She put a cherished drop of Joy perfume on her wrist, which she rubbed subtly against her collarbone and the curve of her neck where it met her ears.

Buttoning up his jacket, he looked off, as if to savor her acknowledgment. "Let me tell you what feels best about all of this. When I was a boy, I dreamed of space. During the summer I would tie small rockets to my wagon, simple homemade sulfur-charcoal compounds I got at the pharmacy near our house in Burghausen, and I would shoot the wagon across the bricked square in the city center. And at night, I would lie on my back with my father in the grass and he would talk to me about the constellations, and I would dream of someday reaching them. So I went to school and I learned the advanced science and my country gave me the chance to hone those dreams, but only so far. I have built a great many rockets, but none of them have ever pointed up. Finally, this one will be aimed not at a city but up, at the heavens."

Smoky turquoise eye shadow on her lids, Maria closed her eyes for a moment, allowing herself to feel fully his sense of accomplishment. "I am so proud of you, Hans."

"America needs our rocket to succeed. I need our rocket to succeed."

He put his big hands gently on her bare shoulders and placed his lips to her head, which fell naturally to the side and back, elongating and exposing the skin along the top of her shoulder through her throat and neck. She closed her eyes and in that moment she thought she was going to be kissed further, down her neck, hands on her, and perhaps because the subject of passion was fresh on her mind, she had the craziest thought about jumping up and locking the bedroom door . . . but he removed his hands from her skin and she opened her eyes and there was Hans, standing behind her, meticulously adjusting his tie, and the thought was gone. She took a deep breath, slowing her heart, relieved to be her calm, steady self again.

"The entire world will be watching and we have just three weeks until launch," he said, turning and walking away. "I have to call Von Braun before we leave. He wants the trajectory work done by the end of next week. We are hiring forty-eight girls to do all the calculations, by hand. Our computer team!"

Maria turned her head and watched him walk out, a man captivated by and committed to his dreams. A moment later, she heard him on the phone speaking engagedly to his boss and friend. As he talked business and science in the next room, she rose and began to slip into her simple but chic black evening dress.

Standing in her bedroom in her partly zipped dress, Maria noticed a crease in the white bedspread on the otherwise perfectly made bed. With its plain new linens and pillows, the bed looked just as it did in Dunnavant's, Huntsville's department store. She gave the bedspread a firm tug and it was instantly taut and straight.

She had left such beautiful bedding back home . . . home, before Nordhausen, before the cottage. There were times when she thought about her grandmother's matelassé coverlet. Oh, how she loved that quilt, its raised stitches a map of the world. When she closed her eyes she could smell that wonderful old house in Heidelberg, the damp breeze off the Rhine through the windows, apples and cinnamon from the spätzle crackling in the kitchen, and she could hear her mother's soft footsteps and see her blue-bordered apron and her flaxen hair pulled back off her sweet, loving face. But of course those kinds of things had to be left. *Had the coverlet survived? Who slept beneath it now?* She did often wonder and the memory of such things gave rise to a sadness, a melancholy that could pour out and fill her like water in a tub if she left open the spigot.

Maria slammed off those thoughts, focusing on the sound of her husband talking about the calculus and chemistry of trajectory optimization. It was a soothing sound that could drive away the demons. True, Hans had designed rockets used by his country as weapons—he did his duty during war—but he was certainly no goose-stepping SS fanatic, those party elite with their infectious talk of destiny who took over Germany's rocket program. He wasn't even a Nazi party *member*, just an intellectual, an academic, at worst, a starry-eyed dreamer. The man never even wore a uniform, save his white lab jacket.

Yes, there was so much for which to be grateful all around her, everything now straight and white and clean. That was the scent of this room, detergent and bleach. It was medicinal, and like his talk of chemistry, and the white jacket, there was something reassuring about that, like knowing there was a doctor around.

She knew her American girlfriends would tease her about her feelings. *Oh, how so silly and frivolous they could be.* But without understanding her past, how could they ever really understand her?

Passion. She knew about that. *Especially* the irrational kind. How many times had she lain under that spotless white bedspread in this bleached-clean room thinking about *him*, the American pilot—James Cooper—with his black hair, and dark eyes, and hands both tender and strong? She knew all about crazy, hot-blooded—*entirely unforeseen*—passion, and she had the secret memories of it, her four days and nights with him in that cottage, to take to bed for the rest of her life. And though it had been twelve years since she had last seen him, she could shape and reshape the images and feelings to suit herself, making them seem fresh and detailed and vivid, like something that could actually happen anew.

Yes, she knew all about passion—and she certainly didn't need it in her real life. She needed Hans. Dear, sweet Hans. He had gotten her out of Germany when the world was collapsing. He had been there for her, and she knew he always would be. He was someone to build a life with, a foundation that was as solid and dependable as the science he loved so much. And she cherished him for that. Hans Reinhardt was a good man.

In a world where unspeakable horrors were kept at bay by the flimsy veneer of civil society, how could her friends really ever understand *anything* without seeing what she had seen firsthand?

Maria opened the Bakelite jewelry box on her dresser, removed the pearl studs Hans had recently given her, and put them on. They were modest but lovely, like her new life in Huntsville, Alabama.

Looking at the colorful comic book images taped to the slightly open bedroom door—rockets and spacemen and mutant alien creatures—Maria knocked.

"Peter, you almost ready?" she asked, pushing open the door and walking into her son's room. He was dressed in crisp white slacks and a navy blue blazer.

"Wow, Mom, you look like a movie star. And you smell good too."

"Thank you, and you look very handsome," she said, and remembered something. "Oh, could you zip the back, honey?"

She turned, shoulders forward, as he zipped up her dress, the brass buttons on his blazer sleeves jingling.

"So are you guys digging a bomb shelter?"

"No, I don't think so."

Finished zipping her dress, he put his face near hers, squinting his eyes. "Have you already built it and you're just not telling anyone?"

"No, Peter. We don't have a secret bomb shelter." These were reasonable questions, so she tried to be measured in her responses.

"I saw workers leaving today, Mom. Tell the truth!"

"My, you have quite an imagination." She straightened his red-and-white repp tie. "But they were installing dogwood trees, not an underground bunker."

"So what happens if the Russians attack? You know with the base here, Huntsville is probably one of their first targets."

"Your father knows more about how to keep us safe than virtually anyone in the country. So you have nothing to worry about."

"Mom, I know I'll be safe. We have drills every week at school, and my dorm has a huge fallout shelter in the basement. And Dad spends most of his time on base, which has safe places to go. But what happens to *you*? This house doesn't have a basement, and if you don't have a bomb shelter, where will you go if they strike when you're alone? Even if you duck and cover, the fallout from a blast will come right through these windows."

"Oh, my dear, you are so sweet to worry about me, but you must stop. Really, Peter, there is simply nothing to worry about."

"She's right, son," Hans said, standing in the doorway. "There is not going to be a war because the Russians know that the United States has superior technology on its side. It would be suicidal for them to try anything. And if they did, and you were away at school, I would take good care of Mom. So you worry about geometry and let me worry about the Ruskies. Okay, son?"

"Okay, Dad!"

"Now put on your shoes and let's get going."

Peter sat on the edge of his bed and began putting on his brown bucks, as Maria and Hans walked together down the hall, past the entryway table with its little stack of mail and several women's magazines, into the living room.

The television was on, sound off, playing an advertisement set in the kitchen of a brand-new ranch house featuring a woman who looked remarkably like Maria extolling what appeared to be the life-changing virtues of using Jell-O brand gelatin.

"Maybe we *should* have a bomb shelter," Maria said, her voice low so Peter couldn't hear her. "The Hendricksons up the street just finished theirs. What *would* we do?"

"We don't need a bomb shelter."

"Half the people in the neighborhood are putting them in."

"Yes, well, they will make good wine storage."

"Hans—"

"There is not going to be a war."

"The Russians have American weapons on their backdoor step now. Right? And they have their satellite flying right over America several times a day. How can you know *what* they are going to do?" She studied him. "Hans. It is not like you to be so dismissive about something so unpredictable. You have insurance for everything."

Hans sighed, realizing she knew him too well to accept that he wasn't concerned. "Cinderblock walls and dirt are about as protective as Chantilly lace."

"But I thought the government is encouraging people to build these shelters."

"Maria, if a nuclear device detonates within a hundred and fifty miles of Huntsville, there is no shelter. And the government is well aware of this."

Maria looked down, eyebrows furrowing, as if her head had become too heavy to hold with this revelation.

Peter charged in. "All set!"

"Wonderful!" Hans said with a clap of his hands, lightening the mood. "Let us go listen to your mother fill this city with beautiful music!"

Hans patted his son on the shoulder and looked to Maria, who was still standing there, processing.

"Mom? You okay?" Peter asked.

Her son's voice snapped her out of her thoughts and Maria lifted her head.

"Of course I am okay." She reached for her violin case on the hall table, next to the growing mail stack, peeked into the polished chrome-framed mirror, and put a smile on her face.

Her skin smooth and glowing like that of a girl in a Noxzema skin cream ad, smile held firmly in place, she turned to face them. "Yes, let us go make music and raise some money for our new symphony."

The three of them headed for the door. But before they got there, the expression on Maria's face was supplanted, once again, by worry.

She wanted to believe that Hans was right, that there wouldn't be a war. But after surviving those dark years in Germany, she had developed what seemed to be a sixth sense that told her when to worry. And this was one of those times.

Abruptly, Peter whipped around and ran back toward the hall table.

"Peter—!" Maria called out in surprise.

The boy grabbed a violin bow from the table and ran back to them with it.

"I think you might need this!" Peter said, handing the bow to Maria.

She laughed, taking the bow. "Thank you."

As the family continued on toward the door, Hans mussed the boy's hair, turning to him. "Your mother's father had a saying about violins and bows," Hans said, with a look at Maria. "Remember, darling?"

Maria nodded. "Every violin has a perfect bow, just like a man and a woman."

"Interesting," Peter said. "So which one of you is the violin, and which one the bow?"

"We'll talk about that later," said Hans, sharing a playful smile with his wife.

THE GIFT OF
PERFECT PITCH

O n Saturday evening, driving east down Clinton Avenue into the heart of the sleepy downtown, the Reinhardts could see the bright lights of the hotel several blocks away. At twelve stories, the Russel Erskine Hotel was not only the tallest building in Huntsville but by far the most glamorous. The site of the first cocktail lounge in North Alabama, the hotel was the venue of choice throughout the region for civic events, debutante parties, society weddings, and important business affairs.

Hans pulled his sleek Oldsmobile 88 up to the front of the hotel under the overhanging marquee. It was lit with lines of brilliant bulbs, just like a Broadway theater.

Hans hopped out, left the Olds with a valet, and joined Maria and Peter at the curb. Peter stood there for a moment, squinting at all the light gleaming in the big plateglass windows along the front of the hotel, a *White Persons Only* sign embossed on one near the doors. Hans put his arm around his son and, the family close together, Maria carrying her violin case by its handle, they walked up the carpeted strip of sidewalk and through the double wood and glass doors held open by doormen.

Inside, the lobby buzzed with people in formal wear and military dress uniform, mingling around the ten-foot-high triple-tiered marble fountain. Water gurgled from the top into a circular pool at the base, the fine mist adding an air of freshness to the room. Near the lobby walls were groupings of deep leather club chairs and dark wood tables and stained glass Tiffany lamps. Ponderous potted ferns were placed throughout. Though the hotel, built in the 1930s, maintained its historic charm, the austerity of the war years had been supplanted by a newfound and distinctly southern sense of sumptuousness.

Peter remained wide-eyed, observing and absorbing everything. Rich rolled carpets with boldly colored Moorish patterning led off to the Blue Room and Gold Room on the left, the Rocket Room lounge up the white marble staircase straight ahead, and through the great doors to the right—the ballroom.

The aroma of roasting garlic-rubbed prime rib wafted invitingly from the ballroom and intermingled with the bittersweet concoction of fine perfumes and tobacco. It was heady and sublime standing in the lobby of the Russel Erskine Hotel on this night.

Directly over the ballroom door hung a large red banner: *Thank You for Supporting Our Huntsville Symphony Orchestra!*

"The chairs are fabulous!" said Carolyn, sliding in next to Maria in the center of the crowd in the lobby.

"Oh, good!" Maria beamed, displaying a touch of relief. "They are all here?"

"All two hundred and sixty-five, and they match perfectly." She turned to Hans. "Your spouse is a genius."

"Brilliant, beautiful, and gifted," he said. "That is my Maria."

"Stop." She slapped his forearm playfully.

"Can you believe the turnout?" Carolyn said as she looked around, purse dangling from her arm, her hair solid as stone. "That's George Wallace over there, our next governor, I'm betting."

"You have done an outstanding job, Carolyn," Maria said. "This is very exciting."

Klaus Bauer, a slight graying man with a violin case in hand, approached Maria and kissed her on the cheek. "Good evening, Maria. You look stunning as ever."

"Thank you, Klaus. I am so glad you were able to join us. Are you ready to play tonight?"

"I have been practicing. Though I fear I could spend the rest of my days practicing and never play anywhere near as well as you." His English was perfect, though his German accent was heavy.

"You are a wonderful violinist," Maria said.

"Yes, you are!" Carolyn added. "We are lucky to have such a gifted violinist join our symphony on such short notice."

"You ladies are too kind."

A mathematics expert who had taught Hans when he was at the university in Heidelberg—an early mentor of sorts—Klaus spent most of his time alone, plotting trajectories. It was lonely, tedious behind-the-scenes work but nevertheless important to the rocket program.

Klaus saw someone waving at him. "See you inside," he said, raising his eyebrows in excitement as he headed off.

"How is school, Peter?" Carolyn bent forward, leaning down toward the boy.

"It's okay."

"Are you taking music classes?" she asked in a sing-song tone. "The HSO is going to need to beef up our string section."

Peter knew he needed to answer her politely, but he always hated when adults spoke to him as though he were an idiot. "I never really took to violin."

"Really?" Carolyn seemed surprised.

Before the boy expressed his true thoughts, Hans stepped in.

"Peter won first place in the Darlington science fair this year. He built a working volcano."

"How wonderful!" Carolyn exclaimed, eyes wide, brows up. "I remember doing that in grade school—a baking soda and vinegar eruption!"

"I used ammonium dichromate," Peter said. "Which contains a common oxidizer, the dichromate, and a reducer, the ammonium, making it thermodynamically unstable when ignited."

"I see." Carolyn's blank face quickly put on a time-honored southern smile—the perfect antidote for awkward moments like this.

"It produced a twelve-foot flame," Peter reported, a simple matter of facts.

Maria jumped in. "Outside, on the playground," she said with a hint of nervous laughter.

"Well, aren't you clever," Carolyn said to the boy, and then turned to Hans. "I wonder where you got *that* talent."

"Yes," Maria said, stroking the back of her son's head. "Peter takes after his father."

Penny wiggled up and joined them, tall cocktail glass balanced effortlessly in her hand. "Well, I think his father should give serious consideration to naming this important new rocket after his mother. 'The Maria' has a nice ring to it."

Hans laughed. "Perhaps the one that aims for the moon. This one is already called 'Juno,' which hopefully conveys its peaceful intent."

Sabine, hair in a tight bun, heavily made up, joined them, a tumbler of whiskey in hand. "I believe we are going to pull this off tonight," she said in her slow accented way, followed by an exhalation of relief.

"Yes, we are!" said Penny, who extended her glass, clinking Sabine's, after which they both drank deeply.

"I hope it's okay to make an announcement about this new rocket tonight," Carolyn said.

"Of course!" Hans exclaimed. "We want everyone to know about the rocket that finally takes America into space!" He lowered his voice a little. "Although truth be told, the rocket is really not so new. We are essentially just modifying the Redstone, which of course is just a dressed up V2."

"Hans! Talking shop?" Wernher Von Braun, also German, dashing and charming in his impeccable tuxedo, joined them. "This is supposed to be a party."

With his robust laugh, Von Braun shook Hans's hand in the firm and casual manner of men who are very close.

"Hello, Peter," Von Braun said, looking admiringly at the boy. "So good to see you, young man."

Peter lit up. "Good to see you too, Dr. Von Braun."

"Wernher, do you know my dear friends Carolyn Propst and Penny Tucker?" Maria asked.

He thought for a moment, then, "Your husbands fly for one of our design teams, right?"

"That's right! On the rocket-assisted takeoff program," Carolyn said.

"My, what a memory you have, Herr Professor," Penny said.

"They are good men," Von Braun said.

"Most of the time." Penny knew how to employ her drawl to make that kind of remark particularly playful. It worked well on Von Braun, who laughed.

Maria saw her friends spot their husbands across the room. The lean men, in their air force dress whites, buzz-cut hair, stood together talking spiritedly, almost conspiratorially, to each other. There was something about aviators, these men who lived to push the limits— they projected an attitude that Maria could pick up even across a densely packed room like this. They displayed all the proper re-spect for rules and regulations, saying "yes, sir" and snapping off sharp salutes to those of higher rank, but inside, there was pure joyous irreverence. A sense that all the trappings of the uniform were but fanciful trivialities to be tolerated for the privilege of fly-ing. You could see it in their cocky grins. Perhaps it was a prerequi-site of the job, Maria had sometimes thought, this true loyalty only to one another, to country, and to the dream of flight.

Von Braun noticed that he was being waved over by an army colonel, but before he left he turned to Maria. "Before I forget . . ." He reached into a pocket inside his jacket and produced a small, flattish gift-wrapped package, and handed it to Maria. "These are for you."

"What is this?"

Von Braun and Hans exchanged knowing looks. "One way to find out," Hans said.

Flattered and unable to contain her expression of curiosity, Ma-ria opened the gift.

"Hopefully someday soon Huntsville will have many music stores," Von Braun said.

"Among other things," Hans said.

"But until then—"

Maria held in her hands two square envelopelike packages, new sets of exquisite violin strings. "Real gut strings. Oh, I have not seen a new set of these since . . . well, since Hans gave me my violin twelve years ago."

Everyone laughed a little, enjoying the moment, as Maria ran her long fingers gently over the packages. "Where in the world did you get them?"

"As it turns out, the army flies fairly regularly to Vienna these days. And you have good connections to the army."

She turned to both her husband and Von Braun. "Thank you."

"Thank *you* for all you do," Hans said.

Von Braun ignored the colonel vigorously waving him over. "*Mögen Ihre Tage mit der Süße eines Liedes und Ihre Nächte mit der Rhapsodie vom Frieden gefüllt sein.*"

Moved by his words, Sabine nodded.

And then Von Braun continued in English for the benefit of Maria's other friends who were lingering. "May your days be filled with the sweetness of song, and your nights with the rhapsody of peace."

As Von Braun began to walk off, he leaned close to Hans. "Six a.m. tomorrow?"

"I will be there."

Von Braun patted his old friend firmly on the shoulder, a shorthand that conveyed the gravity of their work, and then moved on to the colonel, who was waiting to introduce him to a man in business attire. "Hello, Senator Sparkman," Von Braun said, now focusing the full force of his attention on the senator.

"Well, let's get those new strings purring," Penny said, interlocking her arm with Maria's.

Carolyn checked her watch. "You two better hurry." She turned to Sabine. "Help me set up in the dining room?"

"Of course," Sabine said, happy to be of use, as they took off.

Maria turned to her husband and son. "Do you boys mind?"

"Of course not," Hans said. "Go get ready. Peter and I have some people from D.C. to talk to about funding our Mars mission."

Maria gave Peter a kiss on the head, then turned and quickly walked off with Penny close at her side.

Hans lowered his head toward Peter. "Interested in a Coke, son?"

"That's affirmative, sir." The boy beamed up at his dad.

◆   ◆   ◆

Maria sat at a shiny Formica and metal table in the windowless
storage room adjacent to the ballroom kitchen carefully inserting
the new strings into her violin. It was a beautiful instrument, large,
reddish-toned, with a heavy glossy varnish.

Penny stood over her, watching attentively. Behind them, in the
open door, waiters and dishwashers and cooks' assistants scurried
back and forth. Posted near the door was an ever-present yellow-
and-black fallout shelter sign, under its trefoil of three inverted tri-
angles a circle stating "Capacity 50." The stacks of chairs usually
stored here gone, the room was fairly spacious. Tall wire racking,
holding sealed pails of wheat and sugar and beans and the likes,
lined the walls.

"You look like you could do that blindfolded," Penny said as
Maria placed the ball end of a new string into its hole in the tail-
piece, inserted the other end into a tuning peg, and began to tighten
the peg.

"I have been doing this a long time." Maria loosened another
tuning peg and began removing another string. "The trick is not to
remove all the strings at once. You always want to have three of the
four strings in place." She removed the string, placed it on the table
with the other old ones, and began inserting another new one.
"That keeps the sound post tight so it does not fall. This is a hard
lesson for an impatient six-year-old to learn, but I did. 'One at a
time, Maria. Always one at a time.' My father would say to me."

"You started when you were six?"

"Actually, I was three. Music was very important to my father
and he was determined to teach me." She looked off, smiling at the
recollection. "Some children get bedtime stories. My father would
hum Bach to me, the sonatas and partitas for solo violin—major
works and the man knew all six entirely by heart."

"Sounds like you had a very smart father."

"Oh, yes. He was a professor, at the University of Heidelberg. Philosophy, but he was a scholar in several fields—archaeology, history, languages—and was a great thinker about pretty much everything. Although, my mother died before the war and I do think that raising a teenage girl on his own finally stumped him." She laughed as she worked on her violin, remembering. "He would have liked Alabama, I think."

Penny just watched her, intrigued, and even though she wasn't asking, Maria knew she had to explain. "Heidelberg escaped the Allied bombings, but Mannheim, just up the river, did not. It was hit frequently, and one night my father and two of his friends brought bread and medicine to some of their colleagues in the city center, which was firebombed for two nights straight while they were there. None of them returned."

Despite being intrigued and even moved by the firsthand nature of the story, Penny was a military wife, and her father had led an infantry company onto Omaha Beach. As a rule, her sympathies for a German could go only so far. However, she very much believed in trying to judge people for who they were, as individuals, and sitting in front of Maria Reinhardt, watching her delicate but assured hands, Penny could not help but to feel empathy in her heart. The more she had gotten to know Maria since the government had relocated the Reinhardts to Huntsville, the more Penny had grown to like her and admire her.

"You know, I was watching you for a moment back there," Penny said, deftly switching to lighter conversation. "Right before I joined y'all, I was watching you standing there, so beautiful and poised in that gorgeous dress, violin case in your hand. I swear, if Alabama had a princess, it would be you."

"You are teasing me," Maria said, looking down at her hands.

"A little. Sure, that's my nature. But I'm serious." Penny leaned in close to Maria's face. "You've rebuilt a good life, honey. From scratch. A hardworking man, a great son, your music, growing respect in the community. I know it's been quite a journey—for you *personally*—but look where you are, look where you landed. Maria, you are an inspiration."

Hands resting easily aside her violin, Maria was openly touched by Penny's words and remained silent as she thought about them. Yes, a journey it had been, to say the least.

"What do I say?" Penny continued and then began to head for the door. "Break a string?" No, that wasn't right. "How about just— good luck."

"Good luck is something we all can use. You are a good friend, Penny. Thank you."

"You better hurry, sugar, or poor Carolyn will have herself a conniption." And with a smile, Penny walked out.

Tightening a peg on the violin, Maria finished restringing her instrument. Then she picked up the bow, lying atop the table, careful not to touch the hairs, put the violin on her shoulder and under her chin, and drew the bow steadily across the new strings.

The tone was of course a bit wobbly, but she could hear the force and projection promised by the lovely new strings as she began to tune them.

Moving the bow back and forth across the strings, Maria expertly adjusted each of the four pegs, stretching and tightening the four strings—the G, D, A, and E—into tune, a critical and challenging task for even the most experienced of players. With her perfect pitch, Maria could accomplish this swiftly and with ease. It was perhaps the greatest gift she had inherited from her father. Not a trait that always passed through genealogy, it gave Maria great comfort and joy to have this eternal connection to her father.

As Maria made the adjustments, her face softened with an inherent love while the instrument correspondingly came into tune. Maria typically preferred to "play in" a new pair of strings for a few days before performing with them, but given how old her current strings were, causing them to produce a discernible flabbiness in the low timbres, not to mention the growing risk of a thinning string breaking, she was excited to play the new strings, working with any slight tonal fluctuations that might occur as they stretched out to their full flexibility.

Maria looked up, spotting a young black girl in a spotless white uniform standing in the room near the door, listening and watching.

"Hi," Maria said, continuing to play and finalize her tuning.

The girl was shy but mesmerized by the tuning sounds of Maria's violin. Her hair in tight, neat pigtails, the girl was pretty, her intelligent deep brown eyes not missing a thing.

Maria tried again. "What is your name?"

"I like your fiddle," the girl said, staring at it and just standing there motionless.

"Thank you." Hoping she would open up more, Maria pulled the bow while adjusting the E peg. The girl continued to watch. Maria could hear that the E string was still playing a tiny bit flat and she made the most delicate of adjustments to compensate. She knew that no one else would probably ever notice, but Maria always felt that music should be played as flawlessly as possible. Life may be difficult and imperfect, she learned when she was a teen, but music doesn't have to be—that was part of its magic. If you knew how to make it, you could always escape to its protective world where everything could be made just right.

"It looks old," the girl said, eyes darting all over the violin as she studied it from her distance.

"It is. It was made in 1830 by an Italian man. His name was Giovanni Francesco Pressenda." Maria held the instrument up so the girl could peek into one of the f-holes. On the inside back of the violin was an old rectangular label with the information. The little girl's face lit up with curiosity as she leaned forward.

Maria's love for the violin was evident in the gentle but secure way she held it, as one might hold a child. Though Pressendas were certainly known to be fine instruments, they weren't particularly rare, like the expensive Stradivarius violins played by famous musicians at Carnegie Hall, but Maria had played her beloved Pressenda through moments of great hardship and joy, and she treasured it as though it were a living extension of herself. And, in a sense, it was.

"It's got a good sound," the little girl said, fidgeting with a pigtail. "Are those strings sheep gut?"

"They are. That is all I play with, if I can."

"They're the best."

"I think so." Maria was delighted, and surprised, and wondered how this young girl would know such a thing. "I've never seen them around Huntsville," Maria went on. "In fact, I do not know anywhere in Alabama to get them. Do you?"

A voice yelled out from the hallway. "Josephine!"

The girl jumped and turned, quickly heading for the door.

Before she left, she turned back to Maria. "Your E is flat," she said, and was gone.

Maria just sat there for a moment, staring openmouthed in disbelief. She had to check. So she picked up her bow and pulled it across the strings, cocking her head, listening very carefully, and, sure enough, that E was still the tiniest bit flat. Even Maria with her expert-level perfect pitch could hardly hear it, but it was there.

Tickled and amazed, Maria adjusted the E peg again, just a

hair. She thought about going after the girl, but before she had much of a chance to consider that further, Carolyn popped her head in.

"The rest of the orchestra is there and they open the doors in five minutes." Carolyn made herself talk extra slowly but, literally wringing her hands, she was clearly anxious.

A portrait of grace, Maria rose. "That is all the time in the world." She put the beautiful Pressenda back in its case, tossed the old strings in a nearby trash can, and walked out the door, Carolyn nervously in tow.

IN ANOTHER LIFE

Thank y'all so much for coming out tonight," Carolyn said into the standing steel-and-mesh microphone, her voice reverberating through the ballroom. "Your support is providing our great city with a symphony that will be a source of joy and pride as the whole country looks to Huntsville not only to protect our nation but to deliver her future."

A rousing round of applause was enthusiastically offered up by the nearly three hundred attendees in the ballroom. They sat comfortably on the cherrywood and white vinyl upholstered Stakmore A-frame folding chairs, elaborate china and silver and crystal settings before them on twenty-five seventy-two-inch-round tables covered with white damask linens.

At the far end of the room, directly behind Carolyn, sat eight members of the symphony, primarily German colleagues of Hans's, music stands before them, instruments in hand, violin, viola, cello, bass, clarinet, horn, bassoon, and holding the lead violin was Maria, the concertmaster.

Finding that she actually enjoyed the attention, Carolyn continued, very much in her element now. "And if y'all will allow me a few more moments, I would like to recognize some extraordinarily special men we have with us tonight."

While she spoke, a few people continued to filter into the ballroom, others meandered away from the staffed bar at the back, cocktails and place cards in hand, finding their seats.

"Eight years ago, Huntsville, Alabama, was a sleepy little cotton and mill town, until the arrival of one hundred and eighteen German scientists changed our city nearly overnight. We now have one of the army's biggest bases in the world right here, with over three thousand people alone working on guided-missile projects. Rocket City they're calling us!"

Carolyn smiled broadly, pausing for the applause. She had quite a knack for this sort of thing.

"Now, I know some of you have already heard rumors about the big news today," Carolyn continued, excitement growing in her voice. "But let me make it official—our hometown team has been chosen to provide the rocket that will put America's first satellite into space! So please join me in offering special thanks and recognition to mission leaders Arthur Rudolph, Karl Janssen, Hans Reinhardt, and, of course, our favorite son, Wernher Von Braun."

She pointed emphatically at the men, and the attendees not only applauded vigorously, many even cheering, but pushed back their chairs and continued their ovation on their feet, the entire room looking admiringly at the German men.

"Good luck in Florida!" Carolyn's voice boomed.

Finally, everyone finished applauding and sat back down. With a nod to the eight musicians behind her, Carolyn went on. "Now, we have a very special treat for y'all tonight. Eight members of our new symphony are here and will play some delightful chamber music they have prepared, the Schubert Octet, Adagio movement."

And with a flourish, Carolyn stepped away, and the room was

silent. A cough and a cleared throat from the back echoed out. A few china plates in the kitchen clacked together. Finally, sensing the anticipation in the room, Maria picked up her bow—the other members of the group watching her intently—and she began, pulling her bow firmly across the new strings. The other members instantly began playing as well, filling the room with loud, full, and stunningly majestic chamber music.

Though it probably wasn't designed for such, it would have been hard to find a more ideal venue anywhere in the Deep South than the ballroom at the Russel Erskine Hotel for a chamber music concert. With its hand-cut crystal chandeliers, massive scarlet-red drapery with gold ropes and tassels, polished marble floors, and intricate raised and gilded panels, and egg-and-dart moldings and medallions, all along the walls and crowns and ceiling, the formal hall could have been plucked from eighteenth-century Versailles. Likewise, the acoustics were remarkable.

Maria and the other members of the ensemble played comfortably and accurately, as though they had been performing together for years. While the Germans were all highly skilled musicians, and all knew the Schubert Octet quite well, none of them would have ever dreamed when they were younger that they would be in Alabama performing it as they were.

Schubert's work was always much beloved by the members of the orchestra, not only for the classical Gothic Germanic style of his melodies but perhaps even more so for their exhilarating and romantic nature, the tension continually rising and releasing in the unfolding musical narrative. But tonight there was something exceptional, ethereal, in this first performance, and while leading it, Maria gave herself to it fully and completely.

In the audience, a woman in a black taffeta cocktail dress with an impossibly tiny waist closed her eyes, a beatific smile on her face, as she focused on the melody. A man in a slim-cut gray flannel suit tapped one of his penny loafers in time as though he was playing right on stage with the orchestra.

Despite the dress clothes and makeup and carefully set hair, Maria did not restrict her performance in any way, giving in to the full physicality of it, the tornadic force of the music being created, the music she guided, carrying her away from and above all else. Violin pressed securely under her chin, the hundred or so long, taut horsehairs gripping and abrading the four new strings as she pulled and shot the bow back and forth, rising and releasing, building and relaxing, the story of the composition coming to its beautiful, deeply stirring peak, she looked out into the audience as she played and saw it all, them all, and thought again about what Penny had said— from the ruins of war, from death's door, Maria really had made a nice life for herself here in Alabama. And she breathed deeply with a sigh of relief, and she played on.

Looking out into the audience, she blinked, shaking her head at what she saw. At first she thought it was a trick of the music. But as she played and stared, and played and stared, she unmistakably recognized the latecomer who sauntered confidently but quietly through the open double doors.

Still athlete-trim, sable-brown hair neat and short, James Cooper was quite a sight in his dress whites, sharply adorned with medals and ribbons and military decorations. He had a girl with him, probably twenty-two, fresh-faced, maddeningly attractive. As they made their way to their table, they laughed closely and blithely—a little too much so for a few seated people they passed—finally greeting and sitting down next to several other air force officers and their dates.

It seemed unreal to Maria as she played, the entire room watching her, while she watched him from this distance, as though time had come undone and folded back in on itself, some recipe gone wrong in the oven, the past by chance touching the edge of the present. It was a history of which she had never spoken, that she had thought was finally put behind her, at least from consciousness, and now while she performed, in front of an audience that included virtually everyone from her new life, it overtook her.

1945

Cooper stood in the cottage, gun aimed at Maria.

She placed her violin and bow on the shelf near her and then just looked at him, unblinking. "If you're going to shoot me, then shoot me."

"Sit down."

She did not comply.

"I said, sit down."

She simply stood there in her light blue linen dress, bare shoulders back, awaiting her fate.

"Look, I don't want to hurt you."

"Is that why you drop bombs on my head?"

"You weren't personally the target."

"Is that why you aim a handgun at me?"

He glanced over at an upright piano near him and slowly, carefully, laid his .45 caliber Colt M1911 down on top of it.

And as soon as it was down, before he'd even looked back at her— she ran at him and slammed a hard punch right into his chin! He stumbled back into the piano, his open hands banging on the keys.

"Hey!" he yelled, as she threw another punch, but this one he blocked, grabbing her wrist and twisting her arm and throwing her onto the sofa like a sack of flour.

He stood over her, rubbing his dirty face. "Are you trying to get yourself killed?"

Catching her breath, she sat up. "I am not afraid to die."

"Well, I sure as hell am. Now cut it out. Just . . . just sit there and let me think." He rubbed his throbbing chin. "Damn, you've got a hook."

He looked around again, trying to get his bearings, remembering his survival and evasion training, assessing her. What was he dealing with here? Was this the face of the enemy? This skinny, crazy, beautiful girl he'd happened upon while trying to stay alive?

"Just shoot me," she said. "One way or another, my life is over."

"Well, we have a problem then, because I need your help. And apparently you need mine."

He took a few careful steps closer to her, tilting his head a little, looking at her intently. She really was beautiful. Huge wide-set sky-blue eyes, high symmetrical cheekbones, sharp jaw, impossibly smooth skin. He noticed the back of her linen dress was dark with moisture from her dampish blond hair. He could smell the lilac on her body and it was disorienting.

Focus, he told himself. Remember your training. The goal is to get out of here alive.

"My name is Cooper," he said. "Lieutenant James Cooper."

She just threw her head back, whipping around her mane of hair and staring at him hard, defiantly, uncertain of her next move. Moments ago she was ready to die, relieved to die. But instead she now had this man in her cabin, this man with his black hair and square shoulders and penetrating dark eyes upon her, who could lift her and toss her with ease. She was ready for the end, and this strong, dark stranger was standing in her way. Was he going to hurt her? She didn't know and she wasn't sure she cared. But he wanted something from her. He needed her help. And being needed suddenly reminded her, once again, that she was human, and had purpose, which only angered her more.

"Do you have a name?" he asked.

She continued glaring heatedly at him, willing her mouth to stay closed. For to offer that personal information felt like a first step of some kind.

"You know, when someone introduces himself," he said, "it's just polite to respond back."

There was something in his eyes—fear and compassion for her at once—and it touched her, so deeply there was nothing she could do about it.

"My name is Maria," she said, wondering now what was next.

1957

In the ballroom of the Russel Erskine Hotel, Maria played a solo on her violin and then the other seven members of the Huntsville Symphony ensemble jumped in, performing the final climactic part of the movement, the audience enraptured.

At his table toward the back of the room, something drew Cooper's attention away from the fawning girl next to him. He looked up. Was it the music? Was it the impassioned violin soloist? Cooper wasn't sure what was pulling at him, but as he listened to the performance, watching over all the heads in the crowd, he felt something powerful, a force of some kind. There was something familiar. He closed his eyes for a moment, listening. His date put her hand on his thigh, squeezing it, and he turned back to her, eyes open, laughing.

The ensemble group of the new Huntsville Symphony Orchestra finished the dramatic swelling conclusion of the Schubert piece with a precise and emotion-filled chord. Nearly instantly, the entire audience was on their feet, applauding graciously, and with vigor, everyone swept up in the festivity of the night.

The eight musicians all stood, smiling broadly, instruments in hand, and on Maria's cue they bowed.

As the audience cheered and the intensity increased, the musicians took repeated bows. But Maria did not stay until the audience stopped. She walked offstage, violin in hand.

Breathing heavily, she knew she had seen James—but it was clear that he didn't even notice her. Now surely he would not and, emotions churning, she no longer wanted all this attention on her. She melted into the crowd.

What had happened between them in that cabin in the final days of what seemed the end of the world changed her and saved her and destroyed her all at once—setting her on the path to who she was today. Did she dare speak to him again? Did she dare run from the chance to do just that? She didn't know, and just by allowing these thoughts, just by being in the same room with him, she could feel twelve years of carefully honed calm and cool and steadiness fading fast. She felt raw and vulnerable and was certain everyone could see it on her face. Could they all see who she really was now, the Maria she'd carefully hidden away?

She needed a drink.

Maria passed by her chair at the crowded table, nodding at people telling her "great job," and moved toward the back of the room to the bar.

"Riesling, please," she asked of the bartender, pointing at the special bottles of German wine brought in for the occasion. Even her voice sounded strange and tinny to her ears.

The bartender put a white cocktail napkin on the bar and placed her glass of the sweet golden wine on top of it. She could see the tiny streams of condensation running down the slender glass. As Maria reached for the glass, she heard a voice right behind her.

"Can I buy you a drink?" said James Cooper.

Maria froze, her arm extended toward the glass. The bright overhead light refracted in the glass and played across her eyes, causing her to look down. She felt a bead of perspiration growing just below her hairline. She knew she had to turn and face what was behind her.

Maria wiped her forehead with the back of her wrist, grabbed her glass by its long stem, found her most poised and calm smile, and turned.

And there was Cooper, grinning like the cocky aviator he was.

"The drinks are free," she said steadily, demurely sipping her wine through glossy red lips, a picture of beauty and composure.

"The best things in life always are," he said. "Wouldn't you agree?"

A MOMENT IN TIME

Maria and Cooper locked eyes, the rest of the room lost to them.

"What are you doing in Alabama?" she asked.

"I fly planes. A lot of that sort of thing going on here apparently."

"Yes, so I am told."

"And you? What brings you to the land of cotton? Old times here are not forgotten."

"My husband."

"Of course." He motioned his head toward her wedding ring. "Doesn't take a rocket scientist to see that."

Maria squinted her eyes at him, and then, in the subtlest way, a Mona Lisa smile emerged on her face. It was an elusive expression that Cooper seemed to relish and he said nothing to disturb it.

Her slender, elegant fingers wrapped lightly around the stem of her glass, she took a long, deep sip, her forehead down but her eyes up, never leaving his.

Over his shoulder, on the other side of the room, Maria noticed his date searching for him.

"Someone is looking for you."

He did not turn to look. "She having any luck?"

"She is pretty."

"Really? No wonder she's so difficult." His aviator grin exposed teeth as white and perfect as his pressed dress uniform. It was a honed bravado that Maria could see right through, his dark eyes vast and questioning.

She had a million questions for him as well. He knew that, she could plainly see. But before anything was asked, the charged moment was broken when Hans appeared, joining them.

Hans slipped in next to his wife, putting an arm around her. "There you are, darling. Hiding from your fans?"

Maria kissed him on the cheek, steadying herself. "I was catching my breath."

"And a glass of wine—good to see." Hans turned his gaze to Cooper, instinctively noting his rank insignia. "Good evening, Major."

"Good evening, Dr. Reinhardt. I was just congratulating your lovely wife on her riveting performance." Cooper immediately slipped into his dutiful officer tone.

"Have we met before?" Hans asked, looking to Maria and then back to Cooper.

"No," Cooper said. "But your work precedes you. In fact, let me offer my approbation to you too, doctor. If you ask me, America should've brought the V2 to Canaveral years ago. The war is over, right?"

"I like this man, Maria," Hans said with a friendly grin.

"Yes, he is obviously very smart." Maria took a sip of her wine, her gaze over the glass lingering on Cooper.

"Very smart indeed." Hans sized Cooper up, looking at the medals, ribbons, and badges on his uniform to draw a quick and comprehensive picture of his past. "You flew in the Allied campaign, received the Silver Star." It was a question as much as it was an assessment.

"I flew the P-51, eighty-seven sorties. Some of the last ones over Nordhausen."

The irony was charged like static electricity around them.

"Going after the V2," Hans said, nodding.

"That underground factory was not an easy target, by the way."

Maria looked back and forth between the two men, heart pounding, her tension growing all the more difficult to conceal. She was quite aware that, like many other Germans, Hans knew the P-51 Mustang all too well. It had terrorized so many cities, but, in particular, brash American pilots had flown the single-seat fighter-bomber to hit the V2 rocket plant tunneled into the Kohnstein mountain outside Nordhausen, again and again. Simply put, Cooper had been trying to kill Hans, along with his work and his men—but that, of course, was before Cooper was shot down and ended up in her cottage. *What would her husband do if he knew what had happened there?*

"The only problem with the V2," Hans finally said, "was that it was aimed at the wrong planet."

Cooper broke into laughter, and Hans joined him. And somehow the sight of the two former adversaries laughing together made Maria even more disquieted. Men, she thought, no matter race, creed, or country, they seemed to share a code, especially men that had known war.

Her eyes met Cooper's and tried to connect through to something beyond the words being uttered. For twelve years she'd lived her life thinking she would never again see this man, and here he was standing before her in a ballroom in Alabama. There was so much to say. Would she see him again? Did she allow herself the risk even to think about such a thing? Looking at him now took her straight back, images and feelings swirling, like she was being pulled into a vortex.

"You must be in town for the rocket-assisted takeoff program," she finally said to him.

"I am. RATO test pilot at your service. Just got in a few days ago. I'm stationed here indefinitely." He smiled at her.

What did *that* mean? Was he trying to tell her something? No, she was letting her imagination run . . . Oh, this was too much . . .

Cooper extended his hand to her, medals swaying on his broad chest. "It was a pleasure to meet you, ma'am." They shook hands for a long moment.

"Welcome to Huntsville," she said.

Hans put his arm around Maria and began walking her away. "Good evening, Major."

"Dr. Reinhardt—"

"Yes?" Hans said, turning back to face Cooper.

"Why us? Why did you leave Nordhausen and walk right into the advancing American forces? The Soviets would have given you anything you wanted. They'd have let you put a man on the moon by now. Why here?"

What a question, particularly in this setting. Maria could hardly believe he had asked it.

Hans paused, sizing up Cooper again, as if to make sure he hadn't missed something. Finally, Hans smiled at the younger man.

"We knew what we had created," Hans said. "We knew what it had done in the wrong hands and what it could do in even worse. Von Braun likes to say that science does not have a moral dimension. It is like a knife. If you give it to a surgeon or a murderer, each will use it differently. So we knew that no matter what the cost, no matter what the sacrifice, it must go only to a people who were guided by the Bible."

Then Hans turned to Maria. "We really should be getting back to the table, dear. We are being delinquent parents."

Maria watched Cooper take in that last bit of information.

"Our son is with us tonight," she said. "He is eleven going on forty, but we should get back to him."

Maria under his arm, Hans began to walk away. "Enjoy your evening, Major," he said. "I hear the prime rib is superb."

While Cooper stood there and watched them walk off, people congratulating them as they went, his pretty dolled-up date slid up, but to her displeasure his attention was still elsewhere.

After a moment, Maria turned and looked back at him—*James Cooper alive and right here in her town, in an instant everything had changed. What now?*—and then she quickly turned away.

As Maria's glance left Cooper's, it was noticed by someone else, a heavyset man not far from Cooper, at the other end of the bar, air force colonel Mike Adams. A highball of bourbon in his bear paw of a hand, Adams watched all three of them. After the navy debacle, his career was going to benefit tremendously from the mission's new direction, but if things went south because something was overlooked, it was his neck on the line. So a hotshot air force test pilot exchanging glances with Hans Reinhardt's wife was the kind of thing that wasn't going to be overlooked.

FALCONS

H ans at the wheel of the Oldsmobile, his right arm comfortably resting on the back of the bench seat, the Reinhardts drove east, out of downtown, heading back toward Blossomwood.

"I thought it was a lovely event," Hans said, tapping lightly on her shoulder.

"Yes, it was very nice." Maria stared straight ahead, Old Town street lamps flashing on her face as they drove along.

"Von Braun had a very productive conversation with Senator Sparkman. If the launch is a success, Redstone is in line to receive two billion dollars next year. That is twenty-five percent of the army's entire budget. It will be in the *New York Times* tomorrow. No wonder the other branches of the service are taking such an interest in our work. They know where we are heading." He pointed up. "That RATO test pilot had astronaut candidate written on his forehead, didn't you think?"

"Yes, he was very . . . very much a pilot."

"He was buttering you up."

She furrowed her brow at him, then looked away.

"Your friend Penny's dress was a bit daring."

That got her attention. "When did you start noticing my friends' attire?"

"When a bosom is presented for all the world to see, all the world sees."

Her trance broken, Maria laughed. "You are a gossip, Herr Doktor."

"And you were a star tonight."

Hans looked in the rearview mirror, noticing that a dark sedan behind them seemed to be traveling the exact same route they were taking.

Then he turned briefly toward the back. "What did you think of your mother's performance tonight, Peter?"

"You guys were all great, Mom." The boy sat in the very middle of the backseat.

"Thank you, Peter."

"Almost as good as a Bo Diddley concert."

"Bo who?" Maria asked.

"I thought Elvis Presley was your favorite," Hans said.

"Elvis is great. Bo Diddley is better. He's the real thing."

"My word, what are they teaching you at Darlington?" Maria asked.

Peter leaned forward, hands on the back of the front seat. "Mom, do you think I'll be at Darlington in high school?"

"It is quite a privilege for you to attend the Darlington School," Hans said.

"Well, what if I don't want to go, what if I want to live here with you guys—"

Maria could see Hans shooting her a look. "We will cross that bridge when we get to it," she said. "Okay, sweetheart?"

"Well, what if I'm already at a bridge and I want to live at home?"

"Is everything okay at school?" Maria asked, even though she knew she was opening a door Hans would not like.

"Yeah, everything's fine, just sometimes I miss home. I miss you guys."

"That is perfectly natural for a boy your age," Hans said. "And that is why it is so nice to have you home on the weekends. But you must trust our judgment, son. This is a very fine school and you are getting an elite and advantaged education, not to mention making friendships and developing contacts with similarly gifted young people from important families. This will all serve you very well later in life. You will see."

"I know, Dad."

"Good." Hans ruffled his son's hair. "Good boy."

"I just want you to know that I'm getting older, so if I did live at home again, I could take more care of myself. I wouldn't take up as much of your time as I used to."

Maria brought her hand to her mouth and blinked back tears, all of which was picked up by Hans. He could see Maria getting upset once again by this conversation. The subject had to be changed, and fast.

"Some people think rock 'n' roll is just a fad," Hans said loudly. "Something that will be gone in just a few years. What do you think, Peter?"

"I think it's going to be around for a long time. I think astronauts are going to listen to it on their way to Mars."

Hans laughed heartily, relieved to have successfully changed the subject. "Well, we will see about that. In the meantime, when we get home, I have something I want you to hear."

"Dad, I did all my math last night and I can do the English tomorrow night, could I *please* go to the base with you tomorrow afternoon for just a little while?"

"Oh, Peter, tomorrow is going to be difficult, with the static-launch prep and all the trajectory—"

Maria pinched her husband's arm. "Hans, your son is asking to spend a few hours with his father at the office."

Hans looked in the rearview mirror, then he quickly made a turn onto a quiet residential street. "Okay, Peter."

"Thank you!"

"Why are you turning here?" Maria looked around.

"Just a moment." Looking in the rearview mirror again, Hans saw the dark sedan make the same turn, following him.

Hans slowed his Oldsmobile, and the sedan behind him slowed as well.

"Hans, what are you doing?"

He pulled his car over to the side of the street, parking it under a large oak tree.

"Dad, what's going on?" Peter looked around, seeing the dark vehicle behind them too.

"Stay here," Hans said, and he quickly jumped out of the car.

Chewing on a fingernail, Maria watched as Hans waved to the sedan, which had slowed in the middle of the street. After a moment, the sedan pulled over and Hans approached.

Maria and Peter both sat up on their knees, turned around, and stared out the big back window of the Olds.

The driver's window of the sedan went down, and Hans walked right up to the open window, smiled, and exchanged what looked like some friendly words with the driver.

Then, just as unexpectedly, Hans tipped his head to the driver and started walking back purposefully toward the Olds. The driver's window went back up and the sedan drove on, passing Hans, and then Maria and Peter in the Olds.

Hans got back in his car, and Maria started questioning him before he even sat down. "What in the world—"

He shut the door and faced them. "FBI."

"Still?" Maria's hands went up. "What did they want?"

"Who knows? Directions to a diner with some good grits and fried chicken?"

Maria didn't think this was funny. "We have been here for over ten years. We became American citizens. Took the oath."

"They keep up with a lot of their own citizens."

"Genauso wie die Gestapo."

"I understand German, Mom." Peter leaned forward. "And I know what the Gestapo is."

"You design their weapons systems," Maria went on. "Now they have asked you to put the country into space. What more do they want from us? When will it end?"

Realizing it was unsettling Peter to see his mother upset, Hans found his broadest smile for the boy.

"So what did you say to them, Dad?"

"We had a little discussion and it turns out the special agents agree with me, son."

"About what?"

"Rock 'n' roll—just a fad."

Hans and Peter shared a laugh, as Hans started the car and began to drive off, Maria staring out the window, lost in thought.

Maria stood alone in the shadows of her kitchen, a mild breeze blowing in through the open back door, the only light coming from the low-wattage range bulb over the stove and the yellow-white glow from the meters and dials on a boxy ham radio that sat on the kitchen table.

The ham radio emitted a constant sound—a high-pitched beeping, somewhere between a short whistle and a chirp, *wheep-wheep-*

wheep-wheep, like someone endlessly blowing the same high note, an A-flat actually, on a piccolo oboe. *Wheep-wheep-wheep-wheep* . . . It was as steady and unflinching as a sleeping infant's heartbeat.

The sound of Sputnik, the first and only man-made object to circle the earth, filling her dark, clean kitchen, keeping time with the kitchen clock and the southern chorus frogs in the backyard, Maria leaned against the door frame and looked out into the night.

Yes, it was moving that men had used their minds and might to break free of Earth's pull. But who were these men? Maria had heard the whispered stories about what the Red Army had done in Berlin, too many accounts to have been merely fabricated Nazi propaganda. It was hard to feel anything but trepidation at the sound now overhead.

An infinite array of stars, dazzling and blinking, filled the black canvas of the Northwest Alabama sky. Lying in the manicured lawn underneath them, pointing up, were Hans and Peter. Watching her husband and son from her open back door, Maria thought about Hans doing this very same thing with *his* father back in the green rolling grasses of Burghausen.

Suddenly Hans and Peter both jumped up and peered cautiously into a grouping of azalea bushes still in their containers.

"What is it?" Maria called out.

Hans held up a finger to Maria, while he peeked nervously into the thick bushes.

"I think it's a snake!" Peter exclaimed.

"No, I think it's just a cat," Hans said, straightening up.

"Are you sure?" Maria asked.

"Whatever it is, it's gone now." Excitement over, Hans motioned for Peter to come back to the lawn, where they again laid down on their backs and gazed up, laughing and chatting.

They looked so perfect together, Maria thought. Like some

picturesque ad in one of her magazines. But how truly different she felt from those women in those ads and commercials that now seemed to be everywhere—these happy cooking society ladies with their new as-good-as-butter margarine spreads, and the efficient mothers who kept their homes Spic and Span clean while maintaining their youthful Ivory Soap girl skin and their marvelously flattering Coppertone tans, oh, and the pretty wives who did not perspire or in any way offend thanks to their newly formulated five-way-protection deodorants. How in the world did she end up in a picture-perfect life in the middle of suburban Alabama? What would her neighbors think if they knew who she really was? Did anyone, even Hans, really know? There was Cooper.

Hans shot up, arm extended, pointing excitedly at something moving across the sky. Now Peter saw it too and, both of them pointing up, they tracked it together as though it were a bird of prey on the hunt.

Maria took a few steps out and looked up into the sky and she saw it—the Russians' unholy star moving rapidly across the heavens, reflecting the sun's light into the Reinhardts' picture-perfect backyard.

1945

While Maria sat up on the sofa, hair disheveled, bare feet tucked under her, watching, silent as a feral cat, Cooper paced the room, taking a quick inventory. He took the small khaki musette bag with his survival gear, carried it over his shoulder, and set it down near the piano.

Reaching his hand into a front pocket, he produced a gleaming 1895 Morgan silver dollar. A good luck charm from a beautiful girl he'd just met as he was boarding the train for basic training—like an angel, she'd kissed him and slipped it into his hand as the train pulled away—the coin had traveled with him on every single one of his sorties. He breathed a sigh of relief to feel it in his palm once again, flipped it, caught it, and popped it back in his pocket.

He glanced over at Maria, who regarded his coin flipping with disdain, but he just shrugged it off and continued walking the room.

Though the cottage was small and old and rustic, it was filled with fine, even opulent furnishings, beautiful but odd in such a commonplace setting. He walked over to the blackened stone fireplace with its antique forged fire iron set, looking up at a striking painting in an ancient gold frame hanging over the hardwood beam mantel. It was a religious-themed image, the Annunciation to the Virgin, perhaps, painted in the Renaissance style that he had seen in museums.

Moving to the window, Cooper peeled back the curtain a bit and carefully peeked outside. Cooper's outstanding vision was one of the reasons he had sailed through flight school, and it was especially helpful at times like this. Way off in the distance he could see a faint light, a candle or two maybe, coming from what looked like a house.

"What is that structure back there, through the trees?" he asked abruptly, turning to Maria.

She did not respond.

He pointed with his hand. "Up there. It's the only building around, so you and I both know you know what I'm talking about."

Maria's mind raced. Should she help him? And if she did, would he hurt good people to get what he wanted? He had a kind face, and she no longer had unquestioning loyalty to her country, but he was a soldier, an armed soldier. And he had been in a plane that had dropped bombs all over the city. All she knew for sure was that she was fed up with everything to do with this war.

"Answer me, Maria," he said, taking a step toward her. "I need to know what that building is."

She decided that spitting out a word wasn't going to hurt anything. "*Kinderhaus*," she said.

"The children's house? So it's what, a school, a dormitory?"

"Something like that." She looked away, exasperated.

Pacing again, he thought about that for a moment. There were certainly worse places he could have landed. He took a deep breath, feeling some relief.

Then he quickly stepped into the bedroom, grabbed the pitcher of water and a couple of glasses from the dressing table, and marched back to her.

"So what do you do?" he asked, his tone lightening a little.

She didn't respond. She just looked him over, head to boots, as he poured two glasses of water, downed one, and filled the other, which he placed on the table in front of her.

"What do you do?" he asked again.

She looked at the glass he'd set before her, and then she met his eyes. "What do you mean?"

"Why are you alone in the middle of the forest in your little gingerbread house?" He set the pitcher and his empty glass on the table.

Her sharp, strong jaw set, she just stared at him. *What did he want?*

"You're not a witch are you? You know, with the oven and the taste for little children?"

"I teach children music," she said, glaring at him.

"Really?"

"Yes. Really," she replied with sarcasm.

"Wagner, Mozart, Bach, that sorta thing?"

"Yes. That *sort of thing*," she said, mimicking his American phrasing.

"I see," he said, his tone lightening even more.

This was a subject where she couldn't keep herself silent. "You know Bach?"

"Heard of 'im." He sat down across from her, studying her up close now. "You know English."

"Of course I know English."

"Hey, it's not unreasonable to be impressed. You speak better than half the guys in my squadron, not that that's saying much. Why would a German learn to speak English so well?"

"You mean because we are all nationalistic zealots?" she said with sarcasm.

"You're the sensitive type, aren't you?"

"Only fools make judgments about an entire people. Fools and racists."

"Whoa, there." He liked her better when she *wasn't* talking.

"Do you own slaves?"

He gave her a sideways look. "What kind of question is that?"

"Did your parents own slaves?"

"No."

"But some people in your country did. Does that make you a nation of slave owners?"

"So you're trying to make some kind of comparison here?"

"I believe I have made it. You do not know anything about me."

"Fair enough, and you don't know anything about me."

"I know that you were dropping bombs all around a house up there, that is full of children." She pointed.

Abruptly, he stood up, unwilling to defend himself to a kraut, no matter how pretty. He began to walk away, but the satisfied expression growing on her face annoyed him, and he found himself sitting right back down again.

"Well, since you seem to have learned a thing of two about American history somewhere, I'm sure you'll recall that most of my countrymen were so repulsed by what a handful of renegade states were doing that we fought a civil war over it. And the good guys won."

"I know a thing or two about your history. Perhaps more than you, I think."

"I highly doubt that."

"Any black servicemen in your air force?"

He felt his blood pressure rise, his face twitching, as he tried to formulate a smart explanation for why the U.S. military was segregated. There wasn't one.

She went on. "Or in your mind are blacks not even good enough to die for their country?"

"We don't own slaves anymore and we don't turn millions of people into fertilizer!"

"Not everyone thought slavery was right and not everyone is a Nazi!"

"I wasn't targeting a house full of children and you know it!"

They stared at each other, neither talking.

Finally, Cooper took a deep breath. "You know what they make in the factory in this town, don't you?" he asked, his tone measured.

Nothing from her.

So he continued, a little more forcefully. "There's one big factory in this town and I am sure *everyone* around here knows what is manufactured there."

"Yes, I know what is made in the factory."

He nodded. "Ever heard of a store called Woolworth's?"

"Yes."

"Last fall, right after Thanksgiving, there was a little girl named Lucy McNeill, striking red pigtails, freckles, who was shopping with her mother at the Woolworth's on New Cross Road in Deptford, right in the center of London. She was on the seventh floor, in the toy department, and she'd just found this little ragdoll that she'd been wanting for Christmas, red yarn for hair, freckles like her own, button eyes, you know the kind. And she picked it up, and turned to show it to her mother and, *boom*, that's when the rocket hit. A V2 made in the factory and launched from . . . just down the road here. The warhead on the rocket blew apart the entire department store on one of the busiest days before the holidays. They found bodies, a hundred and sixty-eight to be exact, strewn over a five-block radius. The reason I know that ragdoll so well is because when Lucy was thrown the seven stories to the street, hitting the pavement not far from where I was standing a few blocks away that day, she still had the doll in her hand."

Maria was visibly shaken by the story. She had envisioned just this very thing, and the specific account gave shape to her fears.

"What happened to that little girl in London was horrible," Maria said, her voice shaking and cracking. "And I could give you stories too. But I will not. We are *all* living in the ninth circle of hell."

"Dante." He laughed sarcastically. "I'd think Faust would be more your speed. Remember, he sold his soul to make a deal with the devil. Quite German, if you ask me."

She picked up the glass and threw the water in his face. *"Aussteigen! Raus! Raus!* To the forest with you! Go! Go! See how far you get!"

"Hey!" He shot up. "Do you really know what's in the factory? Do you? Do you know what's deep underground, under that tunnel they cut into the mountainside? Do you?"

He ran his fingers across his scalp and threw back his drenched hair.

"Because somehow I don't think you do."

Her lips quivered. He had hit a nerve.

"Yes, everyone knows the V2s are down there. But how do you think all those rockets are getting built? Santa's elves? I've seen the aerial pictures of the camp next to the factory."

"Mittelbau-Dora," she said, her trembling voice giving away her fear. "It is just a work camp."

"Really? Because the pictures I've seen show the cattle cars bringing them in by the tens of thousands."

"That can't be. It's not large enough to hold—"

"The tens of thousands. And every morning they are marched into the factory tunnel, and at night fewer come out. But the cattle cars keep coming. Why does the factory need all this fresh labor? Where is the old labor going? How many workers can really fit in the tunnels? How many workers and how many bodies?"

"You are a liar."

"Really? Are you sure?"

"Liar!"

"Am I lying to you, or are you lying to yourself?"

And with that, tears began to stream down her face. And she broke down and began to cry openly.

Cooper stood there, heart racing, face flushed red, water streaking down his neck, making his shirt stick to his chest, and he just watched her, this beautiful, incredibly smart, vulnerable girl. Any satisfaction he'd warranted quickly disappeared.

He unclenched his fist. What was he doing? Not exactly the best way to gain trust, he thought, berating himself. None of this was covered in his training.

He went over to her, sitting next to her on the sofa, but she moved away.

After a moment, she glanced back at him. "The war . . . it is just a matter of time until Germany is finished, isn't it?"

He responded to her softly. "The Russians are fifty kilometers from Berlin. The Allies have crossed the Rhine. 'The falcon cannot hear the falconer; things fall apart; the centre cannot hold; mere anarchy is loosed upon the world.'"

The words from the Yeats poem had an eerie effect on Maria. She looked into his eyes, shoving her mass of hair back, wiping her face.

"Good," she said. "The end cannot come soon enough now."

"Yes, it's just a matter of time," he said. "How much, and how many more die, it's up to the German people now."

FLIGHT DREAMS

1957

Major Cooper sat in the cockpit and stared out at the horizon, over the expanse of concrete runway tinted purple-orange with the first light of the new day. The military typically didn't fly these kinds of tests on Sundays, but with events seriously heating up with the Soviets, there were no more sacred days of rest for guys like Cooper. He'd been sitting here quite awhile already, G suit zipped up, flight helmet on, and though he certainly believed in having the mechanics complete a thorough preflight inspection, particularly with an experimental jet, he was itching to get this shiny new bird in the air.

He knew, though, that this was no small feat. The Douglas X-A3B Skywarrior prototype was a strategic bomber, large enough to carry a nuclear bomb, but it had to be sufficiently nimble to take off and land on an aircraft carrier. Until intercontinental ballistic missiles were deployed in large numbers, this was how America was going to fight the next war. So while in theory this kind of plane seemed like a good idea, in reality no one was entirely sure if it was gonna fly just right. And it took a certain kind of guy to find out.

"How you holding up out there, Major?" asked the flight safety officer over the speakers in Cooper's helmet.

"Ah, holding up just fine, Tower. Ready to start my day and head up to the office whenever you gentlemen have a green light for me."

"We should have a go for you any minute now. Just hang tight and let us know if there's anything we can do to make your stay more comfortable."

"Roger that. Hanging as directed."

Cooper shifted around in his seat, which was more than a bit stiff. He'd have to remember to let them know about that in debriefing. And, man, the instrument panels could be arranged in a much more practical fashion. The hydraulics meters were a pain to read. Typical. Cooper saw this sort of thing often in test flights of new prototypes. What seemed smart on a drawing board was often very different from what was best in a real-world cockpit, especially during a crisis when a split-second decision meant going down hard in a ball of flames or living to throw back a few more shots of Jack and dance with a few more Jills.

Cooper took in a deep breath of the pure oxygen pumping into his helmet. It made him relaxed and alert, and while he waited for the green light, his thoughts drifted to what was most on his mind right now.

Maria. Maria from Nordhausen, alive and well and married to a pocket protector in Huntsville, Alabama. Who'd of ever thought it? Since those days Cooper had seen the world, flown all over it in tin can bombers and fancy new fighters, captivating new best buddies with adventure-filled stories in ratty watering holes from Kaesong to Kansas City, but there were always those handful of days in Germany about which he never spoke. It was a piece of time that belonged only to him, and to her, and to no one else, and what had happened was not something he ever felt he could adequately explain.

He had thought of her often over the years and on more than one occasion had even considered trying to track her down. He knew people, the kind who could facilitate that sort of thing. But he always shook those ideas away. He had some pretty decent reasons to let the past lie, but he knew good and well his biggest reason was fear—fear of what might become of him . . . of his heart, yes, there it was . . . if he ever did see her again. Yes, you couldn't put the genie back in the bottle, but you could run from her. You could run all over the world . . . until one night you walked into a room in a corner of Alabama and there she was playing her violin, more breathtaking than even in memory.

Did she know how he had felt when he saw her? Could she hear his heart pounding when he was close enough to smell her clean and perfumed skin?

More than anything else, he had always wondered if she had ever told anyone what had happened, either. But just one look at her face and he could see clear as this new day before him that she never had. How could she?

So what now? Well, that was easy. He was gonna live his life. He'd ejected out of enough planes at high altitude, been fished out of the drink with his parachute still smoking, sharks all around— yeah, fate was something you didn't mess with. It was one thing to have a close call, bump into your past, but you didn't go looking for trouble. She was married. And had a kid. With someone very important to his employer and benefactor, the United States government. There were secrets from the past that needed to stay in the past. Yes, he had no interest in seeing her further. In fact, he would make an effort not to. No matter how beautiful she was. In that tight black cocktail dress. Her hair pulled back off her face . . . radiant and soft-hued . . . That sparkle in her eyes . . .

He'd have to frequent more of those college bars.

The voice in his ear startled him. "We have a green light for you, sir. A green light for takeoff on runway zero-niner and a wide-open deck to angels twenty-five. Command has issued you full authorization for flight—you are clear to push the envelope as you see fit, Major."

"Roger that."

The entire sky to twenty-five thousand feet his, Cooper taxied the Douglas Skywarrior out to the directed runway, turning it straight so that all he saw was eight thousand feet of concrete before him and the unfolding dawn above.

Of course, the point of this whole mission was not to use an eight-thousand-foot runway to get airborne. Strapped under the aircraft's wings, all around the big turbojet engines, were twelve cylindrical high-thrust rockets.

"Well, let's see what those Germans have come up with."

And with that, Cooper threw the throttle all the way forward, popped the plastic safety latch, and pushed the red thumb button. All twelve rockets immediately ignited and the plane shot forward, screaming down the runaway for just twenty or thirty yards before blasting into the sky nearly straight up, like a great Roman candle.

"Whoooo!" yelled Cooper.

"You okay up there?" asked the tower. "That was quite a vertical takeoff."

"More than okay. Please give my hats-off to the Germans."

"Will pass that on, Major. Enjoy the day."

That was very much his plan. Grinning ear to ear under his flight helmet, Cooper shot across the sky over Huntsville, breaking Mach 1 with a thunderous banging in a matter of seconds.

◆ ◆ ◆

Knocking on the door. "Mom! Wake up."

Maria opened her eyes.

Peter continued knocking outside the door to his parents' bedroom. "Mom, someone's at the door."

"Just a moment," she said, squinting at the daylight filling the bedroom.

Suddenly oriented to where she was, Maria jumped out of bed, threw on a robe, and opened her door. "Who is here?"

"I don't know. A man and a girl."

She smoothed her hair as she walked. "I can't believe how late I slept."

"Dad said you were up late last night and not to wake you."

"I was, but he was up even later."

"I don't think he went to bed."

Maria saw a throw blanket on the sofa and could smell coffee throughout the house. Hans had made a few pots, after maybe catching an hour or two on the sofa. His usual M.O. She was starting to think that maybe he didn't know they actually had a bedroom in the house.

As she approached the front door, Maria could see through the curtains on the windows to either side of the door two figures standing on her front porch.

She pulled back the curtains on one of the windows and saw a large black man and Josephine, the little girl she had met the night before.

Maria opened the door.

"Morning, ma'am," said the man. He wore worn blue coveralls, and a wide-brimmed hat hung from his hand.

He turned to Josephine, who nodded uncomfortably. Then he

faced back to Maria. "We got your address from the Southern Bell directory," he said with his deep voice. "Hope this not too early for y'all."

"No, no," said Maria. "Not a problem at all."

Maria smiled at Josephine but the girl did not smile back. She avoided Maria's eyes, sheepishly looking down.

Parked on the street in front of the house, Maria saw a dusty 1930s-era red pickup, the back full of used furniture, odds and ends, and several hand-painted wood signs that read *Community Rummage Sale—First Missionary Baptist Church.*

"These strings belong to you?" The man asked as Josephine extended and opened her small, graceful hand, from which dangled four coiled violin strings.

Peter stepped beside his mother in the doorway.

Maria looked at the strings, then to the little girl's face, then to the man, trying to get a bead on what was going on here. Finally, Maria began slowly to nod. "Yes, I believe those were mine. I threw them away yesterday."

Maria watched as the man shot the little girl a potent look.

Then the man turned to Maria. "Why you throw away such fine catgut string?"

"Because I got some new ones, but you are right, they have some good life left in them and I would *love* for her to have them." Maria lowered herself to the girl's eye level. "You keep them, honey."

"My daughter ain't going through nobody's garbage."

"It is not like that," Maria said, about to try to explain further, but again the father shot the girl a strong and charged look. Obviously there had been a lot of conversation about this.

Josephine reached out and took Maria's willowy hand and gently placed the violin strings in her palm. Then the girl quickly turned, raced down the porch steps and across the walkway, and hopped in the passenger side of the red pickup, slamming the door. She sat in the truck, staring off out the open window.

"Sorry to disturb you, ma'am," the man said with a tip of his head.

Maria just stood there, her heart breaking, Peter next to her, as the man left the porch, slid into the truck, and started it.

A kid with a crew cut rode by the truck on a shiny new bike, baseball cards clamped to the frame with clothespins clattering against the spokes.

Maria thought about racing up to the truck—she had so much more to say, questions she wanted to ask. Who was this amazing child who could hear that her violin was ever so slightly off-key? Did this man realize what a gift that was? But Maria knew better than to meddle in the affairs of other people's families.

Her old strings in hand, standing on her front porch in her robe, Maria sighed as the truck drove off down Monterrey Drive, both the man and his daughter looking ahead in silence, passing Mrs. Hendrickson across the street, who shamelessly observed everything while pretending to water her gardenias, her fat tomcat lying at her feet.

Inside the house, the phone rang.

"Sugar, you are a celebrity," Penny said into the phone after Maria answered. "Marlene Dietrich and Grace Kelly rolled into one. Why all of Huntsville is simply abuzz about you this morning."

"Do I know you?"

Penny laughed, and moved Maria out of her sadness.

"I have something to tell you," Penny said with a teasing tone. "Something big."

"What?"

"I can't say. I promised that hussy Carolyn I'd keep my mouth shut until lunch. Not sure I am up to the task."

"Lunch?"

"Great. How's noon?"

"Well . . ."

"Great. I'll see you at the club."

Before Maria could respond further, Penny had hung up. Maria shook her head with a smile and went to find whatever coffee Hans had left.

MAGNET AND STEEL

Maria and Hans, Peter between them, sat together on a glossy hardwood pew in the cavernous new church. A tableau of a perfect American family, they listened attentively to the solemn service, joining in a liturgical hymn.

Maria crossed her legs, adjusted the white knit shawl around her sharp shoulders, and tugged her flower-print teacup dress down over her knees. Content when her family was together like this, she shared a smile with Hans.

St. Mark's Evangelical Lutheran Church on Longwood Drive was just a few blocks from Blossomwood, near an area called Kraut Hill by locals because of all the German families that lived nearby. These families, the scientists and their wives, had founded St. Mark's, the first Lutheran house of worship in this part of Alabama. Since music was such an important part of most of the congregants' lives, the hymn they sang sounded as harmonious as any performed by a professional chorus. Indeed, many congregants had been accomplished singers and musicians in Europe before the war.

Along with the symphony and significant expansion of the city's library, St. Mark's was one of the very first projects the Germans began when they first moved to town, and this beautiful newly completed church, with its towering beamed ceilings and artful stained glass and rich appointments, was a testament to the their industriousness and values.

Maria looked around, seeing many of her German friends, the men in dark suits, the women in proper dresses, children all made to sit straight and still. She noticed a lot of people sneaking smiles at her and nodding, sending their congratulations on the previous night's exciting success.

While singing, Maria felt someone tapping on her left shoulder and she looked to her left, but old Dr. Tiesenhausen, sitting there, looked utterly impassive. She looked forward again, singing louder, and felt the tapping again. She looked behind her. Nothing. Then she heard giggling and whipped her head around to Peter on her right, who just shrugged, suspiciously, Maria thought.

They both returned to their singing, and now Maria slipped her right arm deviously across the back of the pew and tapped on Peter's right shoulder, but before she could retract her hand, he grabbed it—and the two of them cracked up laughing. They held their hands over their mouths, trying to stifle the silliness, which didn't work too well. Hans shot them both a look and rolled his eyes, and they finally straightened up—but not before Peter knocked Maria's knee with his.

Noticing her friend Sabine watching her antics, Maria gave her a broad smile. But Sabine did not return it. Sitting next to her husband, chemist Karl Janssen, Sabine looked stiff and troubled. In fact, both Sabine and Karl looked stiff, sitting next to each other but not touching, both staring straight ahead. Was something beyond Sabine's usual troubles wrong? Sabine was never an especially happy person. She was still having difficulty integrating into the overall community in Huntsville, despite her best efforts. But today, here in church, she looked even more distressed than usual. Maria reminded herself to talk to Sabine and see if she could help. Some of the German wives fit right into America and the South. They were opening German restaurants and starting cultural programs that were welcomed with open arms in Huntsville. Others found it much more difficult to assimilate. But regardless, they all knew that they were fortunate to be here and, moreover, that it was their duty now to make it work, one way or another.

While the baptized congregants, which was most everyone present, came forward, kneeled, and began taking the formal closed Communion from the pastor, a scientist's wife stood at the altar singing "Ave Maria" in German, the Schubert version. A highly acclaimed and rather famous opera singer in Vienna before and during the war, she had a masterful soprano voice, regal and haunting in its power.

The Reinhardts kneeled and Maria watched as Hans opened his mouth and took the Eucharist. The host. The blood. The German words of the "Ave Maria," the Hail Mary, soared, sending a shiver down Maria's spine. Hans had a far-off look in his eyes. He'd been gone when Maria awoke in the morning—and only reappeared before leaving for church. In the car and now during the service, he seemed occupied, more than usual. Was he thinking of heaven—like Maria—or his rockets? Spirituality or science? Perhaps for Hans they were one and the same. Judging by the intent expression on his face, Maria worried he might never come back to the ground.

Out of the corner of her eye, Maria saw Sabine bolt up, excuse herself out of the pew, and, head down, shoulders in, walk quickly up the aisle and out of the sanctuary.

As the "Ave Maria" reached its dramatic crescendo, the German woman's operatic voice reverberating throughout the church, Maria excused herself, stood, and went after Sabine.

Maria looked in the halls, poked her head in the woman's restroom—the "Ave Maria" still climbing in power—but Sabine was nowhere to be found. Had she had a fight with Karl and walked off? That was the only explanation.

Concern on her face, wondering what had happened, Maria stood in the empty narthex of the church, listening as the soprano sang the grand conclusion of the haunting Schubert piece.

Taking it in, Maria paused in front of the church's great bronze plaque featuring the image of Martin Luther. It had been on a monument in the Berlin Tiergarten and, with assistance from the United States Army, the Federal Republic of West Germany had presented the plaque to St. Mark's "as a token of appreciation for the spiritual ministry to the German rocket scientists and engineers who relocated to Huntsville in 1950."

Penny stirred her Bloody Mary with a long celery stalk, pulled it out of the oversized old-fashioned goblet, and took a crunchy bite. As she was chewing, sitting at a table across from Carolyn, she saw Maria making her way through the handsomely furnished Redstone Officers' Club. In her nipped-in-waist bright floral teacup dress, Maria was at once refined and unassuming, not easy to pull off strolling into a room like this. High-ranking men in uniform reflexively gazed at her as she glided by like a prima ballerina in the sleeveless scoop-necked dress and cornflower-blue kitten heels.

Penny waved vigorously and Maria made a beeline to the table. Carolyn rose, enormous smile on her face, grabbed Maria, and kissed her on the cheek.

"Good afternoon, Miss Lovely," Carolyn said.

"Kisses, kisses." Penny blew a couple of air kisses.

Maria sat down. "Well, you two are quite cheaper this morning."

"Chipper, sugar, chipper." Penny slurped the remains of her spicy cocktail through the straw.

Carolyn wiped a dab of lipstick off Maria's cheek.

"Where is Sabine?" Maria asked.

"Couldn't make it," Carolyn said.

There was a pause in the conversation, and a look exchanged between Carolyn and Penny.

"I think you should call her," Penny said. "She didn't sound too cheaper on the phone this morning."

"I will," Maria said, her expression of concern replaced by a little grin at being teased.

Carolyn grasped Maria's arm. "And lunch is on me today."

"No, that is not necessary," Maria said.

"Well, technically it's on the HSO," Carolyn said.

"Let the graft begin!" Penny waved an olive on a toothpick.

The server approached and Penny held up three fingers and mouthed words indicating the she wanted three Bloody Marys for the table. "And this time let's go with the top-shelf spirits. Oh, and a teensy bit more Tabasco?"

Maria searched her friends' faces. What was going on with them today?

Carolyn just beamed, as did Penny, both of them enjoying the suspense they knew they were creating.

"What are you two up to?" Maria asked.

"We had a very good night last night," Carolyn said.

"A *very* good night." Penny sucked a pimento out of the olive.

"To the tune of about—"

"Not 'about.'" Penny cut her off. "Let's be precise."

"Yes, let's." Carolyn folded her hands on the table. "To the tune of *precisely* thirty-five thousand, seven hundred and forty-three dollars."

Wide-eyed, Maria couldn't find words fast enough.

"But who's counting," Carolyn continued.

"You are," Penny said.

"Yes, I am. I certainly am."

Maria did the math in her head. "But that's much more than the ticket sales."

"She can count," Carolyn said to Penny.

"It appears she can. Music *and* math. Quite the gifted girl."

"Quite indeed." Deciding it was time to be merciful and explain, Carolyn leaned toward Maria. "Several well-to-do members of our community, along with one of our nation's representatives to Congress, were so impressed with the Huntsville Symphony ensemble—"

Penny jumped in. "And in particular it's exquisite concertmaster on first violin—"

"That we received donations, *unsolicited* donations. They wrote checks. Checks. I have to open an account for the symphony tomorrow." Carolyn grasped her own hands in joy.

"That is amazing," Maria said. "Truly amazing to have this kind of support so early on."

"Yes—but wait!" Carolyn exclaimed. "There's more."

"More?"

"So much more," Penny said.

"Imagine the following," Carolyn said, a dramatic tone in her voice. "Live from the ballroom at the Russel Erskine Hotel in downtown Huntsville, Alabama, clear-channel radio WBHP, with a fifty-thousand-watt transmitter atop Monte Santo, broadcasting throughout the Tennessee River Valley, is proud to bring you the Huntsville Symphony Orchestra."

"There's going to be a radio broadcast? Really?" Maria asked.

"Really really," Penny said.

"Do you have any idea how many people hear that station at night?" Carolyn asked, and then rambled out the answer. "People listen in from Nashville to Atlanta to L.A.—"

"Los Angeles?"

"Lower Alabama," Penny said.

"That's thousands. Tens of thousands of listeners," Carolyn went on. "And you can be sure we'll have the station broadcast an address where folks can send checks, if they are so inclined. Oh, what this is going to do for Huntsville is simply amazing. Imagine, a city of our size with a symphony of national, even international, quality and reputation."

"And we all thought it was rockets that were gonna put the city on the map," Penny said.

The cocktails arrived, the server placing them in front of each woman while Carolyn and Penny gazed at Maria, waiting for a response. Maria ran this big news over in her mind, realizing the work that needed to be done to prepare the symphony. On any day this was a lot to take in, but after the visit from Josephine this morning and seeing Cooper last night, not to mention the FBI again, her head was spinning.

She hadn't until that moment noticed the man in air force uniform sitting by himself eating lunch at the bar. But as he now caught her eye, and was brought into sharp focus by her racing heart, she became instantly aware that he was looking directly at her, a crooked little smile on his face. It was Cooper.

Carolyn gripped her hands tightly. "So, the event is set for next

Saturday. Now, I know that's not a lot of time, but you can do it, right?"

Maria didn't seem to hear a word Carolyn said. Her focus was on Cooper. Had he come for her? Had he tracked her down? She took an unladylike sip of her Bloody Mary—and then recoiled, her eyes watering. *Whoo, that's spicy!* Even across the room, she could see him stifling a laugh at her.

"Maria?" Penny leaned toward her preoccupied friend. "You okay, honey? You look like you just swallowed a bald-faced hornet's nest."

Maria still didn't hear. *Get a grip,* she told herself. He was an officer in the officers' club. Of course he was here. No big deal.

Or *was* it something else? He could have landed virtually anywhere in Germany, walked into any of a million cottages. And now he was in this town, and she was in this town . . . Was it simply inevitable that they were going to keep smacking into each other, like a supercharged magnet and steel, no matter what they did, no matter what distance was put between them? She felt as though a current were indeed coursing through her body.

"Maria?" Carolyn tapped Maria's hand. "This is Redstone base to Maria. Can you hear us?"

Maria snapped out of it, addressing them both. "I am sorry. It is just . . . great news, truly, great news, but, wow, Saturday. That is soon."

"Do you think the symphony will be ready by then?"

Maria thought about that, and the man that she knew was in this room probably watching her right now, and she opened her mouth to speak, but—

Carolyn cut her off. "Of course, they'll be ready."

Again, Maria opened her mouth, but it just stayed open as she gaped at Cooper. Maria's stomach plummeted as he moved away from the bar. He paid his bill and stood up. Was he going to come over here? Or was he leaving? She couldn't even be sure if she wanted to see him again. But there were things to talk about and this couldn't go on. *She* couldn't go on.

Maria stood. "Excuse me for a moment."

Heading for the bathroom, Maria veered out of the way and swung by the bar area.

Cooper stood, ready to leave, but as he watched her approach, that toothy aviator grin grew on his face.

"Good afternoon, ma'am," he said as she moved toward him. "James Cooper. We met last night."

She stopped and stood right in front of him, toe to toe. "Yes, I seem to remember."

There was a long pause as each waited for the other to make a move. A couple of officers sitting at the bar watched them before turning back to their lunches.

"They make a good Brunswick stew in this club," Cooper said. "Mighty good."

"Yes. They do. And you really should try the hush puppies sometime, Major."

"Thank you. I believe I will."

Well aware that she was being watched by her friends, and perhaps by others, Maria searched his eyes, and he searched hers. There really was so much to say, there were so many questions to ask, and none of it could be spoken here, none of it. Standing near him in public like this, making small talk, so much running through her mind, she felt her skin grow hot. She had a thought and decided to throw caution to the wind and act on it, before she did what was probably the wiser thing—

"You know . . . those hush puppies . . . ," she went on. "They are good, but nothing like the hush puppies at Ruby's, this charming little café in a town about an hour from here called Mentone," she said with unmistakable emphasis on the place and location. "I always eat an early lunch there after I drop my son off nearby at boarding school. Oh, and come to think of it, I will be there *tomorrow*."

"Ruby's."

"Yes. In Mentone." She could see that her invitation was understood loud and clear. "You'll really have to visit sometime, Major."

"I'll keep that in mind."

Her eyes stayed with him for a moment more. "Yes. You should do that. Good day."

And then she moved on, enjoying the long, confident strides afforded by her kitten heels, toward the ladies' room.

Cooper watched her until she was completely gone, unable to take his eyes from her. Then, that self-assured grin on his face, Cooper strolled out of the Redstone Officers' Club.

After a few minutes, Maria returned from the bathroom and rejoined her friends. The server saw her sit and immediately began putting lunch on the table.

"Who's the cute flyboy?" Penny asked.

"Him? Oh, a fan."

Carolyn sighed. "Our orchestra has fans."

"I think Maria has fans," Penny said, studying Maria.

"I think we should be talking about something much more important," Maria said. "Such as Saturday."

"Yes, about Saturday . . . ," Penny said.

"Can you do it?" Carolyn asked.

Maria thought for a moment. *What in the world did she just do?* It was nothing, she assured herself. She had just told someone where she was going to be eating lunch tomorrow, on the off chance that if he happened to be . . . oh, randomly driving around the county in a dinky little hamlet an hour or so out of town . . . Maria put the whole thing out of mind as best she could. "If the men around here can put a satellite into outer space in a few weeks, I think our symphony can be more than ready by Saturday."

"You'll need to perform a piece that everyone knows, that requires little practice, something big."

Maria smiled knowingly. "I know just the piece."

HEAVEN AND EARTH

H eading east along Governors Street, away from the base and toward Blossomwood, Maria drove Peter and herself home in the family's '57 Chevy 150, a practical second car.

"Dr. Von Braun said they had a snake in their backyard too!"

"Peter, I really do think your imagination is wonderful and I am sorry if it's not very exciting, but Mrs. Hendrickson's tomcat has essentially taken over our backyard."

"He said all the construction in Blossomwood is driving the copperheads out of their homes."

Maria laughed in exasperation with this boy. "How was your time on base with Dad?"

"Amazing. He let me do some calculus that went into the trajectory calculations."

"Really? Can you do calculus?"

"Mom! I've been doing derivatives for months already."

She observed him for a moment, smiling to herself. *Where did this kid come from?*

She turned her eyes back to the road. "Well, if that brain of yours can do calculus derivatives, I know you can train it to remind you to pick up your dirty socks and put them in the clothes hamper before you go to bed."

"Mom!"

"What?"

"You're such a mom."

"I will take that as a compliment."

As they passed the downtown area to the north, near the church just a few blocks to the south, Peter saw something on the corner of Madison Street.

"Mom. Look." He pointed to a fairly large hand-painted wood sign propped up against a lamppost. It read *Community Rummage Sale—First Missionary Baptist Church* and above the words someone had drawn an arrow pointing down Madison.

Stopped at the light, Maria read the sign and remembered seeing it earlier. "Isn't that one of the signs that was in the back of that red truck this morning?"

"Yes!"

Maria thought for a moment, racked with curiosity.

"Want to take a little detour?" she asked.

"Can we?"

"You know, Peter, one of the best things about being a grown-up is that you can eat as much candy as you want for breakfast and you can take detours in life whenever you want."

She began to turn the car left onto Madison, driving in the direction the arrow pointed.

"I can't wait to be a grown-up."

She thought about Cooper for a moment. "Of course, you also have to take the consequences of your behavior."

"Can I have candy for breakfast tomorrow?"

"No."

"Such a mom, such a mom."

After driving through downtown, windows rolled down, Maria drove several blocks north of town, paralleling the railroad tracks, through a partly abandoned industrial area with rows of nineteenth-century brick cotton warehouses, windows blackened and broken. Seeing another sign, she crossed the tracks and turned until she ended up on Blue Spring Road.

"I don't see a church," Peter said.

"It must be here somewhere." Maria slowed, scanning both sides of the road for the First Missionary Baptist Church. The houses here in this predominantly black neighborhood were generally small wood structures, some quite old. Many were well kept, others were not—it was quite different from the homogeny of Blossomwood. As they slowly drove on, they began to see cars lining the street, and children, lots of children, running and playing in their Sunday-best clothes and shoes.

"There it is," said Maria, pointing to a large old brick church in front of them, its parking lot filled with people coming and going as they poked through a community flea market.

As Maria slowly drove by the church, she heard, over the din of folks milling about, something that made her stop the car—music, singing, and violin. But it wasn't classical. It wasn't Schubert or Sibelius or Mozart. She wasn't sure exactly what it was but it was violin and it was magnificent.

The windows of the church were thrown wide open—Maria realized that's where the music was coming from—and people in the parking lot were listening to it and enjoying it.

She smiled at her son. "You want to go in?"

"Yes!"

They parked the Chevy on the side of the road and began walking down the sidewalk toward the church parking lot, passing the running and playing children, the music growing louder. They made their way through the rows of tables covered with various items for sale, past an open kettle drum barbecue where people were lined up for what smelled like the greatest slabs of ribs and chicken halves and husked corn in the world. Folks holding Dixie cups of sweet tea smiled at them, several greeting them, making Maria and Peter feel as welcome as they had at any time since arriving in Huntsville. They walked up to the front of the church and stepped inside.

On the altar, in front of a lively audience of several hundred congregants in the old worn-smooth pews, stood a choir. Dressed in long golden robes, the two dozen black men and women swayed and clapped as they sang—and in front of them, playing her violin, was Josephine.

Maria and Peter were captivated. They took a seat in the back row and just listened. How different this was from their Lutheran church. It was spirited and expressive, and the music—Southern gospel, or holy blues—was unlike anything Maria had ever heard. The lyrics were evangelic but performed with a great uninhibited joy that had many of the congregants up on their feet.

And the star of the performance was this young girl. Maria was struck by how a violin could be used in such a way. Josephine's playing had it all, from rip-roaring fast and furious runs to crying vibratos to long, sliding, soulful notes.

The choir broke into a moving rendition of "Amazing Grace" and then stopped abruptly—as Josephine played the song solo on her violin. The entire room went silent as she performed, producing a stirring, heartfelt bluesy sound that the congregation loved, especially when performed by this little girl whom everyone knew, whom everyone had watched grow up playing—as Josephine called it—her fiddle, starting when she was so small she could just barely hold it.

Sitting next to her own child and listening to this little girl performing with such grace and passion, perfection of craft, Maria felt herself becoming profoundly emotional. The juxtaposition of worlds, her church and this church, the formalness and the openness, the different ways of expressing, and thinking about, matters of the heavenly spirit, of everything she had been dealing with, Cooper's return, her past, her life, it all seemed so poignant as she listened to Josephine fiddle with a knowing force that belied the girl's years.

Tears welled in Maria's eyes and she grasped her son's hand, carried away by this epiphany. Oh, how she wished she could have given Josephine her old strings or, better yet, some new ones. But she understood. More than anything, what Maria really wished was that she could talk to her, learn what Josephine knew, share knowledge and skills and pure love for the violin. There was a symbiosis between music and spirituality that seemed so clear right now. What becomes of a gifted little angel like this? And what business was it of hers?

The windows down on the car, Maria drove back into her neighborhood. Sunday afternoons were a particularly special time in Blossomwood, and today was no exception. Fair-haired children ran from lawn to lawn, men washed their new cars in glistening driveways, neighbors sat on mesh lawn chairs, drinking tall glasses of Coca-Cola on ice and gossiping.

Of course, it was also a time when her husband was rarely around and seeing all the other whole families reminded her of this.

Maria approached Sabine's house and saw her in the front yard holding a garden hose, watering some very brittle-looking shrubs.

Maria slowed, thinking about what Penny had said regarding Sabine. Then she drove on to her house, dropped off Peter so he could start on his homework, and went back up the street to Sabine's. Maria parked the Chevy in front of the house and hopped out.

"I think those plants need something besides water," Maria said, bounding up the driveway.

"The soil here . . . ," Sabine said, water gushing from the long green hose. "I do not know soil like this. It is full of acid, I think."

Maria examined the bushes, snapping off a bone-dry twig. A shower of dead leaves fell to the ground.

"They are dead," Sabine said. "I know it. The neighbors know it. And now you know it. I am standing out here watering dead azaleas."

Maria watched Sabine for a moment, realized something was amiss, then walked over to the side of the house and turned off the water.

Sabine just stood there holding the hose, the last of the water dribbling out of it.

Maria walked up to her friend. "Sabine, are you all right?"

"What do I know about azaleas anyway?" She threw the hose to the ground. *"Der Boden hier ist Scheiße! Glaubst du nicht?"*

"We should speak English," Maria said gently.

"I know. I know. Karl says it is the only way I will learn the language and fit in. But sometimes I think it will take much more than speaking Appalachian English to feel like I belong somewhere again."

"Sabine, are you okay?"

"I was up late last night." Sabine knew she couldn't lie to Maria. "In truth, all night."

"Let's go inside."

That sounded good to Sabine. Maria pulled the hose over to the side of the house, dropped it, and they both walked up the front porch steps and into the house.

Though the exterior facades had different motifs, the Janssen house, like the Reinhardt house, was a ranch model. The floor plans of both homes were the same, but in mirror image—the living room in the Janssen house was to the right, in the Reinhardt house to the left, and so forth.

The women sat down across from each other on brand-new matching love seats in the otherwise sparse living room.

"How well do you know Hans?" Sabine asked.

"He is my husband. But how well does any women know a man?"

"Do you ever talk to him about the war?"

It was a broad question, best answered at this point, Maria thought, with a broad response. "Yes. We spoke about those days, years ago. Before we married. Not so much anymore."

"In the early years it all made so much sense. It was *exciting*, was it not? No unemployment. The Olympics. The living space to the east and west. It all came so easy. Everyone was happy again. Remember? Oh—the food, and the parties, the nightclubs." She smiled, recalling, and then spoke with a whisper. "Remember the *Kabarett?*" Sabine blinked hard, fighting tears. "If the men had stopped with Poland and Paris, we would be home now, instead of watering dead azaleas in Alabama."

Maria reached out, putting a hand on Sabine's knee. "Did you have a fight with Karl?"

Sabine thought for a long moment. She clearly had something she very much wanted to share, needed to share. She made a choice.

"I promised Karl that I would not talk about this with anyone. But I need to. Can you give me your word that this stays between us?"

"Sabine. You know you can trust me."

Sabine still looked uneasy.

"Yes," Maria continued. "Of course you have my word."

Sabine stood and motioned for Maria to follow. "Come with me."

The women walked together down the hallway toward the master bedroom. They went to Karl's closet and Sabine opened the door.

"I was vacuuming yesterday and I cleared everything off his closet floor." Sabine moved a heavy shoe rack out of the closet. Then, on her knees, she pulled out more shoes and department store boxes and a clothes hamper and a pile of belts. Maria's curiosity grew as Sabine cleared everything off the hardwood floor of the small closet, shoving it all out into a pile against a wall.

Sabine motioned for Maria to come closer and lean into the closet. "You see?" Sabine pointed to a small round metal insert in the wood. Barely an inch in diameter, it would be very easy to overlook. Slipping her index finger into the insert, Sabine extracted a circular metal tab on a tiny hinge, which she continued to tug firmly until a three-foot-square section of the floor popped up. Sabine removed the square piece of flooring, lifted it out of the closet, and set it against the wall near the pile.

Maria gazed down into a dark hole. She could see the top of a ladder. "What is this?"

Sabine reached into the hole and threw a switch. A bright light came on inside. "Come with me." Sabine started climbing down the ladder.

Maria watched her disappear down the hatch and then began to climb in as well. The metal ladder descended into a corrugated steel tube, about three feet in diameter. It was painted white, reflecting the fluorescent light from below and making the entire inside seem bright and clean.

The tube went down about twenty-five feet. Maria looked up

the ladder and saw the opening nearly two stories above her head. She reached the bottom and stepped out into a room.

With poured concrete walls and ceiling, it was surprisingly large, designed to fit within the perimeter of the house's foundation.

Feeling a damp chill, Maria instinctively pulled her arms against her body and clasped her hands together. She looked around, wide-eyed.

There were neatly made bunk beds, a wood table covered with a red-and-white checkerboard cloth, chairs, and shelves all around the room stocked with a tremendous variety of supplies, canned and bucketed foods, containers of water, a radio, a hand mill, stacks of government-labeled cheese, civil defense–issued ration bars, medical kits, boxes of iodine pills, radiation monitors, gas masks, books, tools, batteries, a pail with a toilet seat, and cases of ammunition. It was a very professionally designed and stocked fallout shelter.

Sabine went to the table, where, on top of the checkered cloth, was a sculpture in green glass of a swan. It was a simple but exquisite piece of art that seemed entirely out of place down here. Sabine picked it up. "He said he wanted something that would remind us that there had been beauty in the world. Something that would survive."

Given not only the discovery but also her recent conversation with Hans about the futility of such a space, Maria was astounded. "You did not know until yesterday?"

Sabine nodded and put down the green glass swan. "If I had not vacuumed his closet, I would not know."

Maria could see the dismay on her friend's face. All this time Sabine had been living over this secret room—just the kind Peter thought the landscapers might be building under the Reinhardt home.

"Why did he not tell you?" Maria asked, her mind reeling.

"He said it was for my own protection." Sabine spoke with a strange tone, a combination of sadness and scorn. "To keep others from knowing in case we need it."

"Does he think you will?" Maria leaned closer to Sabine.

"I asked."

"And?"

"He said, 'Those who live by the sword, die by the sword, and those who make the sword are fools if they do not prepare for the sword.'"

Maria nodded. That sounded just like the kind of thing Hans would say. *But Karl built and stocked a shelter, and Hans did not.*

Maria tried to keep her focus on calming her friend. "Sabine, your husband is simply caring for you. Taking precautions."

"I know. Karl is very good at that."

"Yes, well, there are worse things."

"Have you ever knocked on the floor in Hans's closet?"

"No, I have not."

But Sabine knew Maria well enough to see that Maria was now thinking about it.

"Karl said that when the army finally let us out of the military base in Texas," Sabine went on, "when they transferred us here, the army helped the men get mortgages and it cost an extra five thousand dollars to have the bomb shelters built into the foundation. He says a lot of the German scientists bought them."

Maria didn't want to ask. But she had to. "Did he say which ones?"

"No. And I did not ask."

"Does Karl think it would work?"

"That I did not have to ask. Because if it cost him five thousand dollars, I am certain that he must."

Maria crossed her arms over her chest and nodded slowly. Along with being one of Hans's closest friends, Karl Janssen was a very talented chemist, a rocket propulsion design expert—he would know about nuclear science. And Hans respected him tremendously. *Cinderblock walls and dirt are about as protective as Chantilly lace,* Hans had said about fallout shelters. They didn't need one. Could Hans and Karl really be this far apart on what was a relatively simple matter of science? Or was Hans lying to Maria, just as Karl had been lying to Sabine?

Maria's heart began to race. Would Hans really lie to her? Didn't he trust her? Didn't they have the kind of marriage where he would tell her something like this—especially when he knew she was so anxious about *not* having one?

And did Karl really need to keep this from Sabine *for her own protection?*

Feeling dizzy as she ran all this through her head, Maria reached out to the table, steadying herself. Something didn't add up.

"I wish I had never opened that door," Sabine said. "What if he is right? Is this to be my future? A hole in the ground for forty years with Karl Janssen and cans of sardines?"

Maria struggled to offer something hopeful. It was getting more difficult. "Sabine, the weapons they are making are simply deterrents. It would take a crazy person—"

"A crazy person?"

Maria knew where *that* was going and certainly did not want to discuss German history. "There is not going to be a war."

"My mother used to tell me that Berlin was impenetrable. When the Russian tank guns were rattling our windows, she said the men would never let them in. They would form a wall upon which the enemy would break itself." Sabine had a flash of those days, which she quickly shook out of her head. "Men. They are all animals. Ah, but the victorious are noble, the conquered criminal."

Sabine went to one of the shelves and unfolded a long heavy black plastic bag with a zipper, a body bag. "Look at this. There is only one." She laughed sardonically. "That's Karl, always practical. Of course. If one of us went first, there would be no need for a second bag."

"We all have insurance," Maria said. "That is all this place is."

Again, that dark laugh. "Insurance. Yes." Sabine looked away, sucking in her lips, a fist to her mouth. She looked as though someone were picking around her spleen for a bullet and there was no morphine available.

Finally, Sabine walked over to a large toolbox with German lettering, flipped the heavy latches, and threw open the top. "Let me ask you," she said. "Why would a chemist need an engineer's tools?"

"What do you mean?"

"He would not."

Sabine began removing the contents of the large German industrial toolbox, which was about two feet long, two feet wide, and nearly three feet tall. She pulled out all manner of engineering tools—precision gauges, calipers, micrometers, vises, tapping instruments, hack blades, metal rulers, steel hammers, drills, and bits—most old and clunky, and not in the best condition. Then she pulled out what seemed to be a tight-fitting tray at the very bottom. She placed it on the floor and a couple of dozen chunky galvanized bolts fell from it, rattling.

Sabine reached her hands into the box and removed two fistfuls of bright gold, primarily jewelry, wedding bands.

"Insurance," she said.

Maria peered into the box and saw that the entire bottom section, which had been well hidden with the tray in place, a two-foot-square area, perhaps three inches high, was filled with gold—errant bits and pieces mixed in with some heavy pendants and bracelets and necklaces, but mainly there were wedding bands, thousands and thousands of them.

Maria ran her hands through the gold jewelry, then she looked at Sabine. "There are many explanations."

Sabine gave Maria a look—*please, we both know exactly what this is.* "When your country goes to war, you do your duty. The men joined the party, then the SS. We all know that. They had to, right? It was required to build the rockets. You taught orphans. We all did what was asked, what was required. When your country goes to war, you do not question, right? You do not question, because you may not like what you learn. You do not question because even if you learn, what can you do? What—what can one person do? Indifference, I think, is a warm blanket on a cold night. And this room makes me cold."

Sabine opened her hand, plucked out a wedding ring, considering it closely. She studied an inscription on the inside. "It is Hebrew, right?"

Still trying to digest Sabine's words, Maria looked at it. "Yes, I think so."

Sabine nodded. "We all know certain things that we pretend not to," Sabine said. "All of us. I think it is better that way."

"No. No, I do not believe that. There are horrors in the world, yes, but burying the truth is worse than them all."

"The truth? I think the truth is made by the people with the largest rocket, that is what I think."

Maria thought for a moment. Truth was the backbone of her life and, like science, it was objective. "They were just scientists. What do you mean when you say they all joined the party?"

Sabine studied her face, and then she spoke in a hushed voice.

"Maria, dear, sweet Maria, they were SS officers. All of them. Von Braun was a *Sturmbannführer,* a major. Himmler adored him. The army made it all disappear before we came."

Maria took that in. It couldn't be true. Not all of them. Not Hans.

"Why would the *Wehrmacht*—?"

"No." Sabine cut her off. "Not the German army, the *United States* army."

"This sounds like gossip. Rumor. I do not know where you heard this but—"

"Karl. I heard from Karl. Years ago. But I knew it anyway, of course. After that, I stopped asking."

Looking down, Maria slowly shook her head.

"You did not know," Sabine said softly, sympathy in her eyes, watching Maria struggle with this, watching all the questions building. "You really did not know."

Wringing her hands tightly together, Maria shook her head even more as she tried to process all this.

Sabine knew she had to continue.

"Listen to me," Sabine said, sounding like an older sister. "You know the men left the country with only what they could carry. Our families' wealth, the properties, savings, everything we had, all of it was lost or left behind."

"I do not understand."

"Maria." Sabine grabbed her arm. "*Yes, of course we all have insurance.* Because that is what our men are like." Sabine lowered her voice now, almost to a whisper. "So if you have something in your life of great value, do not ask questions about from where it came. Okay?"

What was Sabine trying to tell her? Maria thought about her modest earrings and needlepoint art.

"I have nothing like that."

"*Maria.*" Sabine looked at her in disbelief.

"*I do not.*" Insistent, Maria lifted her hands and shrugged her shoulders.

Sabine took a deep breath, not wanting to give words to the thought in her mind, but it had to be done.

"I was just a girl when they lined the families up in the square," Sabine said, trying to keep her voice even. "My father told me not to look but of course I did. From my bedroom window high up, I watched them standing there and then sitting there, the luggage all around, in their coats with the stitched-on stars, waiting . . . and when the trains finally arrived, they filed on, mostly quiet, leaving their bags as instructed, and as soon as the trains had pulled out, others would descend on the bags, teams of them, picking through the piles and mounds of it, all the silver going onto one cart, art to another, cash to another—and musical instruments to another. I remember watching as specialists picked over those instruments, particularly the violins, turning them over, peering inside. And out of every town square full of families, thousands and thousands of people every week, along with the occasional painting I remember seeing a few of those special violins carried off. I watched every day for almost six months, until the families just stopped coming."

Maria looked shaken. "But my violin," she finally said, "my Pressenda, is not of great value."

"You would know better than I," Sabine said, not sounding like she believed Maria. "But your husband is just like mine. So there is something. And if you come across it, do not ask. Because you do not want to know."

Maria didn't respond.

So, emphatically, Sabine thrust her hand deep into the box, removed a fat fistful of gold, picked out a few little pieces, and tossed the rest back in.

"Listen to me," she said, urgency in her voice. "If you come across a door, do not open it."

Sabine opened her hand and Maria saw, in her friend's palm, numerous gold crowns and gold fillings, some with a few teeth still attached. The sight startled Maria.

"Because once you do, you will never be able to lie to yourself again."

TOMORROWLAND

Maria dropped her purse and car keys on the entry table and walked into the kitchen. Through the open back door, she could see Peter out in the yard, a large shovel in hand, planting the last of the azalea bushes.

"Peter," she called out to him. "What are you doing?"

"Helping." Covered head to toe in reddish dirt, he grinned like an aviator.

She walked out, joining him. "You are supposed to be doing your homework."

"Finished."

"All of it?"

"All of it."

"What about the English?"

"Mom." He slammed the shovel blade into the ground and looked at her as though *she* were the child. "Five-paragraph essay. Introduction, narration, affirmation, negation, conclusion. A kindergartener could do it."

What could she say to him? Maria just looked around at the pile of empty black containers, watching him carry the last shrub to a freshly dug hole. He'd made a complete mess, of himself and the planting area, but the job wasn't entirely bad.

"Peter, I appreciate the help, really, but we have hired men to do this."

He turned to her, plant dangling from his filthy hand. "Which as you can see is unnecessary."

She just shook her head in amazement at this boy. "There is no arguing with you."

"Everyone says I got Dad's brains."

Pulling the shovel out of the ground, she began digging the last hole a little deeper. "I think that is true."

He dropped the plant and, fists to his hips, watched her dig. "Well, if I lived at home, you wouldn't have to work like this and you wouldn't have to hire men."

"Oh, Peter—"

"Well, it's true, Mom! You know Dad doesn't do this kind of work and you shouldn't have to."

She threw a heavy pile of dirt near his feet and then stopped, leaning on the shovel. "Your father may not be much for physical labor, but he takes very good care of me. You need to know that. He takes very good care of all of us. I know it is difficult to understand why he wants you to attend boarding school, but he really does have your best interest in mind. He is a very good man and I do not want you to ever forget that."

"I know, Mom," he said quietly.

Maria realized her words sounded strangely defensive. She made herself smile reassuringly at him and resumed her digging.

"He said he fell in love with you the first time he met you," Peter said, then giggled a little. "At your christening."

She stopped, wiped her brow. "He said that?"

"Sure did." Peter stuck the plant's root ball in the hole and began pushing the pile of dirt in on top of it.

"Your father and I lived through very difficult times—something we pray you will never experience—and I can tell you that the most important thing in life is family." She paused until he looked up at her, continuing with distress in her voice. "Never forget that."

She looked at him intensely, making sure he understood, and though she tried to resist the impulse to hug him, she lost the battle, throwing her arms around him. Her face up, a smudge of soil on her cheek, she squeezed him tight, and he let her. Oh, how she hated him being away at boarding school. Dropping him off on Monday mornings tore her up inside. And despite her best efforts, he knew how much she hated it. But it's what Hans wanted, and that was that.

Finally, Peter remembered something and squirmed out of the hug. "Mom! What time is it?"

Looking at her wristwatch, she replied, "Seven twenty-five."

"It's almost time!"

He ran toward the house.

"Peter!"

He didn't respond or slow, and so she ran after him.

Just up the back steps, as soon as he set foot in the kitchen, she grabbed his shoulder. "Stop!"

He stood still.

"You have to clean up before—"

"Mom, no! It's almost on!"

Maria took in the sight of her dirt-covered son shifting his weight anxiously from foot to foot.

"All right," she sighed. "Arms up."

He complied and she lifted off his shirt. Then he took off his shoes and socks, then his pants, and, in his white briefs, he went to the sink and washed his hands and face.

She stood there taking in the sight of him, reflecting on their conversation and all that had happened over the last couple of days, until he suddenly whipped back at her with a panicked impatience.

"Okay, go get some clothes on and then you can—"

He was already gone before she could finish.

The setting sun creating a halo of light around her golden hair, Maria raised her chin, brushed some dirt from her hands, and sighed.

JANUARY 1945

By the stone-gray light of the full moon, face down, constantly rubbing her bare hands together, Maria trudged through the light carpet of snow on the path through the woods to her cottage. It was a crisp, clear winter night and she could see the fog off her breath every time she exhaled. She blew into her hands a few times to warm them. In the distance, she could hear the antiaircraft fire trying to pick the Allied bombers out of the skies. These enemy strikes were happening more frequently. And the food shortages at the *Kinderhaus* had become commonplace. Despite the drunken happy talk among the SS men who came through, she knew things were going badly for the German army. She could see the desperation and fear growing every single day now in the men's eyes. There could be no doubt—everything was quickly spinning out of control.

Tonight was especially difficult for the children, but she had succeeded in getting them all to sleep, all except little Mieszko, the fair-haired Polish boy who had taken to Maria as if she were his mother. She read to him and sang to him, nearly every one of the approved German children's stories and German songs. Nothing worked, until she finally broke down and sang a sweet lullaby in her broken Polish in his ear. She knew it wasn't going to help him assimilate into the program, and that could be dangerous for him. But it offered him comfort, and at this point was there really much else she could do?

Although she had grown cold to so much since the war began, just thinking of that poor child brought a lump to her throat. It was all so unfair what these innocent children had to endure.

Maria arrived at her cottage, opened the door, and stepped inside. She stomped some snow from her feet and removed her heavy and increasingly tattered wool coat, and carefully hung it on a hook near the door. She walked into the room, ready to build a fire, but she saw a basket on the table in front of the sofa. She went right to it.

On top of the blanket that covered the basket was a note with her name on it. She picked up the folded note, grinning as she recognized the handwriting, and pulled back the blanket, seeing a small treasure trove of items—several cans of meat, a few bars of chocolate, a bottle of aspirin, nearly a dozen hard apples, and at the bottom, underneath it all, a violin case.

She picked up an apple, brought it to her nose, her mouth instantly watering as she inhaled the sweet fragrance. Oh, how she wanted to bite into it. But thinking of Mieszko, she forced herself to put it down.

She opened the note, reading: *Dear Cousin Maria, I am sorry I was not able to see you on this visit, but I trust you will accept this basket as well as my apologies. As I suspect you understand, the pace of my work has increased precipitously in recent days, and I am overdue at the factory. As much as I will comfort myself with the image of you feasting on what little rations I could bring this time, I know that you will give all of it to the children rather than care for yourself in even the smallest way. So this time I made sure to bring you something that only you could enjoy. Please accept this modest but truly fine violin as a late Christmas present. All my love, Cousin Hans.*

Maria opened the violin case, carefully removing the violin. She held it up, looking inside, seeing the Pressenda label, examining the acutely curved back, admiring the exquisite red-toned varnish. Then she put the largish instrument on her lap and smiled, suddenly warm throughout with the knowledge that, in a world gone mad, she was thought of and loved.

1957

Maria marched up the back steps, threw open the screen door, and rushed directly through the kitchen, past Peter, who sat on the sofa fixated on the television set. She went right to the hall table under the polished chrome-framed mirror and picked up the stack of mail.

The sounds of the television behind her, she sorted through the mail, looking through various bills and solicitations, until she finally came to a letter from Sears, Roebuck & Company Insurance.

Yes, Hans was analytical and responsible, just like most of the other Von Braun men, with their mathematical proofs and scientific verifications, the kind of men who did not like chance and risk.

She looked at the letter in her delicate, slender hands for a long moment. If she opened it, Hans would know. She could look for one of the older bills. Even though she believed he had most of those at his office, there were boxes in the garage. She could get a ladder, and dig through those, and . . . Nonsense. She wasn't going to start sneaking around in her own home. Without further thought, she tore open the envelope in her hands, removed the letter, scanned it, and read:

1830 Giovanni Francesco Pressenda violin
reddish-tint, high-gloss varnish
Value $525, Quarterly Premium $7.50

Just as she had always assumed, it was a high-quality violin, but not worth a bucket of gold.

Maria looked up, catching a glimpse of herself in the mirror, standing there, holding the letter in her hand. She had a smudge of soil on her face. She shook her head at herself, feeling ridiculous. What was she doing?

She wiped her face clean with the back of her hand, put the letter back in the envelope, put it back in the stack, and feeling some sense of closure, she walked leisurely into the kitchen.

A little later, the washing machine purring steadily off in the laundry room, Peter and Maria sat on a sofa, TV trays before them, eating the sauerbraten and cabbage she had prepared earlier in the day and watching *Walt Disney's Disneyland*. Peter was transfixed listening to Walt Disney—dashing but fatherly in a conservative gray suit, moustache neatly trimmed—as he introduced tonight's show, *Man in Space*. Walt spoke earnestly about a special realm of his theme park devoted to things of the future, an area called Tomorrowland, and one of the most popular attractions there, a simulated rocket trip around the moon. He explained in articulate but folksy detail how visitors to the attraction, the Disneyland spaceport, enjoyed thrills similar to what space travelers of the future would encounter when rocket trips to the moon became a daily routine.

Referring to spectacular drawings and mock-ups of spaceships and rockets, Walt went on to explain how scientists had been working to get America into space. He gave a short history of rockets, focusing primarily on the V2 and how it was being used as the basis for the American rocket program.

Then Wernher Von Braun came on.

"Mom!" exclaimed Peter, pointing excitedly at the television.

"I see, Peter."

Von Braun, sounding like a mild-mannered professor, detailed how a trip to the moon and back was going to work. Bringing out a huge glossy white replica of a wheellike space station and rotating it to simulate gravity, he explained how the massive structure would house hundreds and serve as a refueling platform for space travel.

Peter was enthralled by the program, as so many other Americans undoubtedly were as well. Listening to the movie-star-handsome and impeccably dressed Von Braun, explaining in his eloquent German accent how we would all soon be taking trips to the planets, was nothing short of thrilling. Indeed, Von Braun was the perfect spokesperson for America's space program.

But there was no mention, Maria thought as she watched, of what the V2 had done to London and no mention of the slave labor that had built it.

These weren't exactly secrets. She remembered reading vague references to these things when the war trials were going on, right after she'd moved to Fort Bliss in Texas to begin a new life with Hans. But after all that had happened, no one wanted to talk about such matters. All those trials and the horrific history they had dug up quickly faded into the background, a harsh coda to a world everyone wanted to leave behind, including her.

There were new threats on the horizon now, and new dreams. And the V2 was the answer to both. And in fact, as one listened to the smiling Von Braun and Walt Disney chatting before the American public, the V2 suddenly seemed as wholesome as apple pie.

Still, regardless of what Americans knew, or *wanted* to know, about the V2, they clearly had no idea what was under Sabine Janssen's house. Did Von Braun? Because *that* was something about which the American public could never look the other way, even if Walt Disney himself was putting a happy spin on it.

Americans certainly had no idea that the head fuel chemist for the nation's rocket program, Karl Janssen, was not only a former Nazi but an SS officer. Was Von Braun—this kindly paternal man standing next to Walt Disney in front of America—really a high-ranking SS officer? Like those men who had overseen the slave labor that built the V2 and ended up hanging at Nuremberg?

Was her husband?

No. Sabine was wrong about the violin and she was wrong about this too—she must be.

Maria tried to put all this nonsense out of her head and focus on the television. She made herself lean back, like Peter. But she kept shifting and fidgeting as she listened, crossing and uncrossing her legs, Sabine's voice and the handful of gold teeth haunting her mind.

Despite what she tried to tell herself, the sense of relief and closure that she had felt earlier vanished, replaced anew by these irksome thoughts, and she felt crazy. She'd known Hans all her life and he'd always been so sweet to her. Throughout the war, he came and checked in on her whenever he could, bringing food and gifts. He wore always his coat and tie, or sometimes his lab coat, and he spoke only of his rockets and the hardships of the war. Bookish and gentle, just like her father, he was so different from the arrogant officers she met, with their nationalistic agenda and sense of entitlement. Hans always seemed to genuinely care about her.

And he'd always been so forthright with her—more than she was with him, she had to admit. He was just a scientist, he'd told her. So it never even occurred to her to ask him if he had been in the SS—why would she? Furthermore, the Americans would never have brought a Nazi party member into the country, given him and his family citizenship. There were laws . . .

Then again, some of these men were quite valuable to America . . .

So maybe *some* of them had been party members. Maybe some had even been SS officers who built and ran those camps, rounding up families, herding them onto the trains, among other things. She knew about those things. And the more she dared dwell on it, and really think about Karl Janssen, and what she had seen today, the more she could see him in an SS uniform.

But not Hans. The man's life was dedicated to science, to his dreams of space flight, not racist ideology. Hans Reinhardt didn't have a violent bone in his body. Had she ever even seen him kill a spider? No. Surely every wife must wonder about her husband at times, but one thing was simply indisputable—Hans Reinhardt put science over everything. Over nationality, over religion, over passion for anything else, probably even her.

And in that, at least, couldn't she find a kind of peace?

Watching her husband's dear friend Wernher speaking in lofty, impassioned tones about how space flight was man's destiny, she had trouble believing what Sabine had told her.

On the other hand, Sabine Janssen might not know Wernher Von Braun, or Hans Reinhardt, all that well—but Karl Janssen certainly did. And why would Karl fabricate something like that for his wife?

Beads of sweat began to form on Maria's forehead as she fought with herself—*trying to convince herself not to do what she now knew she had to*—and she felt her heart racing. Abruptly, she stood up.

"I'll be right back."

Staring at the television, Peter didn't even hear her.

Maria ran out of the room, down the hall, past several of her flowery new needlepoint pieces on the walls, and into her bedroom. She went straight to her husband's closet.

On the base, near Building 4488, nerve center of the Army Ballistic Missile Agency, in Vehicle Static Test Control Room 1, the men gathered around the primary control panel and looked out the massive plateglass window at a rocket, sixty-nine-feet tall, anchored to metal scaffolding, a test stand, about the same height as the rocket.

The lead rocket scientists—or, as the burgeoning civilian space program was calling them, the aerospace engineers—were all there in the control room. Hans, Karl, Wernher, and about a dozen other of the German men. Joining them in the small room, filled with bulky metal panels and control devices and monitors of all sorts, were several administrators from Washington, including Colonel Adams and, perhaps most important, Senator Sparkman, who was going to get Congress accustomed to keeping its checkbook wide open for the men in this room.

It was an exciting time. Not since the Manhattan Project had a group moved with such speed and commitment to purpose. And even though the test hadn't been run yet, there was a lot of back-slapping and congratulating and discussing of who would be buying frothy German beers at the officers' club.

Finally, the men faced forward, all of them, watching out the window as a technician began the ignition sequence. When the monitors indicated that the alcohol-water mixture and the LOX, the liquid oxygen, were all flowing properly through the propellant's turbopump and the compressed nitrogen was circulating, the ignition switch was thrown and the large rocket tethered to Redstone Static Test Stand 1, about a quarter mile from the control room, began to roar as its engine fired, brilliant orange flames pouring out of the bottom of the rocket.

Fiery gases rushing out of its engine, held down by steel straps and anchored to the adjacent static test stand so it could not fly up, the rocket produced more than seventy-five thousand pounds of thrust, all evidenced and recorded on the meters in the control room—more than enough power to get America's first satellite into space.

The rocket test a smashing success, the men in the room cheered loudly. Colonel Adams shook hands with Senator Sparkman, and both men lit long, fat Cuban cigars. A bottle of bourbon came out, glasses were passed around, and all the men began to celebrate.

This was very different from the multiple disasters the navy had put on with their ill-conceived rocket attempts. Finally, with the Germans, the nation was in good hands.

Still hearing Von Braun and Disney talking about the wonders of the V2 and space travel, Maria threw open Hans's closet door, scooped up the contents on the floor, dumped them into a pile in the bedroom—shoes and dry cleaning boxes and dirty clothes— and examined the bare wood floor for any sign of a metal insert. She searched intently, scanning and rescanning every inch.

There was none. She was certain there was none.

Then she kneeled and knocked on the floor, several times. It was solid. Nothing down there.

She scooted herself out of the closet, tripping and falling and sitting on the floor of her bedroom, looking at her clean, white, sterile bed and the big messy pile she had made of her husband's things. She caught her breath and exhaled a deep sigh of relief.

Her relief was short-lived. As she focused once more on the voices of Wernher Von Braun and Walt Disney and visualized again what she had seen that day, she remembered Von Braun's words. *Science does not have a moral dimension. It is like a knife. If you give it to a surgeon or a murderer, each will use it differently.* But what of the men who made the knife? Could they really divest themselves wholly from its purpose?

Could they really not know how it was manufactured and used?

The violin was not some looted treasure. There was nothing under her house. So why did she still have this nagging feeling that by disturbing the past she'd dug up some serpent that was now uncoiling behind her?

Was it because she was hiding a secret of her own?

DARK CHOCOLATE

The next day, Maria drove up the long circular drive at the front of the Darlington School in Rome, Georgia. It was early in the morning and a thick mist shrouded much of the campus. Boys and girls of all ages in prep school uniforms, books under arms, moved hurriedly along walkways from the dining hall to the dormitories to classrooms. The students came from all over the country and most lived on campus full time. But a few, like Peter, lived in the region and went home on weekends. Maria knew it was probably harder on Peter to straddle both worlds like this, but to not see him for months at a time was unthinkable.

Maria pulled up to the front of Archer Hall, the middle school boys' dormitory, and turned off the engine. The air coming in through the partly rolled-down window was fresh and moist and smelled of North Georgia pines, a heady scent that almost made the two-hour commute worthwhile.

"Remember, next weekend is the school carnival, and your father and I think you should stay on campus for it."

"I know."

"I miss having you home, but your father is right. You will never feel like you belong here if you do not spend more time here."

Peter nodded. He knew she didn't agree with his father, but he didn't want anyone fighting.

"Whatever you want, Mom. Just don't worry. Okay? I'll be fine."

"Okay." She looked at him and sighed. He was getting so big. "Is a quick hug allowed?"

"Sure. Just don't, you know, make too big a deal out of it."

Maria grabbed him around his shoulders, hugging him tight.

Peter saw some of his friends walk by. "Okay, Mom."

Maria swiftly released him. "I'll see you the weekend after next. If your dad has to work, I'll be here to get you. Okay?"

He threw open the passenger side door, grabbed his bag, and slid out. "Okay."

"Have a good two weeks."

"You too."

"I put an apple strudel in your bag."

"Thanks, Mom."

"It is for snack. I want you to eat good meals here."

Peter stood outside the car, looking at her calmly. "I'll be okay, Mom. I love you."

"I love you too."

He smiled as assuredly as he could, slammed the door, and, bag over his shoulder, disappeared into the sea of preteens, boys in blue blazers and gray slacks, girls in seamed skirts and white blouses, all shouldering the heavy expectations of their respective families.

Maria just sat there in the car, watching him go, eating her heart out.

A woman in a smart business suit approached the driver's side of the car and leaned in. "Hello, Mrs. Reinhardt. Good morning." She had perfect teeth and a perfect smile.

"Good morning, Mrs. Johnson," Maria replied.

Even though Maria hardly knew Betty Johnson, the Darlington School director of advancement, the woman spoke to Maria as if Maria were one of her closest friends. Maria wanted to believe this was because of what they called "southern hospitality," but she suspected that Mrs. Johnson was carefully following Hans's important and increasingly public work with an eye to how it might help the school with its fund-raising agenda.

"I saw Mr. Reinhardt on Friday," Mrs. Johnson said. "Congratulations on the rocket! Everyone at Darlington is so excited. Oh, and we'll all be listening to you on the radio leading the HSO! What a couple you two are!"

"Thank you, Mrs. Johnson." Maria could no longer smell the pine trees for Betty Johnson's hairspray.

"Dropping off Peter this morning?"

"Yes."

"You have that 'look' on your face. He'll be fine. They're like puppies, they forget about you the minute you leave them."

Maria wasn't sure if that made her feel better or worse, but she decided it was time to address something else on her mind. "Mrs. Johnson, do you have a moment? I want to ask you for some advice."

"Of course."

Maria stepped out of the car, shutting the door behind her.

"I met this young girl in Huntsville recently who I really think is a violin prodigy."

"Really?"

"Honestly, in all my years playing violin internationally, I do not think I have ever seen such raw talent and potential in a student so young—much less a girl."

"How amazing. Where is this young girl studying?"

"I am not sure, actually."

"Well, you know we have an outstanding music program at Darlington." An extra sweetness now in her voice, Mrs. Johnson slipped into recruiter mode.

"I do know that, of course, Mrs. Johnson. Which is why I brought it up. But honestly, I am not sure this is the place for her."

"We may not quite be on the level of a Juilliard, but if she wants to stay in the south, Mrs. Reinhardt, I assure you, there is no finer program."

"No, I know that." Maria paused for a moment, thinking about the right way to explain this. A group of students ran by. "For one thing, the family could never afford Darlington, you see, they are—"

"Mrs. Reinhardt. You know we have funds for *that* kind of child. We could probably arrange a full scholarship for her through high school."

"I know, and am not sure how the family would respond to that. It seemed complicated, from the very little I even know."

"A full scholarship to the Darlington School? What's complicated about that?"

"I would not even know how to approach it. First, you have to understand, she is a Negro. And it seems her father is very proud. I cannot anticipate that he would accept anything that looks like charity. Do you . . . would you be interested in approaching the family?"

"She's Negro?"

"Yes."

"We're a white school," Mrs. Johnson said, sounding somewhere between annoyed and surprised that she had to explain this to Maria. "We always have been."

"I understand, of course, but Darlington is a private school."

"Yes—"

"So you do not have to follow the state laws. And I just thought that in an extraordinary situation like this, an institution like Darlington that values excellence might be thrilled to make an exception."

"Well, I can tell you with certainty that she wouldn't be comfortable *here*."

"Do you mean *Darlington* would not be comfortable with her?"

Mrs. Johnson laughed. She had a well-honed list of subtle and quite reasonable-sounding ways of handling this topic. Indeed, she referred to the list more and more lately. This wasn't the first occasion she had been asked to consider the admission of a Negro student. But she liked and respected Maria too much to play those games this morning. "Mrs. Reinhardt—of course that's what I mean."

"Okay," Maria said, taken aback by her frankness. "Well, can you recommend any other schools with good music programs that might be more open to her?"

Mrs. Johnson just smiled. "How is Peter doing in math? I hear *he's* a prodigy."

Driving in her Chevy through the northeast Georgia foothills, toward the Alabama state line, Maria rolled down her window all the way. The breeze tousling her voluminous golden hair, the car was instantly filled with the bracing scent of the misty forest. Maria thought about rolling the window back up to keep herself looking intact in the event James Cooper was at Ruby's today. But her mane was already beyond repair and, truthfully, she didn't care. She let her hair fly freely, enjoying the breeze on her face and the way it migrated between her silken tendrils.

Of all the people in her life, she felt that the one person who knew her *true* self was an arrogant boy of a man she hadn't seen for twelve years, someone with whom she really had spent very little time.

Was she kidding herself? She knew that logically, rationally, it made very little sense. But that did nothing to dissuade her.

Maria threw her head back, arms extended on the wheel, her cheeks flush from the breeze. All she knew for sure was that from the second she saw James Cooper walk into that ballroom on Saturday night, their unfinished history had to be addressed.

1945

Cooper paced the cottage, pulling back the flimsy window curtain and peering outside. The orange glow off on the horizon caused by the bombings had subsided, and much of the black smoke had dissipated. Cooper surmised that, over the last few hours, the German troops must have been able to put out the fire at the munitions depot adjacent to the factory, about five kilometers to the east.

He stepped away from the window and took another look at his rayon escape-and-evasion map of the area, folded it up, and slipped it back in the small musette bag, up against the barter kit—a flat, heavy package containing a variety of gold coins and rings, primarily solid gold francs and sovereigns and fourteen-karat-gold wedding bands. The U.S. Army Air Forces put these gold barter kits in the larger Atlantic bailout packs worn by most fighter pilots flying over Europe. Part of Cooper's escape-and-evasion training included coursework in how to seek out, assess, and approach noncombatants in enemy territory who might accept the gold coins and rings in exchange for food, shelter, and safe passage. Cooper was glad someone at HQ had had the wisdom to make sure he had this expensive kit with him right now. Of course, he was also relieved that he had his sidearm and extra ammo with him as well. Getting back into friendly territory alive was not going to be an easy task.

The immediate issue was how long he could safely hide here and when he would need to leave.

Cooper glanced over at Maria, sitting on the sofa, her bare legs tucked up underneath her, motionless, just clocking him in that feral feline way of hers.

Taking another look out the window, Cooper could see the stars now, and judging from their position he knew it was getting late. Morning would be here soon and he would have to make some decisions about his next move. He checked the door, throwing the old brass latch slide bolt. He was tired and ravenous and his body ached in numerous places from the bailout.

He walked over to Maria, sitting in the chair across from her, evaluating her carefully. *Could he trust her?*

"Do you have a boyfriend?" he asked.

"How is that your concern?"

"How long can you stay in this cottage before someone comes looking for you?"

"I do not know."

"Take a guess."

"For three years I taught the children here every afternoon and read to them when they went to sleep in the *Kinderhaus* most evenings. In the last weeks, people are fleeing, there are no more classes, but the children, they are still up there. If I do not go to them, eventually someone will come to check on me, perhaps one of the staff members who stayed behind. What are you going to do?"

He wasn't yet sure. But if what she said was true, he had some time to figure it out. "First," he said, "I am going to eat."

Cooper bolted up and marched over to his musette bag.

"Are you hungry?" he asked her as he returned with the bag.

"No." She looked away in a daze.

He sat back down, bag on his lap, studying her closely again. "You look like you're hungry."

They both knew she was starving, but Maria refused to engage with him. She had found a strange comfort in the dark place where her mind had drifted, already giving herself to some imminent demise that seemed inevitable and even deserved. She looked like she had given up her soul and now awaited the consequences.

Cooper recognized the look. Every man who had been at war as long as he had came to know it. But recognizing it and buying into it were two different matters and James Cooper was not a man to buy into much of anything, especially when it involved emotions. Hell, that he was alive at this very moment was testament to the fact that even something written in stone can be rewritten with enough will and simple smarts. And a touch of dumb luck never hurt either.

"Well, I'm hungry and I don't like to eat alone," he said.

Cooper reached into his bag, fished into a pocket of his folded survival vest, produced a small parachute emergency ration container, and pulled out a thick bar of sweet military-issued Hershey's chocolate. He slipped his fingers into the brown wrapper, pulled the paper off, cracked the bar in half with a sharp snap, put a section of the black chocolate down on the table in front of her, and shoved his section deep into his mouth, taking a firm bite with his back teeth.

Saliva instantly flooded Cooper's mouth as he chewed, and Maria could see the pleasure on his face. He wiped a smear of chocolate off his cheek with the back of his hand.

Despite Maria's best efforts to remain aloof, her mouth watered too. Chewing on her lower lip, she studied him, and the chocolate, knowing how valuable these items were, particularly to a soldier behind enemy lines.

"What were you playing when I came into the cottage?" Cooper asked. "Sibelius?"

She didn't answer, but he knew he was right, and he could see in her eyes that she was intrigued with his knowledge of music.

He went on. "My mother made me take piano lessons starting when I was five."

"I was three," she said with a raspy voice.

"That explains why you're so good. That, and that you're good."

She looked at him for a very long moment. Where was the fear in this man? "Thank you," she finally said, eyeing the chocolate in front of her once again.

"Do me a favor, would you? Eat the chocolate. Watching you staring at it like that is making me twitchy."

"I am not staring."

"Yes, you are." He scooted the half bar of dark chocolate a little closer to her. "Just pick it up."

That did sound like a good idea. And what could it really hurt? She reached out, grabbed the hunk of chocolate off the table, shoved it deep into her mouth, and took a large bite. Her mouth filled with so much saliva as she chewed that a little dribble of chocolate and spit escaped from the corner of her mouth. With the knuckle of her index finger, she dapped up the drool as it ran down her chin. She licked her knuckle, continuing to chew, savoring the luscious cocoa butter and sugar.

"It *is* good," she said, chewing with her mouth open.

"A lot of the guys complain about the rations but times like this—"

"It is very good. Thank you." She shoved the rest of the chocolate bar into her mouth, chewing brashly, entirely unconcerned with manners.

He smiled as he watched her, enjoying how much pleasure this smart, beautiful, broken girl was getting from a simple bar of chocolate.

"There's this little candy store on the boardwalk in Atlantic City," he said, "that makes the most incredible chocolate. Right there, behind the glass, you can watch 'em. They make the saltwater taffy and fudge and such, like everyone else, but the chocolate, dark and bittersweet, they just pour it out onto parchment, dropping in whatever you want—candied ginger, fresh plums, toasted pistachios. I like it plain. You're walking down the boardwalk at night, arcade lights, moonlight, the ocean breaking right under your feet, and you can smell the salt spray, and you're eating this crisp, rich chocolate, round and thick as a dinner plate. You can just walk and walk for an hour like that."

Maria envisioned him walking along that foreign boardwalk, in white slacks and a sports shirt, ocean breeze in his hair, and for an instant thought that he was someone she could like. In another life she would have liked to know him, maybe even be his friend. Cooper was interesting and funny, and the way he looked at her . . .

She was accustomed to men looking at her, and she was familiar with a variety of intents in their glances. But this man was not so easy to read. He had a certain assuredness—she saw it in his actions, the way he made assessments as he marched around the cottage, and mainly from the way he didn't break eye contact with her. She'd seen this kind of confidence in elite soldiers before. But Cooper had something else. She had seen it in his eyes from the moment he had set them on her, a hint of kindness. She could see it in the way he enjoyed watching her eat. She was sure of it. Yes, in another life it would have been fun to walk with him on that boardwalk, eating chocolate and talking, the ocean breeze on them both.

Maria realized she was staring at Cooper, and she became aware that she had what felt like a little smile on her face.

"So you do know how to smile," he said in a teasing tone.

She quickly hardened her expression and looked down at her hands, noticing a few flecks of chocolate on her thumb, which she lightly licked off, like a cat cleaning a paw.

Face still down, she let her eyes wander back up to his.

"I don't know what happened to you," he said. "I don't know what you've done or been through—what your allegiances are or were. And right now, I don't care."

He put his hands on his thighs, leaning forward, closer to her, continuing. "The United States First Army is pouring in from the west right now. They'll be in Hamm by sunrise, Paderborn by tomorrow, and Nordhausen in just weeks. My plan is to survive those weeks. And yours should be to do that too—because once this war is over, everything starts fresh."

"There are some things that, once broken," she said quietly, "never go back together."

"Yeah. I know about those things. And you are not one of them."

She shook her head very slightly.

"You are alive, Maria. And that is a gift, and you have to cherish every precious second of it."

His words and the passion with which he spoke them moved her. She looked away, thinking about those she knew who had lost that gift, had had it taken away in the blink of an eye.

She turned back to him, noticing now the stitched name patch on his chest. "And after this week," she said. "What is your plan then, Cooper?"

He exhaled a laugh as she said his name for the first time. "My family has a farm in middle Pennsylvania. A hundred and fifty acres. Beautiful place. Gently rolling hills of the finest yellow dent corn you've ever seen. A little dairy operation. Horse stable. I think I'd like to settle down there."

"That sounds nice," she said as she envisioned it. "But I must say, it sounds slower than what I thought you might say."

"I know. But after eighty-seven sorties in a P-51, the last one ending in a bullet-strafed cockpit and a last-second bailout through flaming fuselage and heavy antiaircraft fire, I think I'd like to get my feet on the ground and keep 'em there awhile." He rubbed a hamstring he'd pulled when he hit the ground hard and rolled after the bailout.

She nodded her understanding.

"And you?" he asked. "If you could do anything you want when this is all over, what would that be?"

"Oh, I do not know. I have no thoughts of the future."

"I don't believe you. Everyone has a dream."

She nodded slowly. "My dream was to share the joy of music."

He took that in, looking around, focusing on the piano.

"Well, I'll bet you are an *amazing* music teacher. My teacher, Mrs. Mervin, was *strict*, and a big fan of the garlic-stuffed olives. Always ate lots of them right before I sat next to her at the piano."

Maria actually laughed a little. "How unpleasant."

"Yes, it was." Cooper stood up, stepped over to the piano, tapped a few times on the keys. "But Mrs. Mervin sure did love music." He sat down, looked over at Maria, and began to play "Heart and Soul."

He played both parts of the duet, playing with both hands. Then he looked over at her again, grinned, and played only one part with one hand, humming the second part as if calling her over to play it with him.

A whimsical expression crossed Maria's face as she listened to the American soldier in her cottage playing piano and humming. It was a beautiful, sweet sound, and it took her by surprise.

Maria stood. Bare feet gliding over the soft wood, she slowly strolled to the piano, leaned against it, near him, listening keenly. Still humming and playing with one hand, he looked up at her invitingly.

Thinking about joining him in this duet, she reached out to the keyboard, her hand accidentally touching his for a moment. She shared a smile with him and then looked down at the keys. Though the contact was brief, the sensation of his skin upon hers did not fade, causing her heart, involuntarily, to beat a little faster.

She reached her hand out again, and just as she put her fingers on the piano keys, there was a knocking at the door. "Maria!" cried out a German voice.

Cooper immediately stopped playing, insides jumping, every one of his senses slammed into alert mode.

"Maria!" The man screamed out and then pounded hard on the door.

Cooper looked at Maria, and she looked to him, both frozen as each tried to anticipate what the other would do.

"Öffnen Sie die Tür! Öffnen Sie die Tür jetzt!" The man was German military. He tried to force the locked door open.

Cooper and Maria eyed the gun on top of the piano at exactly the same time.

Cooper turned back to Maria—and she swiftly grabbed the gun and fell back a few steps and raised the gun up.

Cooper was stunned. Evidently, she was going to shoot him now or turn him in to this man at the door. Speechless, he slowly started to raise his hands—

Crash! The door exploded in a cloud of splinters and metal fragments as the man kicked it in.

Maria gasped as the soldier fell into the cottage, landing on top of the broken door and its hardware. Taking advantage of the moment, Cooper rushed out of the room and into the adjacent bedroom.

Panicked, Cooper scanned the bedroom, saw a window, ran straight for it, threw the lock, and thrust the window open. He whipped a leg out the window, climbed out, and made his escape.

In the main room, Maria screamed as the German man—a barrel-chested SS officer—held the Colt .45 after easily disarming her.

The SS officer spoke in German, arguing with her, threatening her. Clearly intoxicated, his speech slurred, he reached out and grabbed her arm forcefully, his rage growing. Angry, she pulled her arm from his grasp, trying to reason with him as she backed away, but he just laughed. Despite her obvious protests, he seemed to feel entitled to this visit. Lifting up Cooper's gun, he pushed the magazine release button, caught the magazine as it dropped from the grip, and put it in a pocket. Then he tossed the pistol onto a table and lunged suddenly at Maria, who had backed herself against the wall near the piano.

He threw an arm up against her—pinning her. Then he slipped his hand up her linen dress, yelling incoherent words that were barely audible over Maria's defiant screams. Disgusted and enraged, she fought him tooth and nail, but with little effect except to irritate him further. He retracted his hand to strike her with the back, but he was stopped suddenly. He whipped around to find Cooper— who slammed a fist into his face.

Stunned, the SS officer released Maria and turned to Cooper, shaking off the punch, when Cooper hit him again, sending him stumbling backward, over the low wood table, which smashed into pieces, the half-full pitcher of water on it shattering on the floor, water and glass flying. Falling onto the sofa, the SS officer reached for his sidearm, but Cooper jumped on him, grabbing him by the collar of his uniform and shoving him back into the couch with full force.

The drunken SS officer moaned and flailed as Cooper beat him, his face swelling and bleeding, eyes bulging shut. *Crack!* Blood poured from his broken nose.

Finally, Cooper released his collar, dropping the much bigger man, who fell off the couch to the floor on top of the splintered wood and shards of glass, his uniform immediately wet with the water that had been in the pitcher.

Cooper stood over him, breathing hard, leaning down to get the SS officer's sidearm—when the man grabbed Cooper by the wrist, yanking him to the floor and slapping him across the face.

The SS officer quickly bolted up. Cooper tried to get up too but he slipped on the wet floor and the SS officer kicked him in the ribs. In pain, Cooper rolled and then grabbed the SS officer's booted foot, pulling it out, knocking the man to the ground.

Cooper stood up. Again the SS officer jumped up, his sidearm now in hand, aimed at Cooper's chest.

The men stared at each other for what seemed an eternity. It was over now. Tens of millions of men were fighting one another all over the globe, but for these two the entire war came down to this moment of victory and defeat.

Finally, the SS officer began to smirk and, as if in slow motion, Cooper saw the man's finger pulling the trigger—when a heavy black fire iron slammed into the side of the officer's head, knocking him to the ground.

Maria stood there, the fire iron in her hand.

She walked a few more steps toward the man and looked up at Cooper, her face at once seething and calculating, then back to the injured officer.

He lay on the ground mumbling to Maria in German, his tone

very different now. He wasn't going anywhere, except maybe to a hospital. The fight was over. But seeing Maria's thoughts in her narrowing eyes, he began pleading.

It was clear to Cooper, even without a full understanding of German, that these two knew each other. There was some kind of history here.

Grasping the iron rod firmly by its handle with both hands outstretched in front of her, its pointed flanged tip down, Maria looked to Cooper once more, then to the SS officer on his back on the ground. And Maria made a spontaneous decision. No, there would be no hospital, and reports, and soldiers searching for Cooper. There would be no more of this man's evil.

Seeing what Maria was going to do, the German soldier begged, his eyes wide with fear, but his words had no effect on her. She took a final step toward him, her bare feet just inches from his slowly writhing body.

Maria held the fire iron over him, point down, lifted it up high with both hands, and then, as hard as she could, she plunged it down into his chest.

A pool of blood expanding out underneath him from where the iron point hit the wood floor with a clang, he twitched and died.

Cooper gaped at Maria as she removed the fire iron from the man's torso with a long upward tug, the flanged metal clattering and scraping against his ribs. Then she tossed the bloody implement onto the floor, the comprehension of what she had just done sweeping over her, the realization not only that she had killed a German soldier, an SS *officer*, but that she was a murderer.

TABLE FOR TWO

1957

Calling Mentone, Alabama, a town was generous. It was really just a pastoral bend in the road where Highway 117 crossed over the peak of the ridge and valley region of the far southwestern Appalachian Mountains. Maria slowed as she drove up the mountaintop, approaching the handful of rural shops and inns.

Passing the Hitching Post general store, she pulled onto the gravel parking lot of Ruby's Café, a quaint roadside diner with a wide covered front porch. Right next to the café was the Mentone Springs Hotel, a romantic nineteenth-century Victorian-style house. Behind the café and hotel was a sharp drop with a sweeping view of the heavily forested valley below.

Turning off the car, Maria took a peek at herself in the rearview mirror, smoothed her hair, took a deep, calming breath, and stepped out, crunching across the dusty gravel.

She walked up the front steps, across the wide pine-planked porch, past several big wooden rocking chairs, and pushed through the screened door.

The scent of skillet-fried chicken and pecan pie and Windex hit her as she stepped inside, the wood frame of the door bouncing to a shut behind her. The restaurant had just opened for lunch and was virtually empty—except for James Cooper. In his air force officer's service dress uniform—light blue gabardine trousers, matching jacket with oxidized silver buttons and epaulets, crisp white shirt, dark blue tie—he was rakish and handsome sitting alone across the room at a table among the dozens of empty ones.

Grinning at her, he tipped his head in greeting.

Then he stood and seemed to grow larger as she moved steadily and directly through the empty tables toward him, finally coming to a stop at the seat across from him.

A few ducks caused a brief ruckus outside, and in the distance a train whistle blew.

"Fancy meeting you here," he said.

"Would you like some company for lunch?"

"Please. I think I'm making them nervous just sitting here by myself."

She pulled out her chair, and he came around and slid it in for her as she sat. She folded her hands on the table. "How long have you been here?"

"Oh, since about yesterday afternoon." He sat too, hands folded on the table, not far from hers.

She smiled and they just looked at each other for a very long time.

"So—what happened to that farm in Pennsylvania?" she finally asked.

"Turns out, I wasn't as ready to settle down as I once thought I was."

"But you were ready to become a test pilot and spend your days flying dangerous experimental planes? What happened, James?"

He just smiled at her. What could he say? The truth? That after leaving her in Germany he was never able to feel whole again, never able to meet another girl who made him feel complete, as she had.

"So—you're married," he finally said, eyeing the ring on her manicured hand.

"I am. Anyone serious in *your* life?"

"No. Never quite found the right girl."

Though they spoke lightly, even glibly, it was clear from the way they never stopped gazing at each other that they were talking about a great deal more than their words conveyed.

"If there's one thing I've learned about life from flying," Cooper said, "it's that timing is everything."

There was an obvious subtext to that, and it got to her, and her tone became more serious.

"Two weeks after you left, Hans arrived with American soldiers. He was on the list of scientists whom the Americans and the Russians both wanted—very badly. Von Braun's men raced to the Americans and surrendered to them, and before the U.S. Army got them out of Germany, they let the men get their families. It was part of the deal Von Braun made, and he encouraged the bachelors on his team to get married."

"To fit into suburban America," Cooper said knowingly.

"Nordhausen was in the Soviet Occupation Zone so it was *very* dangerous for Hans to go back there for me. But he did. The American soldiers waited outside the cottage while Hans proposed."

APRIL 1945

In the main room of the cottage, Hans, on one knee, took Maria's hand. Tears flooded her eyes and, fighting them, she looked up, as though seeking an answer.

Through the open door of the cottage, a U.S. Army sergeant, in full battle gear, holding a rifle at the ready, poked in his head, giving Hans an anxious look. They had to go.

Finally, Maria nodded at Hans. And he stood, and they embraced. Wiping away tears in one quick movement of her arm, Maria quickly grabbed a small bag. While she hastily threw in a few items, Hans picked up her violin case.

The sergeant stepped in, waving for them to come, his tense expression rife with the urgency and danger.

Remembering something, Maria rushed to the bedroom, but Hans ran after her and grabbed her hand, stopping her as she reached the bed. They had to leave *right now*.

She froze for a moment, Hans holding her hand tightly, tugging on it. Another soldier stepped in, even more tense than the other, marching right toward them.

She had to go now.

Did she break away and retrieve her cherished possession? And if she did, how could she ever explain what it was? How could she possibly explain from where it came?

In that instant, a million things ran through Maria's mind, and she thought about lies she could tell, but she looked at Hans and right there and then decided that, from this moment on, her life would have to begin with a clean slate.

And with a deep breath, filled with regret but also a growing faith, Maria let Hans take her from the cottage, the two of them holding hands as they ran, the American soldiers jogging behind them, guns at the ready.

1957

Sitting upright, not moving a muscle, Cooper listened to Maria with rapt attention.

"I had minutes to make a decision and grab just one bag," she said. "Hans took my violin. We got in a Jeep, drove south, and made it out. The soldiers arranged for the Red Cross to take the children."

Though he looked as though he had much to say, Cooper just nodded. Finally he found the words he wanted.

"You made the right decision with your life, Maria."

"Hans is my second cousin. He has known me since I was a child, and he always came to check on me whenever he had work at the office in Nordhausen, whenever he could. He is a kind man." She leaned toward him, lowering her voice. "I never thought I would see you again."

"And yet, here I am."

"Here you are."

"And here you are too."

She obviously had something more on her mind than this small talk. And he knew what it was.

"James. Did you . . ."

"No. I was not able to make it back to the cottage. It was impossible. You were smart not to wait for me. You made the right choice, Maria. No regrets."

She closed her eyes, letting that information settle. All these years she'd wondered. Though somehow she didn't feel the closure that she thought she would. She opened her eyes again, still feeling that a door was wide open before her.

Now he leaned over closer to her. "Do you remember—"

"I remember everything."

"Do you remember what we said?"

"In another life. I remember."

He looked around the empty room, in this tiny roadside diner tucked away on an Appalachian mountaintop, and then came back to her. It was just the two of them in the entire world and she was the one who had asked him to come. So he sat now in silence.

"Is that what this is, James?" she finally said. "Another life?"

"Y'all staying at the inn?" asked the gum-chewing waitress who approached their table, pulling a pencil from her beehive hair.

Both thrown, each waited for the other to respond, but neither did. The waitress looked confused.

"We just got here," Cooper said. "Why don't you tell us the specials?"

After listening to mouthwatering descriptions of pit-cooked barbecue and deep-fried okra and local greens with pot liquor and reading their menus with more hearty home-cooked fare, they ordered.

"So how do you like Alabama?" Cooper asked.

"I like it just fine. Lovely house in a lovely neighborhood. The government has been very good to us."

"You don't miss home?"

"This is my home."

"You miss Heidelberg terribly, don't you?"

She looked away, then back to him. "How about you? What do you think of your new base?"

"Hey, they put me in an officer's pad over on Crestwood, pretty much the same as all the other places I've been stationed anywhere else in the world. I swear, even in my own apartment sometimes I have to look at the phone book to remember where I am when I wake up."

The conversation bounced around, covering highlights and tangential anecdotes, on several continents and in various countries, details intimate and reflective and widely varied, their lives' experiences over the last twelve years.

By the time they were halfway through their meals, they spoke with the comfort of old friends. Although Cooper's life had been one of adventure and constant travel and dangerous assignments, and Maria's one of home building, they found they had much in common, predominantly an existential sense that they were lucky to be alive and that one never knew what the next day would bring. It was a peculiar sentiment virtually impossible to express, let alone share, with others who had not lived through years at war—to simultaneously cherish life and feel deeply alone. Perhaps it was due to the beautiful and disturbing firsthand knowledge of man's true nature, something revealed only under the most dire life-and-death circumstances.

"Of everything I have done in my life," Maria said, "I think parenthood is the one of which I am most proud. It changes everything."

He could see what a caring mother she was. "I'll bet he's a great kid."

"He is." Maria reached into her purse and produced a photo of Peter, handing it to Cooper.

"He sure is a good-looking kid," he said, studying the picture.

"Thank you."

"He looks strong. Does he play sports?"

"He runs. But not on a team. Peter is more of a solitary type. Oh, and he is so smart. He beat Hans in chess last week, and Hans did not take it very well." She laughed a little.

"You gonna give him flying lessons? Sounds like you could have the makings of a great pilot there."

"He would love that. But I think I would like him on the ground for now."

He handed the picture back to her and she couldn't resist gazing at it. "He is growing up so fast. Oh, how I miss him."

She put the picture away.

"Why do you have him in boarding school?"

"It is very difficult for Hans . . . he works so much and the work is so vital. And we have Peter home most weekends."

"What's difficult?"

"Hans cannot be distracted and having a child around requires a great deal of attention. And the school is outstanding. The children who attend are from many of the most important families in the country. It is really best for Peter."

"You don't believe any of that, do you?"

She couldn't lie to him. "Getting married is easy. Being married takes commitment, which sometimes includes compromise. Such is life."

She accepted that, so he accepted that. "I see."

Hearing the empathetic sadness in his voice, Maria stirred her sweet tea with the paper straw, poking at the lemon, and took a long sip.

"What about you, Major?" she asked, trying to lighten the tone. "Do you have any pictures of your life?"

"My life?" He reached into his wallet, removed a picture, and slid it to her. "Here's me and my baby having a little rest and relaxation in the South China Sea."

She picked up the photo of him standing next to a sleek fighter jet on the deck of an aircraft carrier. Her face became filled with emotion as she continued to stare at the image.

"What?" he asked.

She laid the photo down on the table, pointing to his plane—to the name written on the side, *Maria*.

"Oh," he said softly, having forgotten that was in the picture. "Yeah."

She tried to read him, to open him up with her questioning expression, realizing how much she had truly meant to him, perhaps in some way did still mean to him.

"You saved my life, lady."

"And you saved mine." She took a deep breath. "But what I did that night was not just for you." Another breath. "I want to tell you something."

"Yes?"

"When my mother died and the war started, my father had a very difficult time and my being his responsibility made it worse."

"Like your husband's difficulties with children around."

She nodded, brushing off her pain about Hans's needing Peter to live away from home.

"But using his connections," she went on, "he was able to help me get a very good position caring for orphans at a nursery in Nordhausen."

"The *Kinderhaus*?" Cooper asked.

"Yes. Originally, it was a place where unwed mothers and SS wives or widows could give birth, and the state would care for the children. But as the war went on, the SS transformed the nursery and others like it into meeting places for racially pure German women who wanted to meet SS officers. The SS told the men it was their duty to make as many children as they could, so the house was very popular."

Her voice had an air of sarcasm. She raised her hands, elbows on the table, and thoughtfully interlaced her delicate, fine-boned fingers, holding her hands together under her chin as though she were praying, or thinking, or both.

"However, that did not satisfy *Reichsführer* Himmler," Maria went on, her tone turning darker. "So, he had his SS systematically kidnap blond, blue-eyed children from the east, mainly Poland, and bring them to the nurseries for Germanization—teaching them German language, culture, and music. The children were told that their parents did not want them anymore. Those that had difficulties assimilating were beaten. Those that refused were sent to the camps."

Maria stopped for a moment, her big, long-lashed eyes fluttering as the story grew increasingly difficult for her. Cooper fought the urge to comfort her, to say anything at all. He knew he needed to let her get it out.

"I was dismayed when I learned this," Maria continued, finding an even tone. "But to leave, initially, meant not only to disgrace my father but also to put him in danger, and by the time he died I could not leave the children. They needed me. I became not only their music teacher but their mother."

The waitress arrived and Maria stopped speaking. Sensing the intensity of the conversation, the waitress quickly grabbed the mostly empty plates in front of Maria and Cooper and hurriedly made off with them.

Maria took a deep breath, setting her hands down on the clear space now in front of her, and forced her mind into a place in the past she had worked hard to forget.

"One of the children," she said, "a sweet little boy named Mieszko, who they renamed Heinrich, had a great deal of trouble learning. He never got over being ripped from his mother's arms on their doorstep in Krakow. All the children had trouble forgetting and complying at first, it sometimes took months to reeducate even the

successful ones, but *Standartenführer* Müller—the SS officer from
that night, a colonel—made Mieszko's life especially impossible,
because he knew how much I liked the boy. And Müller was determined to hurt me because I was not like all those other girls at the
house. I was there for the children. Only for the children. And so I
refused to sleep with him."

FEBRUARY 1945

In Maria's cottage, a light snow falling outside the window, a cozy fire
roaring in the stone fireplace, Maria sat at the piano, playing. About a
dozen striking young children, mostly blond and blue-eyed, well
groomed, nicely dressed like model Aryan children, stood up straight
with good posture while they all sang around Maria at the piano. She
played the "Horst Wessel Song," the stirring Nazi Party anthem,
and the children sang out the words in near-perfect German.

Standartenführer Müller, the SS officer, paced behind them, head
well above all of them, watching Maria intently, grinning at her,
trying to catch her eye.

Uncomfortable with his attention, she did everything she could
to avoid his glances, turning her head down and focusing only on
the children. He didn't like this. He walked the room fiercely, picking up the black fire iron and poking at the fire as he listened.

"*Mit mehr Einsatz!*" he said, emphatically raising the fire iron
high over his head, demanding the children sing with greater commitment.

Maria prodded the children gently and, though visibly anxious,
they complied, singing even louder.

Müller paced with the fire iron in his hand, pleased that his direction was taken but frustrated that Maria refused to acknowl-

edge him and his power. Again, he tried to catch her eye, smiling at her, but she focused her attention on a sad fair-haired boy—Mieszko—standing right in front of her.

As Maria played and the children sang, Müller leaned over their heads, trying to hear what she was saying to Mieszko, but he couldn't. Müller could only see that the little boy was making her smile. Clearly, these two were very close.

"*Sprecht die deutschen Wörter richtig aus!*" he said, directing them to annunciate like proper Germans, raising the fire iron for emphasis.

The children complied. But Mieszko, made nervous by Müller, tripped over the German words. Maria whispered the words to him, but the Polish boy had trouble, tears streaming down his cheeks. Maria reached out an arm and hugged him, comforting him.

Jealous, angry, Müller threw the fire iron to the floor near the fireplace, the clang startling Maria and the children. She stopped playing and they stopped singing.

"*So zeigen Sie Ihre Liebe für Deutschland?*" he asked threateningly, looking only at Maria, questioning their love of Germany.

Finally, very slowly, Maria met his eyes, her expression filled with disdain and disgust. And after a moment, he just shook his head and decisively walked out of the cottage.

1957

Maria sat at the table with Cooper in the dining room at Ruby's in Mentone, Alabama, a resigned sadness in her voice.

"The next day, Mieszko was gone," Maria said. "Müller had sent him to the camp. Mittelbau-Dora. All just to hurt me."

She paused, tearing at the corner of a paper napkin on the table.

He had questions but, seeing the pain this still caused her, he stayed quiet.

"Not a day goes by when I do not think about that boy," she said. "And how I was responsible for whatever was his fate. Not a day, not a night."

"Your husband worked at the camp," Cooper said gently. "Did you ever ask him to see if he could find out anything?"

"He worked in the factory offices. He never visited the camp."

"But the offices, the entire factory, were built into the mountainside right next to the camp. He would have walked by it every time he went to the factory. He probably would have picked out workers."

"He was just a scientist."

"Maria, he was one of Von Braun's team leaders. Don't you think he knew how the rockets were getting built?"

She knew his logic made sense and, given what she had just learned from Sabine, there was no way to try to explain without sounding naïve. "I do not know. I really do not know."

Cooper looked like he had more questions but he could see that his reaction was upsetting her even more, so he moved on.

"Well, what happened to that boy was not your fault, Maria."

"Yes, it was. I could have given myself and saved him."

"Maybe. But what you did in that cottage definitely saved both of us."

She remained unmoved, so he leaned forward, looking up at her face, again speaking softly to her. "I suspected you had history with that officer, Maria. You could have told me this at the time."

"That I committed calculated, cold-blooded murder?"

"It wasn't exactly in cold blood."

"People talk a great deal about values. I hear it a lot in this country. We are told that in the world around us there are good people and bad people. Saints and sinners. But most of us have no idea who we really are, most have no idea what men and women harbor. In all of us live virtue and beast, all of us, and I did not know that, I did not know who I truly was until the moment I stood over that man. Yes, I struck him to protect you. But I killed him not to save myself from prosecution or even to make sure they didn't send soldiers after you. I did it to make sure that pig never hurt another child. It was not an act of passion. I knew exactly what I was doing."

"I know you did." He reached out and put his hands on hers.

She closed her eyes, savoring his touch, knowing that she was understood by this man in a way she was not by any other person.

When she opened her eyes, the bill had come.

Cooper leaned in even closer to her, memorizing her face. She was so damn beautiful. "I thought about looking for you. I thought about it a little, and then constantly. And I guess the truth is, I didn't because I was afraid that I would have found you. I was afraid of . . . this. I was more afraid of kissing you one more time than of never kissing you again."

Maria stared at him. "And now?"

"And now," he said softly, "I pay the bill, and maybe . . ."

"In another life."

"Maybe."

He kissed her hands and then released them. Then he reached for the bill.

Maria sat in the Chevy in the gravel lot, just gazing out the window. It was as though starting the engine would forever break the spell she had just been under. And she wanted a few more moments up here on this mountaintop, a few more moments to relish, a few more moments to herself. She brought her hand to her cheek and took in his scent on her skin.

1945

Cooper completed his repairs on the front door of the cottage. Using wood and hardware from a similar interior door, he managed to fix the frame and secure a door in place. He tested it out, opening and closing the door a few times.

Covered now in dry mud from the terrible task of carrying the body into the woods and burying it, Cooper was filthy.

He turned to Maria, on her hands and knees, scrubbing the blood stain from the wood floor with a large wet sponge. They'd swept up much of the wood and glass, but the stain was not going to be easy to clean.

"It's not perfect," Cooper said, securing the latch on the door. "But it works."

"I once knocked a jar of strawberry preserves on the floor of my house in Heidelberg," Maria said without looking up, continuing to scrub forcefully. "It was the last jar of the season and I was so sure my mother would be mad, but she was not. She was always so kind." There was an aloof tone in her voice, but just underneath it Cooper could hear a great well of emotion.

"She sounds like a nice woman," he said.

"We never did get that stain out of the wood. Never did. I am sure it is still there to this day. Assuming that the house is still there."

Maria plunged the sponge into a bucket next to her and yanked it out, slopping soapy water onto the floor and scrubbing with even greater determination, her hair a shambles, dangling over her face.

Cooper walked over toward her and got down on his hands and knees, right in front of her.

"I think that's enough," he said.

But she just kept scouring the wood floor, moving her hand back and forth furiously, trying to get up the remaining bloodstain.

"Maria," he said, reaching out to her, moving some of her hair back so he could see her face.

The tender sensation of his fingers brushing against her cheek caused her to stop. She froze for a moment.

"When you were walking along that boardwalk in Atlantic City," she said, lifting her head, looking right at him. "Watching the saltwater taffy and the fudge being made and eating your dark chocolate in the moonlight, did you ever see any of this?" She let go the sponge, sat down, and opened both her hands.

"I don't think I ever thought much about the future, really."

He sat down on the floor right in front of her, their knees almost touching. With most of his face caked in dirt, Cooper's clear brown eyes seemed even brighter as he looked directly at her.

"To be honest," he went on, "I'm not sure that you can climb into a plane by yourself and fly five hundred miles into antiaircraft fire to drop a payload in a precise spot and try to get back, if you think about anything more than today, than what's right here and right now. Trying to put things into a greater context, I dunno, I think you can lose clarity, you can lose focus."

He looked off for a moment, thinking about how close he had been to death several times in just the last twelve hours. He felt he had lived half a lifetime in those hours.

Cooper turned back to her, leaning close. "Maria, sometimes you just close your eyes, trust your instincts, and slam the control stick forward. Sometimes you have to trust your gut and not think too much."

"You came back," she said softly. "You did not have to. You could have run off, saved yourself. But you came back and you protected me."

"Of course I did. And you protected me too."

She took a deep breath, studying him. There was so much about her he did not know, yet what she saw in his eyes, heard in his tone, belied all of that.

"And now?" Maria looked up, letting her hair fall back and away from her sweat-drenched face, running her hands through her hair, down the back of her neck, over the tight muscles in her shoulders. "What happens now, James?"

"This will all end soon and the world will start again. You'll see. I don't know how exactly yet, but it'll be better. It's going to be okay, Maria. You're going to be okay."

"You sound so sure." She tugged on the front of her blue linen dress, letting some air cool her skin.

"I am sure because I believe . . . I believe that people can still look out for each other. It's in our nature."

"Kindness," she whispered. "Does that really still exist?"

"Yes. Yes, of course it does. And getting to know you, who I think you really are, in spite of everything we've had to do and the things I suspect you have seen and lived through, I know you believe in that too."

He grabbed her hand and squeezed it and grinned warmly at her. Gauzy light from the rising sun streaming in through the window gleamed off his eyes and teeth.

And for the first time, perhaps since those days in Heidelberg, Maria felt a connection to another human being.

She watched Cooper stand, flecks of dried soil falling from him as he moved.

Retrieving a round throw rug, Cooper tossed it over the remaining bloodstain. Hands on his hips, he surveyed the room, satisfied. Then he turned to her.

"I'm going to clean up," he said, and headed for the bathroom.

Maria sat there watching him, this American soldier who'd fallen from the sky and stepped into her life. This strong, compassionate man who had saved her and cared about her, whom she knew so very little about but still strangely felt that she had known for a very long time.

Maria rose, squinting at the daylight filling the cottage, feeling that this had surely been the longest night of her life.

Wiping her cheek with the back of her hand, she grabbed a broom and dustpan and swept up the remaining wood splinters and soil.

Though her knees were scraped and she was sweating and filthy, she felt a sense of relief as she stood there listening to the soothing sound of the water running in the bathroom.

The door ajar, she could see steam rolling out from the top of the bathroom door frame. Yes, everything looked as though it were just as it was, except for the man in her cottage.

It was more than relief. For the first time in so very long, she felt safe. How strange, safe with the enemy in her house, but there was no denying it. Everything had been turned upside down and perhaps at any moment it was all about to end—but for the first time since she had left her home, she did not feel alone.

Maria walked by the bathroom door, stopping just in front of it. On the white tiled bathroom floor, Cooper's uniform lay in a pile, a little trail of dirt around it. Looking up, through the steam, Maria caught a glimpse of Cooper soaking in the huge clawfoot tub. His arms resting on the sides, fingers dangling, head back, eyes closed, he looked peaceful.

The earth and grime and dried blood removed from him, it was the first time Maria saw flashes of his clean face. She wanted to see it completely.

Steam clouding out above her, Maria edged closer to the door, making out more of him. His wet hair, slicked back off his forehead, looked even darker against the porcelain tub.

Suddenly, he stood, water rushing down and off him into the tub. He picked up a bar of soap and lathered his torso and thighs, splashing himself clean.

Overcome with the need to see his face, to see who this man really was, Maria took another step forward. Perhaps it was because of what they had just been through or the abandon that had come over her, a complete disregard for the world as it was, but despite any consequences she eased the door open.

He sensed her and turned, water cascading down his trim body, his hands up as he combed his black hair back with his open fingers, and he just looked at her in the hazy light, dropping his hands to his sides without shame, and she could see his face and see all of him, and, their eyes on each other, she just stood there and watched him wash.

Then, he sunk into the deep tub again, his head back, his gaze never leaving hers.

And after a very long moment that seemed frozen in time, she took a step toward him.

1957

Maria started the engine of the Chevy and pulled out of the gravel lot, the recollection of James Cooper as fresh on her senses as it had been twelve years before. As she engulfed herself in the past, her body flushed with the exquisite sensation of having and not having, as though trying to satisfy a great hunger with the memory of cake.

She turned the car onto the main road and slowly began to drive off, but as she started to leave this place, she gave one last look toward the café, where she saw Cooper standing on the front porch watching her, looking at her with the same eyes she was just remembering, and it all came rushing back, just as she had visualized in so many daydreams and in those nights lying awake in the clean, white, sterile bedroom, images of him flickering, until she was back to what had happened between them and forward to what might happen again, if by chance or intent she could see him again.

And there he was—standing there on the old porch in his pressed officer's uniform, sun highlighting his dark hair, his big hands open and relaxed, his head turned slightly looking right at her—

She yanked the steering wheel hard, whipped the car over to the side of the road in a sudden cloud of gray dust and grit. She slammed the car into park, hopped out, sprinted across the gravel lot, and bolted up the front steps of the café porch, where she threw her arms around him and they embraced and, his hands to her face, tenderly, they began to kiss.

A swell of warmth rushed from her lips, filling her body, weakening her legs, and the reality of what was happening, her life as she knew it about to be swept away by this sudden all-consuming wave, caused her to hesitate, and she pulled back from the nascent kiss.

Her face still close to his, her hips pressed against his, they stayed like that for a long moment, just listening to each other breathe feeling the warmth and firmness of each other, both afraid to move in any way, cherishing the ache in this perfect moment of shared longing.

"I loved you," Maria whispered. "And I still do."

And with that he forcefully drew her close and kissed her deeply and completely, openmouthed, and she ran her hands up his taut sides and expansive shoulders, finding the exposed soft skin of his neck, her fingers plunging deep into his hair, pulling him to her, kissing him back, their tongues together.

For twelve years she had thought about this moment and here it was, all those years those thoughts standing in when desire came over her and filling her mind when on the rare occasion she was called upon as a wife—thoughts she sometimes invoked while playing violin, bringing her music to transcendent places of profound beauty and pleasure—but what his *actual* touch now did to her was so overwhelming, so far beyond anything she had remembered or imagined or conjured, she knew with certainty that she could not stand here like this with him much longer.

She glanced over his shoulder at the inn just a few steps away, her mind and pulse flying, and just before she lost herself completely, she again pulled back from the kiss.

It was like fighting against a great undertow. Without a doubt, it was the hardest thing she'd had to do since leaving Germany.

"James, I did look for you. Not long after I arrived here, I looked up the number of the farm, and called, and someone answered, but it wasn't you."

"My brother."

"And I did not know if I was more relieved or saddened that it was not you. What could I say? What could there really be for us?"

He nodded.

"Hans is a good man," she said, trying to control her breathing.

"I understand."

And somehow, she began backing away from him.

He just stood there, letting her do what she needed to do, her hands slowing slipping from his body.

"I lost you once," she said, her voice barely audible. "And now I will have to lose you all over again."

She lunged forward, grabbed his face, and kissed him again, and then broke it quickly. "I know this time will be harder, but—"
Overtaken by her emotions, she swiftly turned, bolting down the steps to the car.

Cooper continued to stand there, leaning against a wood beam, watching her car disappear down and around the bend in the road.

Supported by the beam, the mountain breeze on his cheeks, he took in a deep breath, the sensation of her lips on his still present, and he very slowly exhaled as though trying to release her from his core, from his heart, but despite their words and her physical departure, she was still there.

In a telephone booth across the street, a man with a military-style crew cut, in khakis and plaid shirt, a camera around his neck, looking very much like a tourist, aimed his lens at Maria's car, watching her drive off while he spoke on the phone.

"Fine," Colonel Adams said into his office telephone. "Stay with her on the way back into Huntsville and bring what you have to me on base this afternoon." Adams hung up and took a puff on the thick grand-corona-sized Hoyo de Monterrey between his fat fingers.

Concerned, deep in thought, the room filled with rolling, rich Cuban cigar smoke, he made notes from the call in a dark manila folder in front of him on his wide army-issued gray metal desk.

Then he paged through the folder, its various papers and documents all relating to this particular case, until he came to a large photograph, held in place with a big paper clip, of Hans Reinhardt in his SS uniform. He was standing with several high-ranking SS officers at the concentration camp reviewing the camp's gaunt workers, including a few children, in their striped threadbare uniforms, the entrance to the V2 factory in the Kohnstein mountain behind them. In front of the entrance stood a large industrial crane. Hanging from its hook, the body of a dead worker, noose around his neck, could just be made out.

Adams exhaled fresh smoke over the image as he considered it.

BROKEN GLASS

D riving out of the hills and leaving the mountain behind, making her way on the rambling two-lane across the valley just east of Huntsville—James Cooper still very much on her mind—Maria began to sense the earth again, thinking about what lay on this road before her, the reality of her life in the present. And that reality was filled with some deeply troubling questions. Could Hans possibly have known as much about the camp as Cooper suggested? Could he possibly have been an SS officer, as Sabine had implied?

Crossing over pristine Guntersville Lake, she gripped the wheel tightly. Despite Sabine's warning and despite not finding anything in Hans's closet, the questions would not subside. She had built her new life on the premise that Hans Reinhardt was a good man. Was this really true?

Just out of Rainsville, fields of cotton all around, Maria pulled into a filling station, drove up to a pump, and turned off the engine. A cheerful man with neatly slicked hair in a bright, clean attendant's uniform approached her car, a dripping window washer in hand. Maria returned his smile as he walked up to her window and she rolled it down.

"Good afternoon, ma'am! Looks like that front right tire could use some air. Get right to it and if you'll pop the top I'll check the oil for ya. Fill 'er up?"

"Yes, please, thank you so much." Maria pulled the release latch and the front hood snapped open a few inches.

But the attendant didn't move, he just eyed her warily. "Are you a German?" he asked.

"Yes."

The man walked straightaway from the car and marched toward another attendant. Maria watched as they exchanged words that were evidently fairly contentious. The first attendant obviously did not want to service her vehicle. Finally, the first attendant slapped the window washer into the other man's hand—Maria could see him clearly saying "Then you do it!"—and stormed away.

The second attendant approached the car.

He went to her open window. "I'm so sorry about my friend's behavior, ma'am. He's really not a bad guy. He's just . . . How can I serve you?"

Maria didn't need to know what he was. She knew.

"Thank you. I need gas."

"Of course." And the man went for the pump.

Maria turned her head, seeing the first attendant eyeing her from behind the glass of the service station office. He filled his mouth with a wad of chewing tobacco, spitting into a trash can at his feet while he watched her. Despite the scorn on his face, she stared right back at him. Did she deserve to be treated this way? Painted with a broad brush for what some of her countrymen had done? Even for what *a lot* of them had done? Or was this man's behavior, rushing to make a collective judgment, really that different from what was at the root of the evil she had seen in Germany?

All Maria knew for sure was that something had to change.

The mercury-vapor streetlight at the end of Sierra Circle cast a bluish lunarlike glow over the cul-de-sac. It was late and most every house in Blossomwood was silent and dark, except the one at the end of Sierra Circle, where a faint light was still on.

Although it was way past her usual bedtime, Maria stood in her living room among the newly embroidered pieces on her wall and played her violin. There was so much practicing to be done before the radio concert, but her mind was elsewhere.

Stopping occasionally to correct a note and to teach herself a new bow position, she played "Amazing Grace." Captivated by the song and by this new style of violin music, she partly closed her eyes, shutting out the world and letting herself be carried off by the sound.

The front door shut and she looked up, continuing to play.

"Maria. You are up late." Hans walked in and dropped his thick briefcase.

"I could not sleep."

"General Medaris was so pleased with the static test that he pushed up the site scout, so I have to go to Florida tomorrow. What in the world are you playing?"

"Oh . . . something I heard recently."

"I like it."

"Hmm. Me too."

He sorted through the mail on the entry table. "Where did you hear it?"

"A black church in East Huntsville."

That got his attention. "Does this have to do with the girl whose father made her return your old strings yesterday? Peter told me about that."

She stopped playing. "This girl is amazing, Hans."

"That may be, but do you really think you should be spending time in East Huntsville?"

"You would love the music, Hans. I know you would."

"Maria. What are you doing?"

"Doing?"

She stood there, violin hanging from one hand, bow from the other, as though they were natural extensions of her long, elegant arms and hands.

He scrutinized her as if trying to find an answer to his question. Then he chose a tack. "A Negro woman in a city in the southern part of this state refused to give up her seat on a bus last year."

"I read about it."

"She broke the law."

"It was a stupid law."

"That may be but—"

"It was a stupid law."

"Of course it was. But did you read about the four churches in that city that were firebombed? All the houses that were attacked? The violence? Bricks through the windows. Maria—*bricks through the windows*. Do you want one through yours?"

That got to her. Like most anyone else living in a German city in November 1938, Maria knew the sound of broken glass very well. She was only eleven, her son's age now, but she would never forget it, she and her father safe, of course, but outside the glass breaking all night long, and the screaming, as homes and businesses and synagogues were vandalized and set ablaze, and the cheering. That was the beginning.

"Are we still the people who watch, crying, peeking out from behind the curtains, but do nothing?"

"This is different."

"Is it?"

She placed the violin and bow down on the table and went to him with resolve.

"Hans, why is the FBI still following us?"

"I told you, this is just what they do."

He turned away from her, going back to the mail.

"What are they worried about?" she asked, standing even closer to him.

"Who knows? The country is on a witch hunt these days."

"For Communists. And you fought *against* the Communists."

He threw down the mail. "Maria, why are you asking me about this? You know they have always had an eye on us."

"Yes, in the beginning, I understood. But you have more than proven your allegiance now."

"I am telling you, they are paranoid. You have to just ignore it."

She tilted her head slightly as she absorbed that. *Ignore it?* Maria was tired of ignoring things.

"I want to ask you a question," she said slowly. "About your work during the war. I know you do not like to talk about those days—"

"I do not."

"But I have to."

"I thought we had already discussed this," he said in an increasingly sharp tone.

"Twelve years ago."

Hans clenched his big jaw, looking more irritated than Maria was accustomed to seeing him. Then she noticed his eye catch something on the table. He reached down and picked up the opened envelope from Sears, Roebuck & Company Insurance, and he just stood there, holding it, staring at it.

Maria's heart pounded. What would she say? She hadn't prepared anything. How much should she tell him?

Suddenly, Hans dropped the envelope, let out a long sigh, and turned to her.

"What do you need to know, Maria?" he asked.

It took her a moment to catch her breath again.

"Is there something they know about your work during the war that might give them reason for concern?" she asked.

"Like what?"

"Well . . . what do you think?"

"Why do you ask me this?"

"I think it is a natural question."

She had to stop fishing. She headed for a sofa and motioned for him to follow. Reluctantly, he did, and they sat face-to-face.

She continued. "Those men who worked at the camp, that they hung and put in prison at the war trials, did you know them?"

"Maria, that was all a long time ago."

"Well, what do you remember?"

"I knew some of them in passing."

"In passing?"

"They were prison guards and administrators. I was a high-level systems engineer."

"Except for the prisoner collaborators, every single one of those men were SS officers. Were you?"

He put his hands on his knees again, sitting upright. "Was I a member of the SS?" He pursed his lips, thinking. "Before the war, it was a very good time to be a rocketeer in Germany. The party poured money into the program and the fact is, I could never have accomplished what I did, made such profound technological advances—

which America is now using—without the party's support. After
Poland, when the SS took over the program, they poured even more
money in, and we were told . . . we were to join the organization. All
of us. It was not a request. This was a direct order from Himmler
and there was no alternative . . . well, no reasonable one. So yes, I
have a membership number and I believe, once, when some digni-
tary visited the office, I put on the uniform. But none of that ever
had any effect on me. It was a political necessity, nothing more,
which for all practical purposes was meaningless. Which is why I
didn't bother you with it and why I don't bother talking about it and
why this country, along with additional reasons that I suspect are
obvious to you, does not want it talked about either. It is immaterial,
and it is ancient history. So let us now leave it there. Okay?"

She did not seem satisfied.

"Maria?"

"I have one more question."

He did not look pleased, but he acquiesced. "Yes?"

"As a high-level systems engineer, did you not know how the
rockets were getting built?"

Once again, in silence, he pored over her face. "This is important to you."

"Yes, it is."

"Because you need certainty." It was not a question.

"Did you know?"

"This is the last time I will talk about those days. Do you understand?"

"Did you know?"

"I did not know."

She nodded very slowly, taking that in. Then she took his hand
in hers and patted it. "I am going to bed now," she said with a flat-
ness in her voice. She rose, and kissed him on the head.

"I am sorry that it looks like I will be out of town for your performance."

She just nodded sadly.

"*Gute Nacht*," he said.

"Good night."

"Maria?"

She turned back to him.

"Stay out of East Huntsville. Okay? That is not our business."

She did not respond. She just walked away, down the hall, heading for the bedroom.

He rubbed his chin as he watched her go. Finally, with a sigh, he picked up his heavy briefcase and went to the kitchen, so much on his mind.

He set the case down near the table, but instead of getting to work he opened the door and the screen door and stepped outside, leaving them both ajar. He took a few steps out into the yard, taking in the sight of the recently planted bushes. Realizing the job had not been done by the workers, he sighed sadly.

He had a lot to do for his trip, but before getting down to the business of putting the nation's first satellite into orbit, he looked back at his house, the warm light coming from the open doors to his kitchen, where he truly felt a sense of comfort and home, and then he looked up into the stars and, feeling stuck somewhere between earth and heaven, he thought about his wife.

He was sixteen years old the first time he held her, in her white silk christening gown, at the ancient Lutheran church in Landshut. Such a happy day. His cousin on his mother's side, she was an heiress and, despite her father's liberal ideology, she had such a promising future. Like the country, everyone in the family did.

Who could have imagined on that day in 1927 how different things would be for his dear cousin at eighteen, alone and disheveled in that cottage, penniless, her world destroyed, the country going down in flames?

He did what he could for her, as he promised her father and his mother he would. He brought her food, medicine, supplies—even though he knew she gave it all to the children.

Finally, at the end, he took her with him. Beautiful, sweet Maria. She was family, his family, and regardless of everything that had happened and all that had been lost, blood still meant something. He could not bear the idea of leaving her to the approaching Americans, and the Russians . . . he would have slit her throat before that.

She was a link to his past, a rich and noble heritage of Bavarian aristocrats, generations of land barons and castle dwellers, a proud legacy of culture and enlightenment, lost to an impulsive blast of fanaticism and arrogance.

He was so fond of her, partly because she was a link to family but also because he respected and admired her. Maria was a truly amazing woman.

He knew her love for him was never deeply romantic, and he paid that little mind. He had seen and he knew that deep and permanent bonds often grew in arranged marriages when people shared similar histories and values. Indeed, with trust and mutual respect, over time two people could grow together in all ways.

But did Maria trust him?

He could go back in there right now and tell her more. He knew that. But would she understand it? Could she ever understand it?

Maria thought she knew about evil, but she didn't know the half of it. And why should she? He'd made a vow to protect her, to shield her as best he could, and that's what he did, and that's what he would continue doing. For her own good.

Hans looked back at his lovely new house, the warm kitchen light pouring out the open back door and screen door. He saw the light in the bedroom go off, and he thought about his lovely wife climbing into their bed, pulling the white bedspread up around her. Who would have ever imagined on that happy day in 1927, in the grand and ancient Lutheran church in Landshut, that Hans Reinhardt and cousin Maria would end up here, in a humble little house in Huntsville, Alabama? Yet, after everything that had happened, Hans thought, it was a good life. He was grateful for it. And he would protect it.

Hans turned his head back to the sky, so he missed the massive copperhead snake slithering out of the bushes, past the shovel, up the back steps, through the open doors, over the threshold, and into the kitchen of the house—the snake's forked pink tongue flittering out between venomous fangs.

At four thirty in the morning, out for his early run, Cooper jogged quickly down a sidewalk in downtown Huntsville, Maria on his mind. In air force sweats, wet with perspiration, he ran under the bright marquee lights of the Russel Erskine Hotel and continued on.

A sedan pulled up alongside him, slowing. The passenger window went down, and Colonel Adams leaned out over his thick forearm.

"Major Cooper, do you have a moment?"

Cooper turned his head slightly and saw the colonel in uniform, but he turned his head back and kept running. "What's this about?"

"Hans Reinhardt."

"Nothing much to talk about. Met him once at a party. Otherwise, don't know him."

"I believe you know his wife."

Cooper stopped, hands on thighs, bent over, breathing hard.

The sedan stopped. "How 'bout some breakfast, Major?"

PAPER CLIP

Y ou left a working-class family and enlisted as a private before you finished high school," said Colonel Adams, sitting in a diner booth across from Cooper. "Weaseled your way into flight training, two tours out of Leiston, flying ace, shot down over Nordhausen, experimental fighters over Korea—I'm guessing you were recruited for MacArthur's nuclear strike plans over there?"

"I'm not at liberty to discuss that, sir."

"Uh-huh." Adams sipped his hot coffee. "Oh, and test pilot at Edwards in various top-secret jets. I believe you have the makings of an astronaut, son."

"Are you offering me a job, sir?"

"Perhaps."

Cooper gulped down some orange juice and then continued eating his hearty breakfast of eggs and sausage and cheese grits.

"According to your escape-and-evasion report, you received shelter and sustenance from a German civilian when you were shot down."

"I received help from several civilians before I ran into scouts from the advancing Thirtieth Infantry."

"Any of these civvies happen to be a beautiful young German girl, I'm thinking decent violinist with a rocket scientist cousin?"

"I got nothing to hide, Colonel."

"It's not you I'm worried about."

"You don't strike me as a man of great worries."

"Oh, don't let the calm exterior fool you, inside I'm a kitten on needle." He downed a slug of coffee. "I don't seem to be sleeping a lot these days."

"You should try running."

"I doubt that would help very much." He leaned over and whispered for effect. "You see, one of my most important rocket scientists might be headed for some marital trouble, and that just wouldn't be good for anyone."

"You got this all wrong, Colonel."

Adams slid forward a manila folder held shut with a big paper clip, motioning with his head for Cooper to open it. Inside was a picture of Maria and Cooper kissing passionately outside the restaurant in Mentone.

"Air force test pilot kissing the wife of a lead scientist in the United States space program. Some people might not be sure how to interpret that. Some people might look at that and call it love. Which would be quite a scandal, don't you think?"

"She was saying good-bye."

"That's some good-bye."

"You don't understand her."

"I understand that people very often say one thing and then do another. And I make my living anticipating what the another thing might be."

Cooper looked at the photo for a long moment, then studied Adams.

"Hans Reinhardt must have been a very bad guy."

"Whatever he was, he's our guy now."

"He knew everything, didn't he?"

Adams shrugged.

Cooper tapped the photo. "If you guys are putting this kind of effort into keeping an eye on things, you must be pretty tense about something coming out."

"We keep a gander on everyone with sensitive information."

"If he was going to go to the Sovs, he would have twelve years ago. You know that."

"The music never stops but people change partners."

"No." Cooper remembered his conversation with Hans. "He had oversight of the whole thing, didn't he? The entire production line, the slave labor. He knew everything."

Adams didn't have to lie to an officer with top-secret clearance, especially one who wasn't gonna buy it. "Oh, don't kid yourself, son. If we'd lost the war you'd of been shot for the firebombing of Hamburg. Oppenheimer, the Jew, would've run to the Japs, who'd have whisked him and his girlfriend off to a cushy high-tech job in Osaka, while the low-level Manhattan Project crew wound up at the end of Japanese ropes for Hiroshima and Nagasaki. People are busy and they like things spelled out for them in black and white. Trouble is, war is a very gray area."

"You don't believe in right and wrong?"

"I believe in freedom."

"As in giving people all the information and letting them be free to make their own decisions?"

"Free as in living to see another day. Democracy is inexpedient, and when faced with Hitler, Stalin, Khrushchev, annihilation, end of our way of life—and as you are well aware, that is precisely what we are talking about—Americans gladly forgo the fascinating public debate about what our forefathers had in mind, because when push comes to shove, and there's some real shoving going on right now, what Americans really want is security."

"It's not America I'm talking about." Cooper looked out the window, the first light of the new day casting a matte glow across Huntsville. Then he turned back to Adams, waiting for a response.

Adams took a long breath, softening his tone. "She has a good life, Major. This is what's best for her too. If she knew the truth, and I mean really knew it, do you think she'd be able to stay with him?"

"I don't think so," he said quietly.

"She'd run right to you, wouldn't she?"

Cooper sure liked that idea. He leaned back, letting his mind ruminate on the idea of telling her the truth and on being with her forever. The rising sunlight warming the side of his face, he felt a smile growing, but he stopped it and quickly leaned forward, over his plate.

"I don't know what she'd do," Cooper said. "She has a mind of her own and she's pretty damn good at using it."

"Well, be advised, Major. *Everyone* needs Hans Reinhardt to remain an upstanding married suburbanite. Just another guy like the rest of us who waters his lawn after church and plays in the local softball league. Makes a great burger on the backyard grill. Bratwurst is fine if that's his particular predilection. Others may have used his work for political and military gain, but Dr. Reinhardt— like all our other fine German aerospace engineers—is simply a man of science who was never in any way party to the misguided evils of his former leader and his corrupt fascist government."

"That's quite a story."

"People like it."

"What exactly do you want from me?"

"A guy like you, I see you walking on the moon someday. I see high schools named after you."

"I never finished high school."

"What I want from you, Major, is to know that you like our narrative too. What I want is for you to remember who you work for."

"I get it, sir." Cooper pushed his plate away. "And my duty is to my country."

"Good man."

Cooper rose.

"And Major Cooper, the boy . . . he will be in good hands."

"What do you mean?"

"He will be provided for. Looked after. You have my personal assurance of that. This is what's best for him as well."

Cooper just stood there. *Why was Adams assuring him about Peter?* Trusting his instinct, he kept his mouth shut.

"Thank you for breakfast, sir." Cooper walked away from the table, arms up, stretching as he headed for the door.

Gulping his coffee, Adams watched as Cooper jogged by the window outside, continuing his run back to base.

DAWN

Maria heard the sound of the shower turn on and she opened her eyes. Half awake lying there in bed, she saw a quick flash of Hans as he dashed through the still-dark bedroom, down the carpeted hallway, and presumably into the kitchen. Despite having had a restless night of sleep, dipping in and out of strange dreams, she wasn't sure if Hans had ever come to bed. He must be rushing to get ready for his trip, she thought. In the mornings, he often started the shower but instead of just standing there waiting for the hot water, he would zip off to the kitchen, turn on the coffee percolator, and rush back and jump in. That was the kind of thing in which Hans truly took pride. Absolute efficiency. A German trait, yes, but one that Hans took to an extraordinary level.

So why had he left the water running for so long? Maria began to wonder after a minute or so. Certainly it must be hot by now. This wasn't like him.

In her sheer chiffon nightgown, she got up dreamily and, as if floating, made her way into the steamy bathroom. She reached into the newly tiled shower stall and turned the water off.

Just as she was pulling her hand out of the shower, she jumped as a loud piercing clank rang out from the kitchen. Like steel slamming into stone, the noise shook Maria into immediate wakefulness.

She ran out of the bathroom, through the bedroom, and down the hallway, stopping in the doorway of the kitchen, frozen by what she saw.

A large shovel in his hand, Hans stood naked over a massive decapitated copperhead snake.

Her mouth fell open as she stared at the well-fed man, uncircumcised and breathing heavily in the greenish dawn light, and he looked right at her.

"You are safe now," he said.

Dropping the shovel with a bell-like ring on the cold Formica floor, he picked up the four-and-a-half-foot-long snake carcass, with its alternating crossbands of pink and tan patterns, threw it over his shoulders, and walked out the back door, still open from when he'd retrieved the shovel.

Barefoot, Maria tiptoed over toward the broad, bodiless snake head lying openmouthed like those painted hummingbirds on the Blossomwood entry sign in a little puddle of purple blood on her kitchen floor. She leaned over it—and the snake head's mouth snapped at her toes, venom squirting from its fangs.

Maria screamed and jumped back.

The snake head convulsed a few more times and then lay still.

In a near state of shock, Maria peered out the open back door, watching her husband, the carcass draped over him, his white buttocks moving through the mist and across the emerald-green lawn.

Who was this man?

CHARACTER

Having parked the Chevy on Governors Drive, which was already busy with morning traffic, Maria opened the back door of the car, reached into the rear seat, and pulled out a large pile of Hans's dirty clothes. Holding the mass of clothing to her body with both arms, she kicked the car door shut, walked across the sidewalk tucking the clothes under her chin, and with her hip pushed open the front door to the Alabama Dry Cleaners.

After what she'd seen in her kitchen that morning, Maria felt dazed, disoriented, like the world was spinning and she was having difficulty making sense of things as they flew by.

The bell tied to the front door jingled as Maria came through.

"Hey, there," Mrs. Mayfield, the owner, called out from the back. "Good morning!"

Mrs. Mayfield waddled out and helped Maria deposit the pile on the counter.

"Good morning," Maria said, standing there smelling of Hans.

"I hear y'all are gonna be playing for the radio on Saturday." Mrs. Mayfield began counting the articles and dropping them in a big laundry bag.

"Yes, we are."

"I have to say, I myself have never been one for the classical music. I'm more of a country girl myself. George Jones, Ricky Nelson, Patsy. But I just think this is so exciting for the city."

"Yes, well, thank you, Mrs. Mayfield."

"Thank *you*, sweetheart! We're just so lucky to have y'all in Huntsville. And what's good for Huntsville is good for business!" Mrs. Mayfield noted the count in red pencil, tore off a receipt, and handed it to Maria. "How's that sweet little boy of yours?"

"Peter is fine. Thank you for asking."

"Now you be sure to bring him 'round next time you come in."

"I will try."

Maria turned to leave, but Mrs. Mayfield grabbed her arm.

"Oh, before you leave, I wonder if you wouldn't mind signing something for my daughter in Mountain Brook? Her husband rounds at St. Vincent's all Saturday night so she's gonna be home alone listening in and I know she would be impressed by a little signed something from you, if you wouldn't mind."

Mrs. Mayfield ripped off another receipt, turned it to the blank side, and slid it toward Maria, who was having a hard time looking like she was in the mood for this. But she reached for a pencil. "Of course. What's her name?"

"Cecelia. But, oh, let me get you the good pen."

As Mrs. Mayfield wobbled toward the back, the bell on the front door jangled and a businessman walked in carrying a laundry bag.

"Morning, Luke," Mrs. Mayfield called out. "I'll be right with you."

"No problem, Sally," the man replied. "I'll just leave it on the counter."

"That's fine, Luke. Be ready on Thursday after five."

The man tipped his head toward Maria. "Morning," he said. "Gonna be a beautiful day today."

"Yes, it sure looks that way," Maria said.

"You must be one of the rocket scientists' wives."

"My accent betrays me every time I speak."

"You speak quite beautifully."

"Thank you."

And he was gone, the bell jangling behind him.

Mrs. Mayfield returned and handed Maria a pen.

"Thank you so much for doing this," Mrs. Mayfield said as she pulled the laundry out of the bag the man had left, counting and noting the items.

"My pleasure." Maria finished writing and, eager to get going, slid the paper across the counter.

Mrs. Mayfield read the note and smiled but, looking up, she noticed Maria staring at the laundry she had in her hands—a long white robe with a cross badge sewn on it and a white sharply pointed hat with a full-faced mask, the eyeholes cut out.

"I know," Mrs. Mayfield said, scrunching up her face in disapproval. "But our job is to wash the clothes, not get involved in how they're worn."

"Please thank Cecelia for her interest in the symphony," Maria stammered, clearly taken aback. She turned and headed out.

"Have a nice day, dear." Mrs. Mayfield watched her go, then returned to her clothes counting.

Lost in thought, Maria drove the Chevy through the streets of Huntsville. Her hands loosely on the wheel, she stared ahead blankly, driving unconsciously, on instinct, her mind reeling. She had never seen Klan robes up close before, but she knew about them, and the terror they evoked. How could Mrs. Mayfield turn a blind eye to this? Actually, Maria knew exactly how. She had seen so many people just like Mrs. Mayfield, who put their heads down and went about their business while children like little Mieszko stared out at them from behind the barbed wire. Would Mrs. Mayfield act differently if *she* knew what it felt like to be denied gasoline because of her accent? Or Betty Johnson at the Darlington School, would *she* behave differently if she knew what it was like to be hated, deemed an inferior person, simply because of her nationality? What would it take for things to change? What would it take for a good person to do good things?

Then again, was there even such a thing as a "good person"?

She wasn't sure she believed what Hans had said when she had asked him directly about his past the previous night, but she comforted herself with the knowledge that, no matter what others thought, he probably wasn't capable of such things. But now, with the image of him with that shovel . . . she just didn't know anymore. All her life she had known Hans Reinhardt and never had imagined him capable of the kind of violent and primitive act she'd seen that morning. *Who was this man that she'd married?*

Making a snap decision, Maria made a U-turn.

It was crazy, Maria knew this, and even juvenile, what she was doing. But there was only one person she wanted to talk to, one person she felt would be able to help her sort out everything that was going on. She had promised herself she would not contact him and she was determined to stand by that. So somehow she found herself driving over to the off-base officers' housing on Crestwood Avenue and parking her car in one of the spaces across from the half-dozen apartments in the complex where James Cooper lived and just sitting in the front seat of her Chevy and thinking. Yes, as crazy as it was, just being near him in this way made her feel a little better.

What would she do if she saw him? She didn't know. Even just sitting here, she felt that her life was spinning out of control.

It was startling to have seen a side of her husband that she never knew existed. Frightening. On the other hand, he had taken care of her, protected her. What if he had already left and she'd walked in on that snake? What would she have done?

Well, if she couldn't run and she'd been able to get to the back door as Hans had, she would have picked up that shovel and done the same thing. People speculated as to what they would or woul not do in a given situation, but very few could know for sure. J she did. After what she'd done in the cottage to that SS officer, she knew what she was capable of.

The truth of the matter, Maria could now see, was that Hans was much more like her than she'd ever realized. And she was much more like him.

Just then, Maria saw the door to an apartment open and Cooper stepped out. In his flight suit, apparently headed to base for work, he marched toward his car, a Triumph TR3, a little ragtop roadster. As he reached it, an attractive young woman—his date from the event—jumped out of her car and approached him.

Maria slumped down in the driver's seat a little, watching.

In tears, gesticulating wildly, the young woman clearly wanted something from Cooper. He, in contrast, looked calm, stoic. He seemed to be consoling her, but she evidently did not like hearing what he had to say. Abruptly, she ran back to her car, evidently heartbroken.

After a moment, his mind very much elsewhere, Cooper hopped in the Triumph and raced off.

Watching the young woman crying in the front seat of her car, her hands and head on the top of the steering wheel, Maria wished she could go to her—and wished she knew what Cooper had told her.

Finally, feeling herself getting more stirred than she could handle right now, Maria forced herself to start her car and drive off.

The midday sun streamed through the huge floor-to-ceiling windows in precise hazy shafts onto the ballroom floor of the Russel Erskine Hotel. Echoing and cavernous, the room was empty except for a couple dozen chairs at the far end from the doors, and in one of those chairs sat Maria, playing her violin.

Practicing for the upcoming concert, she played the third movement of Beethoven's famed Violin Concerto. Her jubilant playing reverberated powerfully throughout the room. But after a moment, she stopped, head down, dropping the bow to her side. Somehow, it felt like a lie. Her heart wasn't in it.

Raising the bow again, chin pressed to the violin, she began to play "Amazing Grace." Though she continued to sort out the finger work, going sharp and flat as she found her way, there was a great depth to the sound, rich and dark, penetrating in tone, its effect apparent in her performance and on her face. Continuing on with greater intensity, savoring the diverse palate of colors that allowed her to express the true range of her emotions, she felt free and empowered.

Screech—she pulled a note way too sharp, stopping and trying it again several times, not quite getting it right.

"You play like I did when I was seven," Josephine said, standing at the other end of the room, near the service doors.

Maria looked across the room at her. "Not everyone has your talent."

"I don't know about talent. But I sure know about practice."

"What does it look like I am doing?"

"Making trouble for yourself, you ask me."

"I am asking. I would like to be better."

Throwing a look behind her, Josephine saw that she was alone.

"I do not want to cause any trouble for you," Maria said.

"I'm early."

Josephine walked purposefully across the long ballroom toward Maria, her black Mary Janes clip-clopping along the high-gloss floor.

The little girl went right up to Maria, pointing. "You gotta relax your wrist. It ain't a baseball bat."

Maria tried to comply, not entirely successfully. Josephine reached out, touching Maria's wrist to show her how to hold the bow. Maria pulled the bow across her new strings a few times, making Josephine giggle and shake her head.

"Hit that gut like you was skipping a stone across the pond." The little girl made a motion with her open hand. "Skip, skip, skip."

Maria played again as instructed, lighting up at the beautiful, graceful sound.

"There you go. That's real nice. Just keep practicing."

After a few more bars, Maria stopped. "Thank you. I will."

"Fiddle like that wants to about play itself. I think all you gotta do is get out of its way."

"I think that is good advice."

Just the two of them alone in this vast gilded room, looking small as figurines, Maria and Josephine stood there face-to-face, sharing a smile and admiring the pristine antique violin.

"Why'd you come to my church?"

"You saw me?"

The girl laughed. "Course I saw you. You was kinda hard not to see."

"I wanted to hear you play. You are really quite amazing."

Josephine looked at her hands, absorbing the praise.

"Who taught you?" Maria asked.

"My daddy. Now *he's* got talent. How 'bout you?"

"My daddy too. And then nine years in a conservatory."

"I take it that ain't a place where they're growing flowers?"

Maria laughed a little. "You are a smart girl. It is a music school."

"That's it? You just studied music?" Josephine's face was filled with amazement.

"Well, I learned the primary curriculum, languages, math, history, and my father taught me some of that too, but mainly, yes, music. People thought that I might play in a symphony someday."

"That'd been nice."

"Yes." Maria sighed. "It would have been."

"Playing the kind of music you played here on Saturday?"

"Yes."

"That was pretty, real pretty, I thought."

"Thank you."

"I asked them to let me work again this week so I can hear y'all again. And I told my daddy, who's gonna listen on the radio."

"Well, that is so nice to hear. I am flattered."

"That the only kind of music you learned at the conservatory?"

"Well, I thought I knew how to play all the great music from all the great composers. A wide variety. But now I think that maybe I really only learned one kind of music. And I do not think I realized that until I met you."

The little girl took that in, studying this woman standing before her speaking so freely to her.

"You really German?"

"I really am."

"Then it ain't true, you ask me."

"What is that?"

"That you a bad people."

Maria wanted to reach out and hug the girl, more for her own comfort than for any other reason. But she resisted the impulse.

"Josephine, you taught me something today. Can I teach you something?"

"Yes, ma'am."

"It is a great, big world. And you never really know a person until you know what is inside."

Josephine nodded, understanding. "My daddy always says that."

"My daddy did too."

On the other side of the room the doors flew open and a coterie of fashionably dressed ladies marched in—Carolyn, Penny, Sabine, and a particularly well-coiffed older woman, Marjorie Ingram—all clucking about the upcoming event.

Josephine immediately dropped her head when she saw them. "I have to get to work."

"Nice talking to you."

The girl very quickly scurried off across the room toward the service doors, eyed by the ladies who passed her on their way toward Maria.

"There she is!" Carolyn called out to Maria.

"Early as usual," Penny said.

The ladies stopped in front of Maria, who looked at the older woman. "Good afternoon," Maria said, assaulted by a narcoticlike cloud of Chanel No. 5.

Carolyn stepped forward to make an introduction. "Marjorie Ingram, this is Maria Reinhardt."

"My, you're a pretty pony." The bejeweled woman shamelessly looked Maria up and down.

"Nice to meet you, Mrs. Ingram."

"Please call me Bobsie. Believe it or not, I once had hair that was exactly your color. Why, you could be my long-lost daughter." Mrs. Ingram brushed some strands of hair off Maria's forehead. "I thought you were simply marvelous on Saturday night. You are giving this ol' mill town a real touch of panache."

A woman with a camera around her neck bounded into the room. "Hi. Sorry to bother y'all. I'm from the *Huntsville Times*. We're doing a big story on the radio event. Do you mind if I take a few quick shots for the paper?"

"Of course not!" Mrs. Ingram exclaimed, motioning for the photographer to join them.

"Thank you." The photographer marched up to them and started taking pictures, focusing in particular on Maria. "Don't let me interrupt."

"Bobsie is very enthusiastic about supporting the symphony and she specifically wanted to meet you," Penny told Maria, raising her eyebrows in excitement when Mrs. Ingram wasn't looking.

Maria looked over at a silent Sabine, trying to take her temperature. Sabine offered a whimsical shrug.

"What's good for Huntsville is good for the Ingrams," the older woman said. "That's why my family has a long tradition of supporting the arts in this corner of Alabama. Now y'all are gonna need a venue very soon, a performing arts center, a permanent stage, and a place to offer music classes for the entire community. And I'd like to help y'all get started."

"And we would sure love that help!" Carolyn exclaimed.

The photographer motioned for Mrs. Ingram and Maria to stand together. They did and she snapped some pictures, Maria flinching from the flash in her eyes.

"I have some ideas and there are some people I want you to meet, but I know you have to practice so I won't keep you," Mrs.

Ingram said to Maria. "I just wanted to meet the young woman that everyone was talking about. I understand you're going to play the Beethoven Violin Concerto for the radio performance. Oh, I just love that one. And who better to play Beethoven than someone who speaks his native language."

The photographer checked her camera, mouthed "thank you," and quickly headed for the door.

Mrs. Ingram turned and started skittering away too. "I can hardly wait." She began humming the Concerto. Carolyn followed, happy as could be. Sabine tagged along behind them.

Maria grabbed Penny's arm. "Can I talk to you for a minute?"

"Course." Penny called out to Carolyn and Mrs. Ingram, "Y'all go ahead, I'll be with you in a few minutes."

"If there's anything you need," Mrs. Ingram called back. "Any problems with the hotel, anything at all, you just let me know and it's as good as done."

Maria waited for the three to leave the room and close the door behind them. Then she sat, and Penny sat too.

"I have been thinking a lot about the performance."

"Don't be nervous, sugar, you're gonna be great."

"It is not that."

"What?" Penny said gently.

"I think we should open it up to the entire community. To everyone."

"You mean the live performance, in the ballroom?"

"Yes.

"It *is* open to everyone. We're not selling tickets and if we have to we can accommodate standing room for half the city in here."

"You know very well that not everyone in Huntsville is allowed in here."

"You mean Negroes?"

"Everyone."

"You want them to open the Russel Erskine Hotel, the formal ballroom of the Russel Erskine Hotel, to Negroes?"

Penny opened her mouth to laugh, but Maria cut her off.

"It is not a school," Maria said. "It is not a public building. The hotel is privately owned and can allow anyone it wants into the ballroom. No laws would be broken."

Penny considered her friend for a long moment, realizing just how serious she was.

"Maria, there is a time and a place for everything. And while this may be the time for this, the Russel Erskine Hotel is not the place."

"Does the Huntsville Symphony Orchestra belong to the city of Huntsville or just a selected portion?"

"It belongs to the city. And on this I am with you. I am with you. But you listen to me. Redstone Arsenal names a base soldier of the month. Every month. The award is fifty dollars and a free night at the Russel Erskine Hotel—for white soldiers. And fifty dollars and a free night at the Gladys Jane Motel for colored soldiers. You think this hotel is gonna change its policy for Beethoven when it wouldn't even think about it for the United States Army?"

"If the Ingram family was behind it, maybe."

"Bobsie Ingram and her committee have been trying to get the Broadway tours to come to Huntsville for years. She's offered to build a theater. But none of them have ever taken her up because the tours out of New York are integrated, and they aren't going to have some of their actors staying at the Russel Erskine Hotel while the others aren't welcome, and the hotel sure isn't changing its policy anytime soon. Look, I think it's disgusting too, but that's just the way it is."

"Well, maybe someone needs to change the way it is."

"What exactly are you saying?" A very atypical serious expression came over Penny.

"I do not know what constitutes a good person. But I know that if we all continue to look the other way in the face of such things, none of us are. And I know where that leads and I will not go there again."

"Maria—" Flabbergasted, Penny threw up her hands.

Maria spoke clearly and slowly, to be certain her point was well understood. "I am saying that I am thinking about not playing on Saturday night."

That gave Penny pause, her mind envisioning where this could go, and it alarmed her.

"Maria, the symphony can't play without you, and this isn't just about our little project. This is the town we're talking about. They're already promoting it on the radio. The paper has a front-page story coming out tomorrow. Do you have any idea what this kind of controversy could do? This is the base you're talking about messing with. Our husbands' work. Do you understand the stakes here?"

Maria did not respond. Rather, now she considered Penny. Maria was more than disappointed and surprised that her friend offered so little support or even understanding. Maria was angry. And perhaps it was an impulsive decision, but after everything that had happened recently, and the swirl of related emotions, her anger quickly set into resolve.

"Maria," Penny said again, this time more insistently. "Do you understand the stakes here?"

"Completely." Maria Reinhardt set her jaw.

"Penny!" Carolyn shouted from across the room, her head peeking through the open door.

Penny jumped.

"We need to talk about this some more," Penny said to Maria.

"I think I am done talking."

"I'll talk to the girls and we'll figure this out."

Shaking her head as she realized the depth of Maria's resolve, Penny marched across the room toward her very excited friend. She tossed a look back at Maria—sitting alone in the ballroom holding her violin—and then headed out.

A fluttering apprehension rising in her gut, Maria worked to catch her breath. She was making decisions faster than she could think them through and she knew that was dangerous, but a bright light seemed to have been switched on in the distance and she had to make her way toward that light.

The entire room shook with a shuddering sonic boom as a jet shot by overhead faster than the speed of sound.

MIRROR, MIRROR

Sun in his eyes, Cooper pulled back on the control stick of the supersonic jet, whisking it straight up, eight thousand feet a minute, into the stratosphere over downtown Huntsville. Today's assignment was a flight test of another potential carrier-based nuclear strike bomber, an early prototype of the XA-5 Vigilante. It was significantly faster and more agile than the Douglas Skywarrior he'd successfully tested, but the new jet was also much more complex.

After a textbook rocket-assisted takeoff, at about seventy thousand feet, Cooper leveled and then accelerated, firing the afterburner, shooting the sleek sweptwing fighter through the ultrathin atmosphere—the novel aluminum-lithium fuselage increasingly knocking and shuttering around him.

"Redstone base," said Cooper into the microphone in his flight helmet. "She's pitching a bit of a fit up here at angels seventy."

Cooper had trouble holding the stick steady as the plane began to pitch and shake unsteadily. He worked to maintain his calm and to keep control of the aircraft.

"Roger, Major," the air traffic controller responded. "Deck is clear and no turbulence reported. Bring her down until you find stable course and altitude."

"Thank you, base."

Cooper immediately pushed the stick forward, driving the plane into rapid descent.

A cherry-red warning light started flashing, its corresponding alarm buzzing.

"Base, I've got a warning indicator on the engine gear box." Cooper tried pulling back on the stick but was unable to do so. "Uh, I've got a real problem here with the differential pressure."

"Pull up, Major."

"Giving that a shot, base."

"Pull up, now!"

Dizzy from the unhindered fall, more warning lights flashing and alarms buzzing, losing his orientation, Cooper pulled back on the control stick with all his force but could not get it to move.

The controls unresponsive, the plane plummeted straight down, spinning horizontally like a top in what now looked like a free fall. A thin trail of pale smoke wisped out of the tail engine.

The hands on the altimeter whirled wildly, clocking his violent plunge. The g-forces on him increasing, Cooper struggled to get his mouth to produce words. "Controls are not responding."

Smoke began to fill the cockpit. There was going to be an explosion.

"Major—you have to punch out of the aircraft."

Cooper did not move or respond.

"You have to punch out now!"

Cooper's helmeted head started swaying and bobbing, his hands wrenched on the bucking and shaking stick, the horizon spinning. He was losing consciousness.

"Eject now!"

◆ ◆ ◆

The majestic harmonious sound of Beethoven's Violin Concerto in
D major, the only concerto he ever wrote for violin, filled the ballroom of the Russel Erskine Hotel as all two dozen members of the
new Huntsville Symphony Orchestra practiced for the upcoming
radio performance. Now with the growing orchestra all together, a
conductor—a German rocket-propulsion specialist—stood before
them, leading.

In the traditional concertmaster's seat directly in front and to
the left of the conductor, Maria played first violin, the ensemble following her for orchestral leadership.

Maria played an uplifting and technically difficult solo from the
Concerto, backed in harmony by the second violinist, another mid-
level German scientist, and then the rest of the orchestra jumped
in, again filling the room with moving, powerful music as they concluded the piece.

"Great work, everyone," the conductor said, his German accent
very thick. He wiped his brow with his shirtsleeve. "Maria, perfect,
just perfect."

The members of the orchestra were simply delighted with their
new project, and they talked excitedly about it, congratulating one
another and sharing thoughts on sharpening the performance.

"Okay, let's take thirty minutes and then work on the first movement one more time. Horns, let's see if we can get a little brighter?"

While everyone milled about, some individually practicing with
their instruments, Maria walked away from the cacophony and
stepped out of the room to clear her mind, her violin and bow in
hand.

As she walked through the lobby, she noticed a little boy, maybe
five or six years old, standing alone on the white marble staircase
staring at her. He was a strangely beautiful child, towheaded, with

ghostly blue eyes, dressed up in a little sport jacket and white trousers.

His piercing eyes followed her as she walked, making her feel uneasy until, finally, his stylishly dressed mother grabbed his hand and yanked him along.

The boy glanced at Maria over his shoulder as he left, and Maria continued watching him and he her as Klaus Bauer, the second violinist and rocket-trajectory expert, came up to her, startling her.

"You okay with the harmony I am playing in the third movement?" Klaus asked.

It took her a moment to focus her attention on him. "Yes. Yes, it is very nice."

He could see the preoccupation in her eyes.

"You sure everything is okay, Maria?" Klaus asked, his concern apparent.

"Yes, of course. Just a lot on my mind today."

"Well, nothing to worry about. Your playing is breathtaking and they are going to love you on Saturday night."

"Thank you, Klaus."

Maria smiled at the kind-faced, thin older man. She realized that he was leaning toward her, fixated on her violin, which she had resting under one arm like a baby.

And he looked up, realizing that she'd caught him staring.

"It is very beautiful," he said, allowing himself to take in the violin once again.

"Thank you. It is a Pressenda."

"A Pressenda." The way he repeated the word almost sounded like a question. Klaus raised his head and met Maria's eyes and, oddly, gazed at her for a long moment as if trying to ascertain something.

"Well, I am glad all is well with you," he finally said, a warm smile on his wrinkled face.

"Klaus, a Pressenda is a fine instrument, but it is not particularly valuable." It was a statement, and Klaus did not respond to it. And feeling the need for reassurance she pressed the issue, her voice smaller than she had intended. "Right?"

And again, he gazed at her with that look, assessing, and then responded. "That is right."

Maria cocked her head, but before she could say anything further, a front desk clerk noticed her and walked over, an enveloped card in his hand.

"Mrs. Reinhardt, I was asked to give this to you." The clerk handed her the envelope. "You all sound wonderful."

"Thank you." Maria was a bit dazed as she watched Klaus stroll away—had she missed something?—but on the envelope she immediately recognized Hans's meticulous handwriting and that got her full attention. He'd penned her name on the front of the envelope.

She walked by the burbling triple-tiered fountain and sat down in one of the deep club chairs against a wall in a quiet corner of the lobby.

Tearing the envelope open, she removed a greeting card. A red paper cutout in the shape of a heart was affixed to the front of the card. On the inside, the card was imprinted with the phrase "Thinking of You." And below that sentiment, Hans had written in blue pen, "All best wishes with your performance. —H."

Maria stared at the card for a long time, oblivious to the boisterous sounds of the other orchestra members and of the guests and locals enjoying early happy hour in the Rocket Room lounge upstairs. Such an enigma, this man to whom she was married. One minute he could be so thoughtful and caring, a minute later he was distant and analytical. So warm and so cold. And then there was the incident this morning with the snake. The truth was undeniable: although she had known Hans all her life, she really didn't know him. Not in the way she felt sure she knew Cooper.

What was she missing? She had checked the closet. Nothing. She had asked him if he knew about the camp. He said he hadn't. The violin, it wasn't particularly valuable. It was just a relatively common Pressenda. Klaus confirmed that, but then why was he staring at it like it was so extraordinary?

The more Maria thought about it, the more her gut told her that she was indeed missing something.

Reflecting on this nagging feeling that she just couldn't shake, she found herself studying the red paper heart, this symbol of love. *Was she childish to think that she deserved this in her life?*

She tugged at the paper heart, ripping it from the card. She remembered making hearts like this as a child. Folding paper, cutting a half heart, reopening . . . Immersed in these thoughts, she folded the red paper heart in half lengthwise, reopening it, considering the perfect mirror images—and she jumped up, overcome by a revelation.

Maria grabbed the second violinist by the shoulder as he walked through the lobby. "Klaus, something urgent just came up and I have to run home."

"Are you sure you are okay?" the mathematician-musician asked.

"Fine, fine, I just have to . . . I will get back as soon as possible. Should only be a very short while. Can you cover my part until I get back?"

"Of course, Maria, whatever you—"

He didn't finish his sentence because she was already gone.

◆　◆　◆

Maria whipped the Chevy into the driveway, jumped out, slammed the door, ran up the walkway, up the front steps, and into the house.

Sprinting through the entryway past the open living room, she stopped and stood near the hallway for a moment, the bedroom to her right, the kitchen to the left—the mirror image, the reverse plan, of the Janssen house.

She turned and bolted to the left, looking for the approximate spot over the foundation in her house that would be where Karl Janssen's closet was in his.

Maria stopped at the hallway closet near the kitchen, thought for a moment, and then threw open the door.

It was carpeted.

Dropping to her knees, she flung the few items from the closet floor—several pairs of shoes, a couple department store bags, a small suitcase—into the hall. She ran her hands along the carpet and then pounded on the floor with her fist as hard as she could, listening.

Making a split-second decision, she grabbed two fistfuls of carpet and yanked, popping the carpeting off its tacking strips and pulling the entire carpet piece off the floor.

There was the wood floor—and the tiny metal insert.

INSURANCE

The fallout shelter was indeed the exact same design as the Janssens', poured concrete walls, twenty-five feet in the ground, down a brightly painted corrugated steel tube, and designed to fit within the perimeter of the foundation. Many of the provisions and rations and supplies were identical as well. But the personal touches were different.

Hans had made the bunk beds with lovely quilts and plush pillows. He'd stored some flowered china plates and stainless flatware. A cobalt-blue water pitcher sat on a stained oak table. Too big to make it through the entrance, the table must have been partially constructed down here. So much effort, Maria realized. And where had he gotten all these items? Not at Dunnavant's. He must have gone shopping in Birmingham or Nashville. One thing was clear: Hans, like Karl, felt there was a high probability that the shelter would be used.

There were several boxes of linens and apparel. How strange it was to riffle through the shirts and jeans and undergarments he had picked out, purchased, and stored for her.

On the shelves were dozens of books, definitive science and

medical reference texts, as well as works by Thomas Mann, Hermann Hesse, Martin Heidegger, Friedrich Nietzsche. And there was sheet music, for violin. Stacks of it. From Bach to Brahms, Schubert to Mozart, hundreds, maybe thousands of sheets. What looked like examples from every so-called important work. And mainly there was Wagner, every dour piece he ever wrote.

This was to be the end for her, interminable years playing Wagner on her violin, in attire that pleased Hans.

What was most definitely not in the shelter was an industrial toolbox like Karl Janssen's.

Maria had turned over and examined and searched through virtually every object—the books, the supplies, the mattresses. She'd even tapped on the table legs and inspected the walls. There was nothing hidden away in the shelter.

The only "insurance" Hans Reinhardt seemed to have put away was his work. On one of the shelves, next to all the sheet music, he'd made copies of the blueprints of his rockets, design plans, test results, fuel mixtures. Most of them were neatly stored in clear plastic folders that were clipped into large three-ring binders. Hans had documented and archived his life's work, preparing it for long-term survival. Maria wondered if he had done so not only to save his knowledge for posterity but also to use it as barter in the event he had to start all over again for another government.

Throwing a large binder open on the oak table, Maria paged through all the plans and blueprints, until something in one of the plastic folders made her stop and stare—a small old rectangular label that read *Joseph Guarnerius fecit Cremonae anno 1741 IHS*. It was a stringed-instrument label. For a Guarneri. Most likely a Guarneri violin.

Maria leaned over, looking even closer at the label through the carefully sealed plastic sleeve. Brown and weathered, the label was in excellent condition. And from what she knew, it sure looked real.

A label from a Guarneri.

She had seen a few Stradivariuses in her life and had once played an Amati that had belonged to a wealthy Czech friend of her father's. But an authentic Guarneri she had never seen. They were so rare, and so incredibly valuable.

What in the world was Hans doing with a Guarneri label?

She thought about it for a moment, and then realized—

"*Scheiße.*" Maria did not like the use of expletives, but when they did on rare occasion slip out of her, they did so only in her native tongue.

CROATIAN WOOD

The bespectacled proprietor of Nashville Fine Violins had worked a long day and was ready for dinner, so he turned around the *Open* sign in the window to read *Closed*, quickly stepped out the front door of the small house on Music Row that was now home to his business, shut the door, and locked it. Marching briskly down the front walkway, keys in one hand, briefcase in the other, he passed his business signage in the front yard and got into the car parked in the driveway.

As he started the engine, he noticed in his rearview mirror the 1957 Chevy speeding down Seventeenth Street, then slamming to a stop and parking right across the street from him, next to RCA's new Studio B. Probably another nutty Elvis fan, he figured.

But as he backed up, he saw a woman jogging from the Chevy, up his driveway, violin case swinging from her hand, waving her arm for him to stop.

She ran up to his car window and, warily, he rolled it down.

"Please do not leave yet," Maria said.

"I'm sorry, ma'am. I have to get home. We open tomorrow at nine."

She snapped open the case and removed the violin and held it up, thrusting it toward his open car window.

"Is this a Pressenda?"

Recoiling, he looked at her uneasily, not sure what he was dealing with here. But he couldn't resist taking a little peek at the old instrument.

"No. That is not a Pressenda."

"The label says it is."

He looked through an f-hole at the label and shrugged. "Yeah, that's a Pressenda label, but that's not a Pressenda."

"Well, what do you think it is?"

He leaned farther out the window. "It's really beautiful. Definitely Italian. Early eighteenth century, I'd bet. Probably made by a student of the Cremona school. I'd have to take a closer look at the varnish texture, comparative designs, wood characteristics. Like I said, nine a.m." He reached for the crank handle to roll up the window.

"What if I told you it was a Guarneri."

He laughed. "I thought you might be crazy when I first saw you running up here."

The conviction on her face did not waver. She shoved the instrument through the open car window—and as he had no choice but to give it a very close look, he stopped laughing.

Inside the shop, the proprietor stood behind a counter, Maria on the other side, both looking at her violin, which rested on a felt blanket on top of the counter. Next to the violin, the proprietor poured through several books and auction catalogs, comparing the violin with pictures of similar ones.

"How do you know for certain that this is not a Pressenda?" Maria asked.

"Because *that* is a Pressenda." He pointed to a lovely violin behind him in a locked glass case. The varnishing was thin and yellowish, the front and back plates were acutely curved, and the overall proportion was smaller and wider than her slightly larger, more subtly worked reddish instrument.

While he flipped through pages, making comparisons and growing increasingly excited, Maria looked around the store. Along with many fine violins and violas for sale in the glass counters, there were others in various states of repair behind him. On the walls were numerous photos of men and women in formal attire holding their instruments—classical musicians—as well as eight-by-ten signed publicity photos of country musicians, most also holding violins.

"Well, ma'am, your instrument matches all the comparisons exactly. The flaming patterns on the back plate are classic Guarneri. This is clearly Croatian maple, all he used. Look at this craftsmanship." Realizing what he had before him, the man ran his fingertips lovingly along the neck of the violin. "There are only a couple hundred of these left in the world, and I thought they were all accounted for." He paused for a moment, not sure whether to say what was on his mind. "You know, a lot of fine violins disappeared from homes in Europe during the war."

"How would you return one?"

"I don't know that you could. They're not like paintings, with long records of provenance."

"What about insurance policies? Some kind of records must have been kept."

"Remember, a violin was not viewed as a commodity, it was a cherished heirloom, passed down through families and regularly played. And even if someone had taken out insurance, he'd have to be around to cash it in. In fact, the only records I've heard of that survived were kept by the Nazis, cataloging the fine instruments they . . . acquired from these families."

Maria just nodded, understanding it all more than she wanted to.

"I don't know where you got this, but I can tell you that it's an authentic Guarneri."

"And the label?"

"I'd say someone opened up the instrument, very common for repairs, and put in a different label. You see that a lot. But of course only on cheap instruments with fake labels purporting to be something better. This is a very valuable violin you have here."

"How valuable?"

"Hard to say exactly without the label, but certainly more than a similar Stradivarius, probably tens of thousands. Maybe more."

"And if I had the label?"

He exhaled a nervous little laugh. "Well, depending on the year, it could be into the millions."

"Say the year was 1741."

"A 1741 Guarneri . . ." His voice cracked at the thought. "That would be priceless."

"Do me a favor. Try putting a price on it."

TURNING POINTS

Illuminated by the diffused undercabinet fluorescents, the violin before her, Maria sat at her kitchen table, very much alone in her quiet dark house. She felt as though she could hear her father in the night, speaking to her the way he would when she was a child in that warm home in Heidelberg. She remembered how he spoke of musical breakthroughs, turning points after which nothing was ever the same. Oh, how she wished he were truly here for her in Alabama tonight.

All this time, Hans had been hiding the violin in plain sight. Even more, he was having his insurance put to good use. How practical. How Hans.

Maria thought about those terrible fearful days in January 1945 when the basket with the violin arrived, when the war was lost and well-connected men like Hans and Karl scrambled to make exit plans, to ensure their futures. And she knew that in those days a violin like this could have come to a man like Hans only from one of those families, one of those families who had cherished it—one of those families who had performed his rocket-building work.

Whom had the instrument belonged to? How many generations? Who had been determined to learn to play it and how many dreams had been fulfilled?

Sabine was right. And Maria understood now. She understood it all. Now that she had found the door and opened it, she could no longer lie to herself.

And the more Maria thought about it, the more her insides swam as though she were becoming sick. It was one thing to steal money, but to take a musical instrument was to take memories and experiences, moments from human lives, to take a violin was to take years of love and expunge them, as though they had never existed.

How could she ever play it again?

The sun was barely up but the knocking on the front door was loud and incessant. Still in yesterday's clothes, her hair a mess, Maria went to the door and opened it.

"Where have you been?" Carolyn asked, bounding past Maria and into the house, bringing a powdery waft of cosmetics fragrance along with her. "Do you have any idea how worried we've been about you?"

"I am sorry." Maria closed the door. "I suppose I should have called you."

"I'll say." Arms crossed, Carolyn stood in front of Maria in the entryway. "Entirely out of the blue, you suddenly decide you're not going to perform unless we turn the event into a civil rights protest?"

Maria tried to walk away but Carolyn blocked her. "Then you walk out of rehearsal. Never return. Don't pick up the phone all afternoon or evening. Penny and I came by twice looking for you last night. Sabine finally got in touch with the base and if you weren't here right now we were going to call Hans. We didn't want to worry him but—"

"No, do not call Hans."

"Maria—what is wrong with you?"

"I really am sorry. I have a great deal on my mind." Maria walked away.

"What are you talking about?"

Carolyn assessed her friend, telling herself to soften her tone and find some sympathy but, her neck on the line, she couldn't bring herself to be sweet right now. She ran up to Maria, getting in her face again. "We have important people coming from all over the area—Chattanooga, Birmingham, Montgomery—they're coming to hear you! You! These are potential donors."

Exhausted, Maria slumped down and just looked at Carolyn, with her astonishingly perfect hair and thoughtfully coordinated shoes and clothing and accessories. There was nothing Maria could find to say to her right now.

Pacing the living room, Carolyn grew even more apoplectic from the silence. "I just don't understand what has suddenly gotten into you. This is a chance to put our city on the map, and you want to use that for some personal agenda? I don't know exactly what you went through and you don't have to tell me. I don't even want to know. I believe we all deserve a fresh start. But holding the town hostage because of your demons isn't going to save a bunch of syphilitic sharecroppers and it's not gonna save you."

Maria's eyes narrowed as though she couldn't stand to look at this woman. "How can you live with yourself?"

"I say this to you because I know that I can because you are one of my best friends and I care about you and you know that. I know I am being blunt, but what you're doing is just downright selfish."

Hit hard by these words, Maria barely heard the phone ring and ring. "Excuse me," she said to Carolyn as she finally picked it up.

Carolyn tried to calm herself as she watched Maria listen to what appeared to be some difficult news.

Visibly besieged, Maria put the phone down.

"What is it?" Carolyn asked.

"I . . . I have to go."

"Go where?"

"I will call you later, I promise." Maria quickly began to gather her things to leave.

"Maria—!"

Maria spun around. "Leave my house now, Carolyn!"

HEART AND SOUL

The Chevy sped through the semicircular drive in front of the hospital and pulled into the parking lot, fairly empty this time of morning.

Marching swiftly down the bright corridor, passing tired hospital staff coming off the night shift, Maria looked at the numbers on doors, until she came to the one she had been given.

Without hesitation, bracing for what she would find, she simultaneously knocked and eased the door open.

In hospital gown, standing and looking out the window, his back to the door, Cooper turned.

"Wow, the nurses here just get better looking every day," he said, that crooked little grin growing on his stubbly face.

She caught her breath. Little lacerations covered his face and arms, just like when she'd first seen him twelve years earlier.

"What is it with you, Cooper? You are supposed to fly the planes, not jump out of them all the time."

She moved into the room and they could not take their eyes off each other.

"I'm glad you came," he said gently. "You doing okay?"

She ran to him and hugged him, and he put his arms tightly around her too. It was something she so badly needed. Then she pulled back and punched him hard in the shoulder.

"Hey! What's that for?" He recoiled his head a little.

"For almost getting yourself killed," she said, her hands on her hips.

"As you can see I'm fine." He rubbed his shoulder.

"And for making my life so complicated."

"Sorry to break it to you, but I don't think it's all me."

"Yes, if not for you I think I would be just as pitiful, but at least I would not have to know I was so pitiful because I would not know there was a way not to be."

"Oddly, I think that actually makes sense."

"Yes, it does seem to."

"Should I take it as a weird compliment or just your neurosis?"

"I do not know. Perhaps we should both be in hospital gowns."

"That could be fun."

"Stop it." She met his grin with her own.

He reached out, took her hand, and pulled her toward a chair. He sat in the other and scooted it close to her so that their knees touched.

"Really, Maria. I'm glad you came. I saw the article on you and I'd be lying if I told you I hadn't read it a few hundred times already."

She saw on his nightstand a copy of the *Huntsville Times* with a huge above-the-fold photo of her holding her violin. Next to her story was a much smaller one featuring a photo of a pouting Nikita Khrushchev and the headline "Soviet Leader Brags about Missile Superiority, Challenges U.S. to 'Shooting Match.'"

Looking up and closing her eyes, she felt the anxiety rush over her anew.

"Now don't go getting a big head," he said. "There's little else to read around here besides *Beowulf* and *Better Homes and Gardens*."

"I told them I was thinking about not playing unless they desegregated the ballroom and opened it up to *everyone*."

"Because . . . your life isn't complicated enough?"

"Because it is the right thing to do, James."

He stared into her eyes, really seeing her. "You are truly the most amazing human being I have met in my life." He put a hand on her thigh. "Yes, of course it's the right thing to do, and an incredibly brave thing too."

"Do you think I am crazy?"

"Entirely. And I think that's why I love you too."

She took his hand and squeezed it. "What do I do?"

"I can't answer that for you. There's only one person that can."

"I know."

He glanced over at the big front-page story on Maria in the paper. "You realize what would happen if you didn't play because of this?"

"It has been brought to my attention."

"I mean, this could affect the base and by extension the launch and—"

"You are not helping."

"Plus your entire life would become regular fodder for town gossip. The way people talk in a little southern town like this . . . Look how fast you found out about me."

"What do you mean? I got a call saying that you were here and that you were asking for me."

"You got a call? From whom?"

"I don't know. He just said he was with the hospital and that you wanted to see me."

Cooper ran his fingers through his thick hair. She could see his mind working.

"What?" Maria asked.

"You know what?" Cooper stood up. "Let's take a walk."

"You want to go for a walk?"

"Absolutely."

"To where?"

"Have you seen the hospital cafeteria? Oh, it's really so lovely. You really must see it."

She looked at him strangely as he headed quickly to the door, but she complied.

In the hall, he motioned for her to follow him. But she saw a sign for the cafeteria and realized it was in the opposite direction.

"James—" She pointed to the sign.

But he tugged her arm. "Actually, I want to show you something else."

A little farther down the hall, Maria looking entirely confused, they approached the recreation room. Cooper pushed through the double doors and Maria followed.

"Okay, what is going on?" She stood in the middle of the room, surveying a Ping-Pong table and some card tables.

He went to an upright piano against a far wall, sat, and started to play—the one song he still knew fairly well, "Heart and Soul." Like he had in the cottage twelve years earlier, he played just one part of the duet. She laughed a little, listening, remembering, her heart melting, and she slowly walked over to the piano bench, sitting right next to him, and began to play the other half.

Their shoulders and hips against each other's, their hands intermingling on the keyboard, they played like that for a while, deeply enjoying each other and this respite from the world.

"I didn't ask for you to come," Cooper said, continuing to play.

"What do you mean?" She played on as well.

"I'm so glad you're here but it wasn't me."

"Then why am I here?"

"I think because we're friends, and someone thinks you're a loose cannon. Which you kind of are."

"I do not understand."

They stopped playing and he turned to her.

"Maria, Sputnik is just a useless hunk of metal, a beeping after-thought to the true peril—the rocket that threw it up there. You aim that thing a few degrees northwest, and you have an interconti-nental ballistic missile that can be launched from Novosibirsk, de-livering whatever you want in less than twenty minutes to New York, D.C., anywhere along the Eastern Seaboard of the United States. Don't you see? Hans and Von Braun and company aren't trying to launch a satellite, they're trying to show the Soviets that we also have a viable ICBM. Because if the Russians don't think that war means mutually assured destruction . . . well, I don't have to tell *you* about the evil aspirations that live inside people."

"So you have been asked to talk some sense into me?"

"We have had the deterrent for years, but using German rockets is touchy stuff. However, people also want to move on, and Von Braun's outreach to the public has been outstanding, but, yeah, the slightest controversy or scandal right now could blow the whole thing. I'm sure they don't want Hans distracted and I know they don't want the country distracted. I have some buddies in the 101st Airborne. They were sent to Little Rock a few weeks ago with the *entire division* because nine colored kids are trying to attend school up there, and apparently even that wasn't enough to protect those kids and control the city, so Eisenhower federalized the entire ten-thousand-member Arkansas National Guard. We have a nervous and ambitious nuclear-armed enemy who right now has a window of opportunity. Meanwhile, America is at war with herself."

"And I have to choose a side."

"I'm afraid you do. Yes. I'm afraid you do."

She put her face in her hands, so many questions running through her head, but they just left her weary. "All my life I have been tending to obligations. When I was a teenager it was the *Kinderhaus* in Nordhausen, then this marriage, now a symphony. Where am I in this, James? Where am I in my own life?"

"You are an incredibly powerful woman, and despite a lifetime of challenges that would leave most people cowering in the hangar or punching out early, you have always met those challenges on your terms. You're a fighter, Maria. And there are many ways to fight."

As she took that in, he grasped her hands. "You know, I have to choose a side too."

"And?"

"And I choose you."

"That could be a very unwise career move."

"I love my country, but if the world is going to end, I want to be with you. And if it's not, I want to fight by your side."

"Sounds like we are both loose cannons."

She put her hand to his face and kissed his forehead.

"I do not know, James. I do not know. What is the right answer here?"

"There may not be one. Sometimes you just close your eyes, trust your instincts—"

"And slam the control stick forward," she said teasingly, remembering his words from years ago.

Cooper laughed, captivated by that beautiful whimsical smile of hers. Then he sighed.

"The truth is, Maria, life often comes down to a coin toss."

"So maybe we should flip for it."

"Heads you stay and play, tails we run off and have a mad, passionate life traveling the world together."

"Tails sounds pretty nice."

"We'll have to live on love. I don't have much money to offer you."

"Oh, I do not think we would have to worry about money."

"Really? Well, this is sounding better and better."

"Until the military catches up with you."

"I'll tell you what. I have two weeks of leave due. I'm going to reserve a room at that inn in Mentone starting on Saturday night. If there is a concert, I will be there, and right afterwards I will drive to Mentone. If you want, join me. If there is no concert, and you want, meet me at the inn."

"And after that?"

"After that . . . we'll flip for it."

"I will think about it."

Next to him there on the piano bench, she put her head on his shoulder and let out a deep breath. And they sat like that in silence for a good long while.

"The space race, the cold war," he said. "It's all just one big dance, you know."

"It does feel that way. Germany and Russia started as allies, then Germany attacked Russia, who became America's friend and is now her foe."

"But right is right, Maria. Right is right. Try not to think about everything else too much."

"And do what?"

"Make your own music and dance along."

He stood up, took a few steps back from the bench, and began humming "Heart and Soul." Then he extended his hand to her.

Looking up at him, her eyes filled at once with adoration and sorrow, she stood and took his hand.

He slipped his other hand along the side of her waist to the small of her back, bringing her close, humming very softly, his cheek tenderly to hers, his warm breath upon her ear.

"Sometimes," she whispered, "I lie in bed and wonder what would have happened if only you would have come back for me."

"I always thought I would see you again, Maria. In my heart, I know I always thought I would. In spite of the years and everything that happened, I never really could let you go."

"If I can't come, James . . . If I don't come . . . you have to, you have to let me go. Promise me you will. Promise me."

Ever so slightly, as though pained, he nodded. And Cooper in a hospital gown, Maria in yesterday's clothes, they danced together in the rec room, lost to the world.

REDEMPTION

Maria stood over the open violin case resting on her dressing table. Such a beautiful object. But it was no longer simply her beloved violin, no longer just a musical instrument. The misgivings fluttered anew every time she thought about reaching for it.

She closed the case, heartbroken, turned, walked out of the room, down the hall, and into Peter's room. She went to his closet and, from the top shelf, removed a violin case.

The two dozen members of the Huntsville Symphony Orchestra played with even greater focus. The radio event almost here, and spurred on by the wave of recent publicity, everyone was clearly excited about the performance. Using her son's instrument, Maria sat in her first-violin chair near the conductor playing with her usual commitment and impeccable craft, helping to lead the ensemble. It was late in the day, and they had all been playing for quite a while, but no one allowed the exhaustion to show in his or her work. And because of the grueling session, no one paid close enough attention to realize that Maria was not practicing with her extraordinary instrument.

While they practiced, a team of uniformed black employees carefully set up rows and rows of chairs throughout the ballroom. Several white hotel and event managers oversaw the operation. From high-society weddings to political galas, the Russel Erskine was famed for its attention to detail, and this event would be no exception. To be sure, given all the focus and the exceptionally large crowd that was expected—there was seating for over five hundred and standing room for another several hundred—the hotel was determined to execute a flawless and memorable event. Some were even using the word *historic* to characterize the first public performance of Rocket City's new symphony.

The lure of the story too good to resist—*Germans start both world-class symphony and America's space program*—several journalists from the region were expected, including Don Whitehead, a Pulitzer Prize–winning columnist for the *Knoxville News-Sentinel* whose work was also carried by the Associated Press.

As Maria completed her solo from the Concerto, backed by Klaus, the second violinist, the rest of the orchestra joined them and they concluded the piece.

"Great job, everyone," the conductor said, his hair damp with perspiration. "Let's take fifteen."

As the members of the orchestra relaxed and took a much-needed break, gregariously exchanging ideas on the performance, Maria quietly put her son's violin in its case and headed out of the room.

Through the big floor-to-ceiling Palladian windows, Maria noticed a familiar red truck in the parking lot, and she could make out Josephine's father sitting in it, presumably waiting for his daughter.

As Maria approached the doors, she saw Penny, arms crossed, leaning against a wall, watching her.

"I need to talk to you," Penny said as Maria came near.

"I know, I owe Carolyn a phone call."

"No, you don't."

Maria took a moment, not sure she really wanted to get into another heated discussion right now, especially with someone she had begun to trust. She felt so alone in all this.

"Please, Maria." Penny motioned with her head toward the kitchen doors.

"Just so you know, even though I am practicing, I have not made up my mind about anything yet."

Penny walked toward the kitchen doors. "Please."

Passing several waiters and maintenance workers and Josephine, who looked concerned, Maria followed Penny into the empty storage room adjacent to the ballroom kitchen. Penny closed the door and turned to her.

"Don't play."

"What?"

"Don't play on Saturday night."

Maria leaned against the shiny Formica and metal table, and cocked her head as if she couldn't hear right. "What exactly do you mean?"

"I owe you an apology. A huge apology. I can't speak for anyone else and I won't, but for myself . . . I am embarrassed, and I am sorry."

As these words sunk in, Maria pulled out a chair and sat. "Penny, there is no need to—"

"No, let me finish." Pacing in front of the wall just under the yellow-and-black trefoil fallout shelter sign, Penny tried to gather

her thoughts. "We . . . I have been so caught up in the symphony and all the sudden attention that I lost sight of myself. I lost my values. While you, this newcomer to town, see something wrong and you want to stand up and do something about it, and the people who are supposed to be your friends try to push you around for their own benefit."

Penny stopped right in front of her. "Maria, what I'm trying to say is, you inspire me."

Surprised and deeply moved, Maria could not find words. She stepped forward and hugged Penny, who returned the embrace.

Maria finally released her. "That is the nicest thing anyone has ever said to me."

"I meant what I said to you in this room last weekend. You have it all, honey. And you are my friend and I will stick by you."

"Oh, I do not have it all. I really do not."

"You got more than most, sugar, I can tell you that."

"So if I tell them I won't play, do you think the hotel will open it up to everyone?"

"I don't honestly know. It's a pretty serious game of chicken we'll be starting. All I know is it'll get a lot of attention. Good and not so good." Penny tucked flyaway strands into her beehived hair. "But if you want to do this, I will stand right by your side throughout."

"You are such a good friend."

"One thing you need to think about. If we do this, are you sure everyone will come? Are you sure *anyone* will come? Have you asked?"

A hand to her forehead, Maria realized that hadn't even occurred to her. Here was one of the downsides of acting so quickly on her impulses.

Then she remembered. "I need to go talk to someone right now."

Maria threw open the storage room door.

◆ ◆ ◆

The red pickup backed up, beginning to leave. Maria jogged to it across the asphalt of the parking lot on the side of the hotel. Josephine, in the passenger's seat, turned and stared wide-eyed through the back window of the cab. Her father, his head out the driver's window as he backed up, saw the woman trotting toward him and threw the old vehicle into park.

She approached his window, out of breath.

"You okay, ma'am?" the man said.

"If we can get the hotel to open up the event . . ." Hands on her sides, she tried to catch her breath. "Would you come?"

He looked her up and down and then turned off the truck.

"Wait here," he said to his daughter, opening his door.

"Dad! I want to come!"

"Josephine!" It was a tone that required nothing further.

"Yes, sir."

The girl sat, face forward, as he got out of the truck, slammed the door shut, and strode several paces away. Maria followed, walking right up to him.

The large man towered over her. "What kind of game you playing at?"

"It is not a game."

"You asking me if I would like to be a guest at this hotel?" He pointed to the building.

"I am."

"The Russel Erskine Hotel?" He started to laugh. "Why not ask me if I would like to sprout wings out my behind and fly over it?"

"You did not answer my question."

"Yes, I surely did."

"I am thinking about refusing to play."

Abruptly, he stopped laughing, taking a step closer to her.

"You see black people escorted into schools by soldiers and so you thinking you just gonna turn our local hotel here into your personal protest?"

"It is not like that."

"No? You tell me, what's it like?"

"I am trying to do the right thing. It is as simple as that."

"Right thing."

"Yes. If I am to play in the city's symphony, I think it should belong to the entire city."

"And where do you come to thinking like that? You decided that things didn't go so well in your country so you gonna come over here and set America straight? That's right noble."

"I understand that the threat of violence can be intimidating, but I—"

"Violence. What you know about violence?"

"Enough. I think I know enough."

"What I think is that you got some kind of something you need to fix, and you need to take a long, hard look inside yourself before you go trying to save other people."

"Maybe I just think it is a shame that the world does not know about a child as talented as yours."

He noticed Maria looking at someone behind him, and he turned and saw Josephine sticking her head out the driver's side window. "Josephine!"

The girl retracted back inside the truck and he shot his head back to Maria. "You know nothing about my daughter or the hateful things that happened to her mother. I won't have Josephine end up dead too. Now you stay away from her, you hear?"

Maria's shoulders dropped. "I am sorry," she said quietly. "Maybe I *was* playing at something that is none of my business. I just think it is a shame. For everyone."

"The world don't want to know about my little girl."

"Some of it, maybe much of it, I do not know. But she said that you told her not to judge a person until you know what is inside, and I think that is wise advice. Because I can tell you there are some very good people in the world. I happen to have a friend in there right now who is one of them, so I know. Sir, for your daughter, take your own advice."

He sucked in his lower lip, then blew it out, her appeal finding its mark and his expression softening.

"You seem like a nice lady and Josephine says you got the makings of a pretty decent fiddler. You looking to make something right, ain't you?"

He moved his face very close to hers, speaking in what was almost a whisper. "I know where you at. You between two places and you stuck in the mud and you sinking fast."

"Yes." Her voice was barely audible.

"You want salvation? Look into your *own* heart. Be honest with yourself. You got to do your time, save your own soul, before you go looking to save someone else. Ma'am, you want redemption? Play your fiddle. Stand up there and face all those people and play it like you never played it before." Emphatically, he pointed at her chest. "Start there."

And he turned, strolled up to his red pickup, glowing with the long golden light of the receding southern sun, hopped in, and drove off. And Maria just stood there in the big, empty parking lot of the Russel Erskine Hotel in downtown Huntsville, she just stood there alone on the blacktop, hands down, palms forward and open, as if waiting for something to come to her, thinking about what he'd said as the sun pulled back and away behind the old cotton warehouse across the street, and she made a decision.

REPAIRING THE WORLD

At dawn, Maria walked resolutely along the tree-lined path through the greenway next to the gaping Tennessee River. Strolling through the mist, she passed army officers and Redstone personnel, a few accompanied by service dogs, all out for their morning run. A gray osprey meandered overhead, fishing the quaggy eddies at water's edge.

Later in the morning, Maria drove into bustling downtown and picked up the dry cleaning from Mrs. Mayfield, including her long black gown, pressed for the event.

On her way to the car, she noticed several people standing in front of the appliance store next to the dry cleaners. They were watching something captivating on the television sets in the big display window.

Maria approached and, on the half-dozen new television sets in the window, she saw Wernher Von Braun sitting and talking to a recognizable reporter on a launching pad in Cape Canaveral. Next to Von Braun sat Hans and Karl. And behind them, extensive work was being conducted on a long, slender modified V2 rocket, presumably the topic of the conversation.

Later in the day, Maria wandered the Ayers Family farmers' stands tucked away off Memorial Avenue in a shady grove of white oaks, filling her basket with just-picked seasonal produce and fresh eggs. In their big straw hats, the farmers greeted Maria as she looked through their beautiful fruits and vegetables.

She spent the late afternoon in the dappled shade of her backyard, watering the new bushes and planting some herbs she'd picked up at the farmers' market.

In the evening, she cooked and ate alone in the kitchen, and then later, after cleaning, she sat on the sofa looking over sheet music, humming to herself as she read.

Throughout it all, though she made a point to put her mind and body into as restful a state as possible, she spent a great deal of time thinking about the telephone. She walked by it and glanced over at it, next to the stack of mail on the hall table under the chrome-framed mirror, but it just sat there, silent. Would Hans call? He usually did if he was gone this long. She knew how difficult it could be to get an interstate long-distance call out, and she imagined that he was incredibly busy with his vital and time-sensitive work, but she also assumed that Hans could use his government connections to set up a call if he wanted to. And if he did, what would she say to him?

Maria finally fell asleep on the sofa listening to orchestral jazz on the radio, on a station out of Memphis, and at some point in the middle of the night made her way to the bed.

She was awoken in the morning by the sound of the phone ringing, but by the time she finally got herself out of bed and answered it, the caller had hung up. Was it Hans? She had no way of knowing for sure and no way to contact him if she needed to or just wanted to. He was out there, certainly thinking about her—but ultimately, *she was on her own*, just as she had been in the cottage twelve years ago. Actually, she felt, even more so.

Much of the afternoon was spent at the hotel meeting with the orchestra while the broadcasting equipment was set up and tested. Workers and technicians came and went, setting up large metal-mesh microphones on stands in and around the orchestra, including one directly in front of Maria's chair.

Huge flower arrangements were brought into the ballroom, the bar was stocked and set, additional chairs were placed along the walls, and all manner of last-minute items were checked and re-checked. A large truck was readied in the main parking lot on the side of the hotel to serve as a control room for the broadcast.

On Saturday, Maria slept late and, after lingering over the wholesome lunch she made for herself, she took a long, hot bath, shaved her legs, and carefully did her hair and makeup, finally slipping into her black evening gown.

The doorbell rang.

Calm and collected, Maria opened the top drawer of her dresser and carefully removed the clear plastic folder with the old rectangular Guarneri label. She reached for a small black leather tote bag that she had packed, unzipped it, placed the folder inside, and zipped the bag shut.

Then she reached for the violin case on her dressing table .

She popped the case open, considered the Guarneri one last time, and closed the case.

Carrying the Guarneri violin in its case and the small bag, Maria walked out of the bedroom and went to the door, where a driver was waiting for her. In her driveway sat a shiny black sedan, engine running, owned by the city, all arranged by Carolyn, who wasn't taking any chances.

Maria stepped out onto her front porch, case in one hand, bag in the other, and headed for the car.

In the backseat, as the sedan pulled out of her driveway and into the cul-de-sac and drove off out of Blossomwood, past newly planted azalea bushes and carefree fair children playing on milky white sidewalks with their brightly barking dogs, the bag beside her, Maria rested her fingertips carefully, protectively on the violin case sitting on her lap.

She thought about the families, the mothers and fathers and children, in their tattered coats with the stitched-on stars, standing and then sitting around their luggage in the town square, and in hundreds of other town squares, thousands—she knew about them, they all knew about them.

She closed her eyes, her hands on the precious violin, and she tried to imagine to which family among the thousands it had belonged.

Maria's eyes opened wide, Blossomwood rushing past her in a blur, perhaps for the last time.

It was no longer just a violin. It was not just wood and glue and animal parts. It was a direct link to lives, and she was not going to let it sit in silence, its true identity hidden away unless it needed to be sold or bartered for who knew what purpose.

This was a powerful, valuable, living thing, and somehow she could use it to repair the world. Of that she was certain. But could she use it as well to repair her heart? Because she knew she was, indeed, going to have to do that first.

Despite Sabine's warning and everything she herself had worked so hard to build and believe—this house of cards built over a secret fallout shelter—she had to be honest with herself. Josephine's father was right, and as painful and unthinkable as it was, she had to start by being honest with herself about Hans.

His office at the factory had been right next to the camp. He was a team leader with oversight of the entire production line. His colleagues were tried and hanged—simply because they did not have the special knowledge that he had. The Americans had covered up and were still covering up.

The uniform. The violin. The secrets.

How could she build a life with a husband who was lying to her? How could she stay with a man who had been a party to evil?

Head turned, gazing out the window at her world flying past her, Maria sighed. she would play her violin and she would go to Mentone with James Cooper—and she would tell him about their son.

In crisp white dress uniform, medals shined and straight, Cooper stepped out of his apartment and headed toward his Triumph, a bounce in his gait, a small, worn duffel bag swinging from his hand. He tossed the bag in the trunk of the little roadster, its top down, hopped in behind the wheel, popped on his Ray-Ban aviators, and sped off toward downtown, the wind slicking back his thick cropped sable-brown hair.

DREAMS OF HEAVEN

People poured into the front doors of the Russel Erskine Hotel early Saturday night. Dozens of smartly attired parking attendants and doormen opened car doors and directed guests across the red carpet and under the dazzling marquee lights. *Welcome, Huntsville Symphony Orchestra. Live on Radio WBHP,* read the marquee. A long line of vehicles snaked around the entire hotel block.

Driving through the nearly full parking lot, around the side of the hotel, under the bright street lamps and security lights, the city's shiny black sedan pulled up to the cordoned-off area in front of the main service entrance. The driver hopped out and opened the back door of the car.

Legs long and high-heeled, Maria stepped out. She tugged her figure-hugging black dress down over her seamed stockings, tossed back her thick honey-blond hair, and with bag and violin, chin high, walked past the radio station truck, up and across the concrete landing, and into the service entrance.

The sound inside was nearly deafening as waiters and workers flew by her, and the fluorescent utility lights were searing. Maria squinted and raised a forearm to her face.

Penny quickly grabbed her, wriggling her through the back corridors of the kitchen, past people who greeted her, others with trays of food and drinks dodging her, until they arrived at the storage room.

Inside, Penny closed the door and there was quiet, the commotion outside reduced to a low, steady hum.

"Jimmy says that when they send you to war, ninety-nine percent of your time is spent waiting—it's the one percent that counts. I think this is one of those one percent nights."

"I think it has been a one percent week."

Penny stood before her friend, reached out, and gave Maria's reedy forearms a light squeeze. Maria could see the joy and excitement gleaming in Penny's eyes.

"We have a packed house out there," Penny said. "People are already starting to stand along the walls. But you say the word, honey, and I'll march right back out that side door with you. Right by your side."

"I know, and I appreciate that. But I am ready to play."

"Okay. The symphony will be meeting in the Blue Room in five minutes. I'll let you warm up, and then I'll be back."

"Thank you, Penny. For everything." And now Maria reached out to Penny, squeezing her hand. "You inspire *me*."

"Now you stop that. You'll make my eyelash extensions slip right off."

As Penny reached for the door, she remembered something. "By the way, there is a flyboy sitting alone in the front row, off to the left near your chair, who looks remarkably like that handsome fan of yours from the club."

Although Maria made a concerted effort to keep her face dispassionate, her heart pounded hard and fast and she began to feel dizzy. She willed herself to breathe in calmly.

Penny knew Maria well enough to pick up on her reaction, and she studied her closely.

"Anything you want to talk about?" Penny asked lightly.

Clearly there was, but, sighing deeply, Maria thought the better of it.

"Do you ever wonder if there are some things better not talked about?" Maria asked.

"Things that we know but pretend not to?"

"Exactly."

"I do. Unless it includes salacious behavior, in which case you can and must describe it *in detail* for a dear close friend who you *know* you can trust."

Maria cracked up laughing. "Maybe later, Penny."

"Ooh, I just know this is gonna be delicious."

Penny rubbed her hands together in delight and then, with a wink, she waggled out of the room, closing the door behind her. Maria rose and went to one of the wire rack shelves against a wall behind her. She scooted forward a thirty-pound pail of hard winter wheat, placed her small bag behind it, and scooted the pail back.

A hush fell over the packed ballroom as the twenty-four members of the Huntsville Symphony Orchestra filed in from the lobby, through the main doors in the back. And then the room broke out with spontaneous roaring applause.

Heads turned, everyone watching, as the ensemble members walked by all the well-dressed people, many in military uniform, standing along the sides and back. The ensemble marched single file to a center aisle between the rows of seats, continuing down the aisle to their chairs at the other end of the room. Those seated in the audience applauded even louder as the procession of musicians passed them.

Carrying her violin and bow, Maria strode in at the end of the line, followed finally by the conductor.

"The Huntsville Symphony Orchestra is filing in," the smooth-voiced announcer said into the large microphone in front of him, at the table near the orchestra where he sat.

The orchestra members stood in front of their seats, waiting as Maria and the conductor found their places.

"And there they are," the announcer said. "Conductor Felix Meyer and violinist Maria Reinhardt."

The musicians sat.

The room quieted down and the orchestra members picked up and readied their instruments, drawing bows across strings, blowing random notes on horns, everyone settling in. Maria looked over the orchestra until the discordance ceased and all the members were still and in position.

Exchanging a glance with Maria, who nodded, the conductor tapped his white wood baton five times on the metal stand in front of him, and then he raised the baton. Everyone in the entire ballroom, sitting, standing, working, every single person was silent as the conductor held his baton in the air, frozen, every eye in the room focused on it, none with more intensity than Maria's.

But in that moment when Huntsville, Alabama, held its breath, Maria dared to glance down and out, and in what seemed a fraction of a second she saw him, sitting there alone, dashing as ever in his white air force uniform, that grin on his face, looking right at her and connecting with her as if they were the only two people in this room, the only two that existed and had *ever* existed, and the future, everything and anything beyond here and now, was as unfathomable as the magnitude of the universe.

The conductor lifted his baton, and Maria and the orchestra, all at the same moment, in perfect harmony, began to play.

1945

Steam filled the bathroom, causing Maria's sleeveless blue linen dress to stick to her. Thin lines of moisture tracked down her neck and shoulders through dried perspiration and caked dirt.

Eyes still on Cooper in the tub, she unfastened the top button of her dress, then, slowly, she unfastened the one below it, and the one below that, and the one below that, sliding the right shoulder strap off with her left hand, the left strap with her right, the dress dropping to the floor. She unclasped and slid off her undergarments.

When she was a child in that wonderful old house in Heidelberg, the damp breeze off the Rhine though the windows, the spätzle crackling and the sound of soft footsteps, she'd lie in bed under her grandmother's matelassé coverlet, its raised stitches a map of her life to be, but she saw none of this world. No war and death, the destruction of dreams.

The map was flawed, the house destroyed, the world as she thought it would be—gone. There was nothing but her body and her soul.

Her bare feet on the cold ceramic tile, the rest of her skin exposed to the warm steam as she moved through it toward him, her body tingled from the varying sensations. Her heart plunging blood forcefully to her extremities, making her draw breath with increased pace, muscles at once tightening and dilating, she could feel fine little hairs standing up on every part of her.

At the tub, Maria stepped in.

Standing in front of Cooper, her wide, lean shoulders back, long, lithe arms down, she bent her knees, sliding into the water, feeling at once vulnerable and powerful, lost and found. She threw water onto her face, running her wet hands through her long hair, her head back.

Cooper moved forward toward her and reached out, his large hands tenderly cupping her cheeks as he brought his face close to hers, their lips brushing and quivering, and he kissed her fully, his hands sliding down her neck, to her shoulders, arms, his thumbs and palms slowly over her breasts, open hands over her tight waist, sliding back and down and pulling her up close, against him. She sighed, her sound deep and low.

Their noses nearly touching, he just shook his head in the slightest way as though he could not believe how beautiful she truly was, and she could feel his hands trembling on her more and more, and suddenly he raised her up—those large hands that had lifted her and tossed her like she had been a bag of flour— her ankles crossing behind him, her hands sliding over his expansive hard back as he steadily and slowly lowered her, their eyes locked, and her head going back again, involuntarily, fingers gripping his shoulders, the exquisite pain transcended by the incomprehensible pleasure of being full with him and the bond, her mane of hair hanging and swaying, face up and mouth open, his lips on her neck and throat, and she could feel his breath hotter than the water all around them, as he raised her and then lowered her still, her arms wrapping around his neck, hands grasping his wet dark hair, and lower still, both of them crying out . . .

1957

Loud and big and epic, the sound of Beethoven's Violin Concerto filled the packed ornate ballroom. The conductor gesticulated wildly but rhythmically with his baton, reaching a fevered pitch, swept up in the zeal of the orchestra as they played with the greatest precision and passion, the musical story reaching a sustained crescendo.

Most people in the audience had never before heard music performed like this and they were moved, many stirred in a way they had never before known. Mouths were agape in amazement and joy and disbelief at such beauty.

Penny, Carolyn, Sabine, Bobsie Ingram, and their husbands, as well as many congregants from St. Mark's, sat toward the front, near Cooper, in reserved seats, along with reporters, out-of-town donors, and high-ranking officers from the base. Like everyone else in the audience, they were white.

Along the back wall of the room, next to the service doors, stood Josephine with a few hotel and event workers, all black.

Maria stood and—as the conductor thrust his baton at her— she began her solo.

1945

Maria and Cooper stepped out of the tub, clean and renewed. Maria threw the door wide open and the room was soon bright and cool. Standing on the tile floor, facing each other, they shared a towel.

As Cooper dried Maria's hair, smoothing it out with his hands, still he could not take his gaze from her. Seeing her so close and clear like this, fresh-faced, he was simply entranced by her.

He fanned out his fingers into her damp blond hair, gently pulling her forward and leaning toward her, running his nose along her soft cheek to behind her ear, taking in the pure scent of her. She exhaled audibly with the pleasure of being treasured.

Slowly drying her body with the towel, he was overcome once again, and he swept her up in his arms, the towel still partly around her, and he kissed her deeply, carrying her out of the bathroom.

Towel falling open and hanging from his arm, under her, he took her into the bedroom and laid her down upon the bed, sliding up beside her, his large hand moving again to her face and through her damp hair and unhurriedly down her while he kissed her, discovering her all over again.

And that is where they spent much of the day, and evening, in that big bed in the cottage in the woods, their lovemaking boundless and complete and seemingly without end, with regard for no country or creed, only for each other. For in a place of supreme darkness, where all that it had once meant to be human and civil was gone, they had found a precious bond, an affirmation of the goodness in people, proof that love could still exist.

The early-morning light illuminating the bedroom, Cooper and Maria lay intertwined on the disheveled bed. Though exhausted, spent, they seemed to glow, looking serene and content.

"When I was a little girl," Maria said quietly, her head on his chest, "I would lie in bed in the mornings and play a game where I would pretend that I had the power to stop time, and I would imagine all the things I would do, running around with everyone just frozen."

"What would you do?" Cooper asked, stroking her hair.

"Oh, all kinds of naughty things. I would steal cookies and ride my bike all through the house."

"Bad girl, you."

She laughed at the recollection. "Sure would be a nice power to have."

"Sure would."

And they were quiet again, just lying there, eyes wide open, thinking, absorbing each other.

"There's a tree on my farm in Pennsylvania, this old ancient oak, biggest tree you've ever seen, up on a hill in the middle of the land, and at sunrise you can go up there, the low clouds all around, and sit in this tire swing and sway back and forth, through the fog, back and forth. It's just like flying, and after meeting you I think I know for certain now that's all the flying I'll ever need in my life again. You'd like this farm, Maria. You'd like it a lot."

Her head still on his chest, she closed her eyes and smiled, moved and delighted by his words.

And ever so softly, running her fingers lightly along his body, she began humming.

"I love Beethoven," he said.

"'Ode to Joy.' I learned it when I was nine. I have played it a thousand times. But I think for the first time in my life I understand what it is about."

She rolled atop him and kissed him lightly on the lips, looking into his eyes.

"My father used to say that every violin has a perfect bow," she said, crossing her hands on his chest. "Some violins are played for generations, until they find their bow. Do you believe that, James?"

"When my cockpit was on fire and I punched out, I thought for sure I was done. But my chute opened and the wind blew and I could've landed in a thousand places. I don't know what I believe— except that I am alive, and I am here, and now that I've found you I don't want to lose you."

He reached up and held her face and kissed her. As the kiss grew, there was a loud knocking on the front door.

They both bolted upright.

Cooper jumped out of bed, went to the bedroom window, and peered sideways through the curtain, arching his head.

"SS," he said in an alarmed whisper.

More pounding on the front door. *"Fräulein, können Sie bitte auf-machen?"* The voice was civil but demanding.

Running around the room, frantically searching for clothing, Maria began to panic.

Cooper stood still, silently indicating with his hand and expression for her to relax and stay calm.

"Nur eine Minute, bitte!" Maria called out, as sweetly and casually as she could.

Fumbling with the buttons on the dress she had tossed on, Maria ran out of the bedroom, into the main room, where she grabbed Cooper's musette bag and threw it to him in the bedroom, where he was standing, naked, holding his gun.

She went to the front door. Would they notice it had just been repaired?

More knocking.

Maria forced herself to breath and opened the door.

In the bedroom, Cooper listened as two SS officers asked Maria if she had seen *Standartenführer* Müller. And as he leaned forward, head cocked tensely, he could hear there was more. Something about an American pilot.

His back against the closed bedroom door, Colt .45 held just below his chin at the ready, Cooper could feel a bead of sweat running down his face. Had they adequately cleaned the blood from the floor? Were there any remnants of the dead officer's uniform in sight? Would Cooper's boots that he'd left near the fireplace be noticed?

Cooper heard Maria tell one of the soldiers that of course he could get a glass of water, and Cooper heard the man coming closer, his jackboots clip-clapping hard along the wood floor.

Cooper tightened his grip on the pistol, running his plan through his head, ready to shoot both men dead in an instant.

Listening then to the soldier put an empty glass on the table, he thought about how to kill the one closest to Maria without shooting her.

But what then? How many more would come? How many rounds did he have? How long could he fight them before they finally grabbed her for harboring him?

His heart pounding, Cooper heard the men leaving.

"*Auf Wiedersehen und Danke*," he heard Maria say, and although she tried to sound nonchalant, he could hear the terror in her trembling voice.

The men left. The front door closed. And Maria strode as calmly as she could back to the bedroom.

She threw open the door, saw him standing there, and she just lost it, overwhelmed by so much emotion, throwing herself into his arms and sobbing.

"They found your parachute," she said.

Cooper held her tight, the gun still in his hand, both of them knowing how dangerous it was for him to stay.

1957

Maria stood before the room playing solo. Guarneri firmly atop her shoulder, face pressed to the chin rest, she drew the bow with utter conviction up and down at just the right angles, searing over the new strings, a sense of longing in her expressions.

Every face in the room was focused on her. All across the region people listened to her. But there was only one person of whom she was aware, and she met his eyes, looking out to him sitting there in the front row as she played on with increasing physical commitment, as if conjuring the joy in the composition would spill over into her own soul, as if bringing to life the love she still felt for James Cooper and letting everyone know about it would set into stark relief all that was hateful and wrong and prejudiced, allowing everyone to see it all clearly, stirring them to change, as if playing with all that she was could bring back that little boy.

Tears began to well in Maria Reinhardt's eyes, just as they had when she had played in the cottage twelve years ago, right before James Cooper walked into her life.

And looking out at him now, she could see the promise of the rest of her days and nights spent with him and, using her violin as a conduit for one of Beethoven's greatest expressions of jubilance and passion, she envisioned that life.

In the shadowed back of the packed parking lot of the Russel Erskine Hotel, a large black man sat alone in the cab of his old red pickup truck, head back, looking out at the brilliant stars, listening to Maria on the radio. His callused hand rested on a fiddle case beside him on the bench seat.

Maria, still standing, was now joined by the entire symphony in the glorious conclusion of the performance. As she gave herself to the music, playing with even greater force and fervor, her hair broke free of its pins and spray, flying around as she moved her head in the building rhythm.

Struggling, fighting as if to transcend something holding her back, Maria kicked off her shoes—to the amazement of the conductor and many in the audience—and, in stockinged feet, she played on. Completely unrestrained now, her true sense of abandon unbound, she felt connected not only to Cooper and those for whom she played but to all those lives . . . those people and families and generations who played this violin, who played their fiddles, from Nordhausen to Montgomery, Krakow to Tuskegee. Memories and dreams and moments from human lives passed through her as though she were a bridge between what was and what is, and none of it was lost.

Beads of sweat flew from her forehead as she whipped her head even more wildly, and though fatigue was apparent on her face, Maria pressed on, the violin a part of her now, like her own bone and sinews and hair. Oh, how wrong she had been all these years to try to repress her feelings. She decided right here and now to always know what was true. What she would do with it, she would take day by day, night by night, starting with this night, when she would leave for Mentone with this man in white before her, who had come to take her away.

Fighting tears, everything foggy through them, she looked over Cooper's shoulder—and she saw Hans, standing against the wall, a large bouquet of red roses in hand.

He had come.

He smiled at her, as he had so many times, and she felt as though her bow would slip, screeching across the strings, and she would stop playing and the world would gasp as one, everyone knowing her secrets.

But she played on, drawing strength from some inner well that she knew was nearly drained, she played on knowing that the longer she played, the more she could put off having to come back to the reality that now awaited.

How could she just run out on him? This man who had known

her all her life, who was her family? But how could she stay with him? She could not live her life with someone she could not trust.

A difficult choice before her, Maria Reinhardt led the orchestra into its finale, the entire audience, near and far, breathless.

1945

In the main room of the cottage, Cooper, dressed in civilian clothes, gathered a few of his supplies, reviewed his silk map, and tucked it into a pocket.

Maria stood near the piano, watching him, her heart breaking.

"I can keep you hidden here. I know I can," she said.

"It's too dangerous for you," he said, checking the clip on his gun. "We've been over this."

"The Americans will be here in just weeks. You said it yourself."

"And if I am discovered, you will be too, and I won't do that to you. I have sixteen rounds. Not enough to fight off the reinforcements they will send."

She went to him. "James—"

He put his finger to her lips. "You are going to be okay. You are strong. You can do this."

Reaching into his front pocket, he withdrew his Morgan silver dollar, holding it out before her. Then he took her hand. "Come with me," he said.

He marched her into the bedroom, and he went to the bed and slipped the coin under her pillow. "This will keep you safe. And bring you dreams of Pennsylvania."

She bit her lip, trying to stop the rising emotions.

Then he took her back into the main room and produced the gold barter kit, handing it to her.

"Now listen to me. You take this, and you buy food, whatever you need, for you and the children, and you keep yourself alive. I will come back for you. I will."

"James, if something should happen, to either one of us—"

"Nothing is going to happen."

"I was ready to die and then you dropped from the sky, if that is not proof we belong together . . . So if not in this life, then in another."

She took the gold barter kit and he threw his arms around her, holding her tight, this woman to whom the wind had blown him.

Setting her jaw tight, taking in the feeling of his embrace, setting it to memory, Maria raised up her head, meeting his eyes.

And they grasped each other even tighter and kissed, deeply and passionately, one last time.

Cooper finally broke away, took a breath, and headed for the door. He opened it and turned back to her.

"Wait for me," he said.

And he was gone.

1957

Outside, in the parking lot of the hotel, where scores of cars sat silent under the faint him of the street lamps and security lights, a heron on its way back to the river squawked serenely overhead. Light poured out from the big Palladian windows, and the dull roar of hundreds of people applauding could be heard.

The ovation continued and continued, unabated, and through the windows hundreds of people could be seen standing on their feet and clapping their hands and cheering.

The door to the service entrance flew open and Maria ran out, heels dangling from one hand, violin and bow from the other. In her tight black dress and stockinged feet, she dashed across the concrete landing, the heavy door pounding shut behind her, and she sat down on the edge, feet dangling over, and she cried.

Drained by her performance and overwhelmed by all that had happened over the last week, over the last twelve years, her life in time of war and reconstruction, love found and love lost and love found, she no longer had the reserves, or the inclination, to remain detached, and it all poured out of her in sobs.

I know where you at. The memory of Josephine's father's words rang in her ears. *You between two places and you stuck in the mud and you sinking fast.*

Yes, it was true. So true. Where was she in her life? Where? She had to make a choice and she had to make it now.

Like raindrops, tears fell upon the violin on her lap, so she picked it up, instinctively putting it to her shoulder, and, as was her nature, she started to play.

Legs dangling in the breeze off the river, sitting alone out there in the night, a silent sea of cars before her, she played not Beethoven or Bach or Sibelius. Maria began "Amazing Grace."

With the bow moving in long, steady cadence, the soulful sound seemed to resonate throughout the parking lot. In the back of the lot, the black man stepped out of the red pickup.

"You were good tonight," said Josephine from behind Maria.

Maria stopped and turned around and saw the girl, in her pressed white uniform, standing in the open service door.

"Oh, nowhere near as good as you," Maria said.

Josephine walked out on the landing.

"I don't know about that."

Maria wiped her eyes. "You are very kind."

The girl sat down next to Maria.

"Why you cryin'?"

"Oh, I am being silly, I think."

"I know a thing or two about silly. You can tell me."

Maria put her arm around the girl. "I know. You are a very special person and I am so lucky to have you as a friend."

Penny charged through the door. "There you are! Everyone is looking for you!"

Carolyn followed, winded. "Maria! The press is waiting for you in the Blue Room. What in the world are you doing out here?"

"I am sitting, with my friend."

Josephine started to get up but, not wanting to give up the comfort, Maria kept her arm on her. "Can you sit with me a little longer?"

Josephine nodded, feeling very safe and secure next to Maria Reinhardt right now. As the girl smiled up at a rather flustered Carolyn, the door burst open again and several more people rushed out onto the landing.

Klaus, violin and bow in hand, approached. "Maria, are you okay? You ran off before the applause was over."

"I am fine. I just needed some air."

"Well, enough air!" Carolyn said, standing right over Maria and Josephine. "Let's get in there and talk to the reporter from the AP."

Maria did not move. "You know, I think I would like to just sit here for a while."

"You want to just sit at the service entrance?" Carolyn bellowed, until Penny grabbed her and glared at her and yanked her by the arm.

"Leave her alone," Penny said. "This woman just left Alabama in a state of awe." Penny leaned over toward Maria, speaking gently. "You take all the time you want, honey."

Continuing to just sit next to Josephine, violin and bow on her lap, Maria looked out and saw the first audience members trickling into the parking lot. She heard the buzz of the crowd surging, and looking through the windows at everyone standing and milling about, she realized that the ballroom was about to hemorrhage people into this parking lot, and two of them were surely looking for her right now.

One of them she spotted across the lot, easy to see in his crisp dress whites, leaning, arms crossed, against his little Triumph ragtop. Cooper just stood there grinning and waiting.

The other one was somewhere in this crowd.

More people poured out into the lot, searching for their vehicles, the chatter growing. Maria knew she would have to act soon.

A photographer jogged up to the landing and a flash went off in Maria's face. Squinting from the sudden burst of light, with more people pooling into the open area below and in front of the landing, she saw a tall fair man with a large bouquet of roses walking between the cars and coming straight toward her—Hans.

She looked back over at Cooper, still standing there, arms crossed, waiting for her.

And as a groundswell of people now flowed into the lot, she took a deep breath and, from the shadows, Josephine's father stepped forward, up to the platform, carrying a fiddle case.

He lifted the case up to his daughter. "Josephine, maybe Mrs. Reinhardt would like to play with you."

"Really?" The little girl lit up at the suggestion.

He nodded, mainly to Maria, a response to her appeal to him. "Thank you for the advice," he said.

"Thank *you*."

"Sam. My name is Sam."

"Thank *you*, Sam."

The girl turned to Maria, violin and bow in hand. "I know something we both know. Want to play?"

"It would be my honor."

With Carolyn and Penny and everyone on the landing watching, Maria placed her violin on her shoulder, against her chin. Josephine followed. And at exactly the same moment, they lifted their bows in the air and, smiling broadly at each other as though they had been playing together for years, as one they began.

The poignant sound of "Amazing Grace" played masterfully on two violins pierced the night.

Throughout the parking lot, they froze, keys in hand, hugging good-bye, chattering on about tomorrow's brunch, standing in front of cars, searching for cars, sitting in cars with doors open, one by one and then all at once, the people of Huntsville stopped in their tracks and listened.

Something was happening.

And slowly, as though bound by a spell, they began to move toward the music, toward the landing, men in felt hats, women balanced on high heels, heads up and eyes narrowed in the bright security lights, hundreds of people snaking in between the cars came forth as one.

Engrossed in their performance, Josephine and Maria stood. Smiling happily at each other, the little girl and the woman played with an off-the-cuff freedom, riffing on each other's work as musical equals, the heartfelt, spiritual, bluesy sound of "Amazing Grace" soaring over downtown Huntsville.

Standing on the landing looking out, Maria could see Cooper at his car, watching in amazement, and just below her, in front of the landing, there was Hans, flowers in hands, admiration on his face.

As Josephine and Maria reached the powerful climax of their duet, people packed into the open space in front of the landing, they jammed in between the cars nearest the landing, hundreds and hundreds now all pouring in to hear the little girl playing with Maria Reinhardt by the back service entrance.

They emptied out of the hotel lobby, came out of nearby restaurants, parking attendants and police officers and passersby, hotel workers and waiters, black and white, all listening and intermingling and all trying to get a peek, everyone wanting to know—

Who was this little girl?

As one, Maria and Josephine pulled the final note across their strings and then lifted up their bows, laughing together with pure joy, and the diverse crowd assembled there in the parking lot of the Russel Erskine Hotel, all together as one, broke into raucous applause.

And now, with Josephine by her side, Maria did what she had not done after the performance inside the hotel—she took a bow. Then, with encouragement from Maria, Josephine did too. Then they both took one together.

The crowd cheered, and Maria could not seem to stop smiling, especially at Josephine, who was poised beyond her years with all the attention.

Several flashes went off as photographers took pictures and reporters made notes.

Finally, the crowd settled down and began to disperse, everyone talking about the performances, both in the hotel and out. What a night for this city, one that was to be talked about for quite some time.

Josephine looked up at Maria. "I better get back to work before someone notices I'm gone."

Maria laughed at her joking. "I think more than that may have already been noticed."

They shared a long look where nothing was said but much exchanged.

"I'll see you again soon?" Josephine asked.

"Count on it."

Watching the little girl head off into the service entrance, Maria heard a voice that she knew as well as her own.

"I have not seen you play like this since the family reunion on the Königssee," Hans said, standing right next to her, flowers in hand. "You were twelve years old and already a virtuoso. Do you remember?"

"I was eleven and gawky as a newborn giraffe." She faced him, speaking flatly. "And I had such a crush on you."

He extended the flowers to her. After considering them, and him, she took them, her nose down, taking in the pleasant fragrance.

"You came all the way from Florida to reminisce?" she asked.

"I came to see my wife."

"It is not like you to put anything above your work. Wernher insisted, correct?"

She had a coldness to her voice, an unsentimental distance, that he rarely, if ever, heard.

"I am here because I do not think a husband should keep things from his wife."

Maria's mind reeled. Had he spoken to Karl in Florida? Something had changed. She could hear it in his forthright tone.

As cars pulled out of the lot, headlights on, several people engaged in loud conversation walked by, smiling up at them.

"You were wonderful tonight, Mrs. Reinhardt!" one exclaimed.

"Both performances were amazing!" another shouted up. "Congratulations!"

Maria smiled politely down at them and then returned to Hans. She stared at him, unable to find words. She looked out into the lot, over all the departing vehicles, and off in the distance she saw Cooper, still standing there leaning on his car, waiting unwearyingly for her.

As much as she wanted to leave right there and begin her life fresh with James Cooper, she knew she had to give Hans a chance to answer a single question.

"Hans, why are you here?"

All his life he'd known this woman and he knew exactly what he had to do right now. He had to tell the truth.

"You opened the letter from the insurance company."

"I did."

"So you have questions, and I am here to answer them."

She decided to let him talk. "Okay."

"Your violin," he lowered his voice. "It is worth more than you saw in that letter. Considerably more."

"Hans, I know."

He absorbed that and knew that he was not the one to be asking the questions now. "Oh. Oh, I see."

She moved her head closer to him, turning it slightly, as though searching for something in him. "You said that your work had to go only to a people who were guided by the Bible. Hans, do you believe in the Bible?"

"Oh, my dear . . ."

"Do you?"

He didn't want to lose her, but he would not lie to her. So he said nothing.

"Hans, *do you?*"

"I am a scientist."

"How can you live a moral life if you have faith in nothing beyond that which you can see?"

He felt her eyes burning into him and knew that he had only this one last chance to speak to her the truth.

"I believe in space. I believe that is mankind's destiny." He took a step even closer to her, his voice soft and vulnerable in a way she'd never quite heard before. "There was a time when, perhaps, I let my conviction in this splendid dream justify the means used to achieve it, and in that I am the same as the men who believed themselves entitled to an exclusive destiny, the same as men who today believe as much, but it is my hope that I can use my special knowledge, and my fondness . . . it is my hope that I can mend some of what was done by helping America and can draw on the fondness I have for you, Maria, my lovely, sweet Maria, to build something that makes my life more constructive and meaningful being lived than not. I believe in space and my dream is enduring, that I will not deny. But also, what was done was shameful and I believe in being ashamed. Do you not see? I am who I am today because I believe in remorse, and it will last my lifetime, and so, yes, in that way, I suppose I do believe in the Bible."

Repentance was something she felt in her own way too, and his acknowledgment of it moved her deeply, because when she thought about it and listened to his tone and looked in his eyes, she knew what he said was true.

"This is why I work as I do, and why I am here . . ." He extended his arms, opened his hands. "Tell me how to make the world better. Tell me."

"Peter comes home. Immediately."

"Peter comes home. Yes. And let us go there too. And we can talk about the violin."

This was the moment, and Maria knew it. She had to make a decision. She raised her head, looking for Cooper.

"Maria," Hans said. "Let us go home."

"I have some ideas about how the violin might be used," she said.

He smiled broadly at her. "I am sure you do."

"Beginning, perhaps, with a music program here in Huntsville."

"I want to hear about it." He extended his hand. "Let us go home and talk about it."

And after a long moment of consideration, she took his hand.

"Maria, we have known each other a very long time," Hans said. "But do you think you can ever learn to open your heart to me?"

"My heart has always been open to you," she said softly.

"Do you think you can open it fully?"

They looked into each other's eyes for a long moment, both aware of what he was asking, and he could see the uncertainty. So he decided to stop asking questions and take action.

Hans took his wife in his arms and kissed her on the forehead. He pulled back, considered her reaction, and then he kissed her on the lips.

"We must make things right with the past," he said. "And then put it behind us. Memories do fade. Particularly when new ones are made."

Maria just nodded slowly, tired, her heart aching.

They strolled across the concrete landing to the stairs and, hand in hand, they walked down them and across the nearly empty parking lot.

On their way, Maria looked across the lot for Cooper, but he and his car were gone.

Suddenly, she stopped.

"What is it?" Hans asked.

"I have to get something." Going back to get the bag, she headed across the lot, up the steps of the landing, looking out one more time.

The only vehicle she could see remaining in the back of the lot, in the shadows, was an old red pickup truck.

CODA

Sunday, at a particularly beautiful dusk, Maria drove the Chevy up Highway 117, around the pastoral bend where the road crossed over the peak of the ridge, slowing as she approached the center of Mentone. At Ruby's she parked and turned off the car, filled with Peter's belongings from Darlington.

She and Peter stepped out and crossed the parking lot to the café's porch.

"Have a seat and wait here," Maria said, pointing to a big wooden rocking chair. "I will be right back."

"Okay, mom."

Peter sat rocking, watching his mother as she walked next door to the Mentone Springs Hotel.

Inside, Maria went straight to the front desk, where a kind-faced older gentleman smiled warmly at her.

"Evenin', ma'am," he said.

"Good evening. Can you tell me if James Cooper has checked in?"

"Major Cooper?"

"Yes."

"I'm sorry, ma'am, Major Cooper has gone."

"So he was here?"

"He was. You just missed him, in fact. He checked out about half an hour ago."

Her face dropped and she looked at the floor as though she would find some kind of answer there. "I see."

"Are you okay, ma'am?"

"Did he say where he was going?"

"No, he didn't. He was very . . . quiet."

Maria walked slowly from the desk, lost in thought, looking outside through the big front windows.

A middle-aged woman, hair up, marched toward the desk, something in her extended hand.

"Tom!" the woman called out to the man at the desk. "Someone left this in the Riverview Suite. Do you think it's a tip?"

The man at the desk took the item from the woman and studied it for a moment, eyebrows raised in amazement.

"Ma'am," he called out to Maria.

"Yes?" Maria responded.

"I don't imagine you know if Major Cooper had a Morgan silver dollar."

Maria felt her heart drop. She swallowed hard. "1895?"

The man turned to the woman. "I don't know why he left it, but something like this is special. Where did you find it?"

"You'll never guess," the woman said.

"Under a pillow," Maria said quietly.

"Now, how did you know that?" the woman asked with a curious smile.

Maria did not respond. She just stood there, dazed.

"Why don't you take this, ma'am?" The gentleman extended the coin to Maria, who slowly approached and took it.

Holding the silver dollar in her hand, running her thumb over the cold shiny metal, she felt as though she were transported back twelve years, back to that cottage.

He *had* come. *James Cooper had come back to the cottage for her.*

And he didn't want her to know, didn't want her to have regrets, didn't want to destroy her life, because that's the kind of man he was—the kind of man who could be counted on, who just half an hour ago had done what he had promised and had finally let her go.

Still speechless, stunned, Maria looked up, realizing the two hotel employees were staring at her.

She began to walk away, down the hall.

Passing a couple of doors, she approached one that was open, a cleaning cart in the hall in front of it. A small plaque next to the open door read "Riverview Suite."

Holding the silver dollar tightly in her hand, Maria peered into the room and then stepped in. She looked around at the wonderful antique furnishings, the big fireplace, the oversized clawfoot tub in the bathroom, and the embroidered white drapes that matched the spread on the romantic canopy bed.

The bed was almost completely made, except for a single pillow, lying askew.

A profound bittersweet feeling running through her, she walked over to the bed, in her mind flashes of what could have been but what in this life would not be.

Maria stood alone in that room in front of the embroidered spread on the romantic canopy bed, and she began to cry, the tears flowing down her cheeks in rivulets. She put her hand to her mouth and let it all pour out, twelve years of love and longing, and a lifetime of missed possibilities, all washing over her.

◆ ◆ ◆

Walking slowly back across the lot, up the steps of Ruby's, the sun now set, Maria pulled a rocking chair over near Peter's, and she sat next to him. Rocking, she was quiet and sullen.

He scooted forward in the chair, looking at her closely, and although she had made an effort to pull herself together, Peter knew his mother well enough to tell when something was wrong.

"Mom, what's going on?"

She held the silver dollar out to him and then placed it in his hand.

"What's this?"

"I am going to tell you."

CAPE CANAVERAL, FLORIDA, JANUARY 31, 1958

"Thirty seconds to liftoff," said the technician, announcing the launch countdown for all the men in the control room and all those listening in around the country and around the world.

Colonel Adams, Hans, Karl, Von Braun, and the several army officers and other German rocket scientists crowded in the room leaned forward over the control panels, gazing intently out the thick plateglass window. The results of all their efforts, from Nordhausen to Huntsville to Cape Canaveral, sat on the launch pad below—the seventy-foot-tall, six-foot-wide, sixty-four-thousand-ton four-stage rocket Juno I, with her very special payload atop.

"*Explorer 1* beacon is active and operating," another tech said, and the constant *beep, beep, beep* of a small satellite in the top stage of the launch vehicle transmitted over the control room speakers.

"Ten seconds."

The men were silent as they watched, steam now rising from beneath the rocket.

"Five, four, three, two, primary booster is ignited, and—liftoff! We have a liftoff! Juno I is a go!"

Massive flames firing out from the main engine, the rocket began to rise, moving faster and faster, following its carefully planned trajectory up into the sky.

In the control room, the glass window vibrating, the men began to applaud, and then—as the rocket disappeared into the heavens—they began to cheer.

Beep, beep, beep, the satellite continued on.

Standing in front of a table before a packed room of reporters, Von Braun, Karl, and Hans, all three of them ebullient, held a life-size replica of the four-foot-long, thirty-one-pound *Explorer 1* satellite over their heads while photographers snapped shots, several of which would end up in newspapers all over the country and one of which would make the cover of *Time* magazine.

NORDHAUSEN, MAY 1945

On a bright, sunny spring day, Cooper, neat and sharp in his officer's uniform, knocked on the cottage door. There was no response.

He looked around at the forest, fresh with new growth, observing the *Kinderhaus* up on the hill, but no one was in sight.

Finally, he opened the door of the cottage and went in. He threw open the curtains, letting in light.

Cooper tried to ascertain if Maria had left. There were few clues. But then he went to the recessed shelf in the living-room area where she kept her violin. Discovering that the instrument was gone, he felt his heart drop.

He went to the bedroom, looking around, approached her pillow, lifted it up, and there was his silver dollar.

Holding the pillow close to his face, he inhaled, taking in the scent of her, and sighed.

Cooper picked up the silver dollar and sat on the end of the bed, the coin in his hand, staring ahead.

ACKNOWLEDGMENTS

If there's one thing I'm learning about writing books, it's that you don't do it without a tremendous amount of help.

A huge thank-you, once again, to my incredible editor, Katie Gilligan, and all the fine folks at St. Martin's Press and Thomas Dunne Books, particularly Sally Richardson, Matthew Shear, Tom Dunne, Pete Wolverton, Matt Baldacci, John Murphy, Anne Marie Tallberg, Sarah Goldstein, Stephanie Davis, Elsie Lyons, Nick Small, and Melanie Fried. Thank you to Roslyn Schloss for the amazing copyediting. And thanks to my friend and agent, Daniel Greenberg, as well as to Beth Fisher and the entire team at Levine Greenberg. And many thanks to Jerry Kalajian at IPG.

Thanks also to Amy Charles and Susan Hall for the early reads, Cecilia Price for the music lesson, Professor Susanne Kelley for help with the German, and everyone at Kennesaw State University.

A tremendous thank you to my friends, fellow writers, parents, and my children, Sophie, Charlotte, and Eli.

And as always, my deepest gratitude to my wife, Elizabeth—thank you for your ruthless notes and enduring support. I love you.